THE FAMILY HISTORY

THE
FAMILY HISTORY

A NOVEL

Jean Jardine Miller

JM
PUBLISHING

Library and Archives Canada Cataloguing in Publication

Jardine Miller, Jean, 1945-
The family history / Jean Jardine Miller.

ISBN 978-0-9731376-5-1

I. Title.

PS8619.A735F35 2008   C813'.6   C2008-901686-6

Cover and text design: Design and Copy Consultation Services.
Cover illustration from *Black Lion Wharf,* etching by James McNeill Whistler 1859.

Jardine Miller - publishing what is significant to today
Shelburne, Ontario L0N 1S4 Canada

A tribute to my own nineteenth century ancestors who worked on the Thames and whose lives inspired this story.

July 2006

It was amazing, Holly thought, to be able to type in a name and click through a few screens to find the names of yet another set of great, great grandparents.

She hadn't really been too enthusiastic when Julie first told her about how she was researching her family history and suggested Holly see what she could find out about hers so that they could put together really extensive family trees for the children to have when they were old enough to understand the importance of roots. Holly wasn't at all sure that her roots were especially important to her or her children, and told Julie that all she knew about either side of her family was what she had written in the front of the children's baby books and that her mother was not very forthcoming about her own ancestors or those of Holly's late father. Julie figured this was probably due to the possibility that there were a few hurriedly arranged marriages and untimely births involved – the sort of thing less enlightened older generations still tended to think shouldn't be freely discussed. Holly's mother was, in fact, the result of a wartime romance in England, in the early 1940s, and had been brought up as her grandparents' youngest child, unaware that her older sister, Grace, was really her mother.

Unaware, that is, until she caused a family crisis, at age fifteen, by asking for her birth certificate when she had to apply for a passport to go on a school trip to Norway. Holly had never mentioned this to her in-laws – well, there had been no reason to, and the subject hadn't ever come up – so she told Julie the story, as her mother had related it to her, and Julie said that it was amazing how many such cases you turned up once you started looking into your family history.

They had been sitting together in the bleachers, during this conversation, watching their sons' minor baseball game. Since Julie's nine-year-old Ryan hit the ball out into centre field, at that point, allowing his cousin, Jamie, to make a quick dash to home plate to score the winning run, they became too busy congratulating the boys to continue the discussion. As everybody, collecting together kids and equipment, headed for their cars, Julie shouted over to Holly that she should see if she could get together enough information to start tracing her family on the genealogy sites on the internet. Holly nodded and raised her hand to indicate assent and turned back to deal with Jamie and Carolyn who were arguing about whose turn it was to sit in the front seat.

A couple of weeks later, when Paul had taken the three children to a Sunday afternoon Jays' game, Julie decided that she was going to introduce her to the world of internet genealogy, whether or not she was ready. Holly's father, who had died when she was twelve, was a second generation Canadian whose grandfather had emigrated from England in the early 1900s which meant that, since they knew that he had been living with his family in Lancashire before that, they should be able to find him on the 1901 census of England. They went to Ancestry.co.uk, took the two weeks' pay-per-view option and found the family quite quickly on that census and the preceding ones. Julie said that a visit to the 'LDS site' would give them access to parish records to confirm birth and marriage dates, and Holly was introduced to the International Genealogical Index or the IGI.

Holly had not been entirely convinced that she wanted to get involved when she and the children left Julie's and Paul's house after supper that evening. Julie had loaded her up with a family history program to install on her own computer and another disc with all the information she had compiled on her own family history. She recognized that Julie's own interest in tracing her family tree had only come about in the months since Justin's death and she thought it was something that Holly, too, might find absorbing, so she gave her sister-in-law a quick hug to let her know that her concern was appreciated and hurried the children out to the car because it was a school night and past time to get them home and in bed.

Tracing ancestors, previously unknown to her, proved quite fascinating after the slow start she had eventually made, at Julie's prodding, several weeks later and she had, after exhausting leads on her father's side, begun investigating her mother's family. To work the same way Julie had shown her when they found her father's grandfather on the 1901 census, she needed the name of at least one family member born before the census was taken, which meant asking her mother and, since her mother was not exactly into talking about her family, that was probably not such a good idea. Holly's mother had left England and come to Canada in the early 1960s, maintaining minimal contact with her family and would, Holly knew from previous experience, definitely get annoyed if she asked about them. On hearing of Grace's death in a letter from her half-brother just two years before, her attitude had been, what she would have termed herself, as of the 'good riddance' variety. Holly had decided, instead, to try going first with what she did know. Surprisingly, she struck lucky. She had no idea whether her maternal great grandparents had been born before or after 1901, but simple mathematics indicated that their birth dates had to have been somewhere around there. She remembered her father once pointing out to her mother how Nana, after years of heading the return address on birthday and Christmas cards, with Mr. and Mrs. E. Kentson, had written 'Mrs. Maud Ellen Kentson', indicating that Grandad Kentson had died. She remembered the incident because her father, himself, became terminally ill before the next Christmas came around and, when he died, in one of those strange twists our minds make at such times, hers had registered the fact that her mother would now be writing only her own name on Christmas card envelopes. So, she had Maud Ellen somebody and E. Kentson, both born sometime around the turn of the century and marrying, probably during or after the First World War, although, since she didn't know how old Grace was when Mom was born in 1941, that wedding day could have been into the twenties. If that were the case, she was out of luck, she knew, because it was not likely to have been transcribed for online records yet. Without a lot of hope, she went to Free BMD and entered the name Kentson, selected 'London' and the years 1890 to 1920 and, surprisingly, came up with a marriage record for 'Kentson, Edward' in the third quarter of 1915, the last name of his bride – 'Smith', and the page and volume number recording their marriage, which had taken place in Stepney. She clicked on the linked page number and, there it was, 'Smith, Maud Ellen'. They must have been in their eighties, then, when she was a child receiving those cards. Anyhow, if they were old enough to marry in 1915, their names and families had to be on the 1901 census.

At that point, she'd decided to wait until she was sure she had time before paying up again to go on Ancestry to check the census records. She'd only used her last pay-per-view subscription for one day and then hadn't had a chance to get back to it. Besides, it was *time for bed, anyway. The morning rush to get the kids to day camp and herself ready to do her morning on the office duty roster would be upon her only too soon.*

Tonight, both children having gone to sleep without finding reasons to stay up any longer and a weekend ahead currently free from both appointments and the duty roster, she was back working on Edward Kentson's family. She knew it was more likely that they'd married in Maud Ellen's church or local registry office, whatever... That would be where her family would show up on the census records but the name Smith, obviously, would present quite a challenge. She'd decided to work on the assumption that Edward, too, lived in Stepney and to try searching there first, figuring that, if she failed to turn up anything, she could try London generally, although she knew that the areas further east were in Essex. Thank goodness for good old Edward having an uncommon name. Had it been Kinley or Kinsella or plain Kent, she'd have had a problem. As it turned out, of the three Kentson families that selecting London as the county and Stepney as the town turned up, there was only one with an Edward – aged six, second son and fourth of the seven children of John and Martha Kentson of Poplar; not Stepney. It had to be him. She'd scribbled down the names ages and places of birth of the parents and children, plus a couple of lodgers, in case they turned out to be useful – my God, where did they all sleep? – as well as the address, then checked for Edward Kentsons in Essex and, just to be sure ran a check without entering any county or town. She'd come up with two adult Edwards, a three-year-old Teddie, living in Lincoln, and an Edward, aged '5/12ths', in Chatham, Kent. There was an outside chance that the three year old might have gone to London and met and married Maud Ellen in 1915, at age seventeen, but it was hardly probable in the middle of World War I. He was more likely to have sought adven-

ture by adding a year to his age and joining up early to fight for 'King and Country' – the phrase which would not yet have become an euphemism for cannon fodder in the summer of 1915. The infant would have been only fourteen and the adult Edwards – well, both would surely have been far too old for Maud even if they had relocated to London, by 1915, and met her. John and Martha's six-year-old Edward Kentson of Poplar had to be her great grandfather – Grandad, who'd died some time in the late nineteen seventies, causing Nana to write 'Mrs. Maud Ellen Kentson' instead of 'Mr. and Mrs. E. Kentson' on the return address portion of her envelopes. John and Martha then were her great, great grandparents.

Checking her notes, Holly had then entered the details given for Edward's father – John Kentson, born about 1866 in Southwark, and was returned a John Kentson, with those details exactly, on both the 1891 and 1871 census records, at the top of the list. Truly amazing… She'd find out what happened in 1881 later. For now 1891 would confirm the 1901 details – not so many children, of course – and 1871 should give her information on John's parents.

In fact, 1891 provided clues to great-great grandmother Martha's pedigree, since John and Martha and their eldest child turned out to be living with Martha's parents. Then, in 1871, John was living, not with his parents, but with his grandparents, presumably his maternal grandparents, since their name was Walkerston, not Kentson. So, amazingly, she had not only acquired Edward's mother's last name, but his father's mother's last name, too, without having to go back to the statutory marriage records. The Walkerstons – both parents and children – were born in Woolwich, Kent, and must have moved sometime between 1862, when the youngest son, Henry, was born in Woolwich, and 1871 to Southwark, wherever that was, then to Stepney. She'd have to see if she could find a map on the internet to *check out these places where her ancestors had lived. She was pretty sure they were all either East End of London districts or riverside areas nearby. Southwark – yes,Shakespeare lived there, and they reconstructed the Globe Theatre somewhere there on the south side of the river, and Marlowe was killed in a riverside tavern in Southwark, wasn't he?*

She struck out on both Kentsons and Walkerstons on the 1861 census, but found Samuel and Phoebe Walkerston living in Woolwich, on the 1851 census, with their children, also named Phoebe and Samuel, neither of whom were listed as living with the family in 1871. Phoebe, born in 1848, making her only eighteen when John was born, had to be his mother, then. Perhaps John, as a first child, was named for his father. She should try John Kentson born – say, 1845 plus or minus five years, and see what she came up with. Top of the list – an 1851 census entry showing a John Joseph Kentson, aged three and living in Woolwich, Kent. Clicking through to the record, she found the rest of the family – John Joseph Kentson, his wife, Rebecca, and their two children, John Joseph and Emma Mary, aged three and four respectively...

June 1856

Johnnie Kentson crawled through the bushes until he was as close as he could get to the parade ground without somebody seeing him and chasing him away. Ever since the Royal Artillery had come back from Crimea in the winter, he'd been coming up to the Barracks, as often as he could, to watch them drill the horses or practise shooting and throwing shells on the common. This afternoon horses were being drilled and he lay down flat on his stomach and watched as the soldiers lined up their mounts. Maybe they were practising for when the Queen came – a man in the beer-shop had said she was coming to Woolwich again, to see the Sebastapol bells this time. She'd come to greet the troops as soon as they'd been brought ashore from the ship in February. Half the town had turned out to watch. All the local lightermen had been hired to bring them to shore in their barges. Johnnie wasn't quite sure why the soldiers were being unloaded to lighters as if they were cargo – maybe because of all the kit. Anyway, it was good as far as he was concerned because his pa had let him come on the lighter and he'd been right there in the stern, with Pa and Eddie Jones, with the soldiers sitting on the straw bales he'd helped Pa put down for them. They'd kidded him, telling him he'd better make sure his pa didn't drown them all when they were so close to home, after sailing all the way home from the Crimea. One had asked him if he was going to be a lighterman like his pa when he grew up and that was when he decided he was joining the cavalry as soon as he was old enough. Pa, of course, had told them that all the men in their family were lightermen working mostly up at the London Docks and around the Pool, but he was down here to handle transporting vegetables to the city and hops to the breweries. He even went on to tell them that he didn't work the boat so much in the winter, because of his bad chest, and mostly hired it out to jobbers, like Eddie, who didn't have barges of their own. But he took this job, of course, because he wasn't going to deny his son the opportunity to witness history and help transport the troops home from the war. Then, one of the soldiers had given Johnnie the button off a dead Russian soldier's tunic that was now one of his prized possessions, displayed on the little shelf over his bedstead, along with his flint arrowhead, lucky rabbit's foot and the spent shells and cartridges he'd collected on the Common where the Artillery drilled.

"You ain't 'alf goin' to cop it, Johnnie Kentson."

The voice behind him broke his reverie and Johnnie turned his head. "Not as much as you are, Sam," he said indignantly. "Whatcha following me around for, anyway?"

"Saw you when I come out the playground, din't I? You was crossing over Wellington Street an' I shouted to you, but you didn't 'ear me. So I run after you."

"But you'll get Phoebe into trouble with your ma again."

"I keep telling them that I don't need Phoebe to meet me. I can walk 'ome by meself."

"Maybe, but it's not fair getting your sister into trouble. Come on, let's go back and see if we can catch up with her before she 'as to go home without you."

"But I want to watch the soldiers."

"You'll 'ave us chucked out, anyway, if you don't shut your gob," Johnnie said, rising to his feet. He pulled Sam up and turned him in the direction of the road. "Come on – race you to the alley."

By the time the two boys reached the infants' school, there was not a soul in sight. Johnnie sighed. He agreed that Sam was old enough to walk home from school by himself. Nevertheless, Sam's mother didn't think so and his sister, Phoebe, was supposed to walk up from the girls' school to fetch him. Johnnie's own sister, Emma, who was Phoebe's bosom friend, usually went with her. He and Emma had gone to the infants' school together because their ma had decided, since she had to look after the beer-shop when Pa was away on the river and couldn't walk Emma to school, she could wait until Johnnie was old enough for the two of them to walk there and back together. Poor Phoebe hadn't even gone to the infants' school because her ma thought she was more useful at home helping to look after her little brothers, but the authorities had got them to send her to the girls' school when the family was tested to decide what they should pay for Sam to go to the infants' school when he was five. Phoebe was often kept at home, though, when there was only enough money to pay for Sam to go to school or, sometimes, to look after Will and the baby, Georgie, when her ma had a lot of stitching to do for the slop tailor she worked for. When that happened Phoebe would have to go back and forth four times a day with Sam, trundling Will and Georgie in the little wooden cart their pa had made when she and Sam were babies. Emma would walk up from the girls' school, or meet them along the High Street, and tell Phoebe what they'd been doing at school. Today, Emma and Phoebe would have walked up from the girls' school to meet Sam and, finding no Sam, would be on their way home without him and, if he didn't get Sam to them before Phoebe gave up trying to find him, she'd get clouted once again by her ma, who always blamed Phoebe, rather than Sam, when things went wrong, because she was the eldest.

"Come on, Sam," Johnnie said, "if we run all the way, we'll catch up with them. You *know* it's not fair to let Phoebe get into trouble, again when it's all your fault."

"Only if we can stop on the bridge and watch the train."

"Only if we've caught up with the girls first."

They ran through the narrow streets, found the train had already gone by and ran across the road from the bridge, then down Union Street to Gough Yard and across to the alley that led into the High Street beside the New Packet, the beer-shop kept by Johnnie's ma and pa. At last, Johnnie sighted the girls on the other side of the road. Emma must be going all the way home with Phoebe, he thought, or she'd have been indoors getting their tea ready. He glanced into the open door of the beer-shop and saw his ma handing a filled jug to old Mrs. Wiggins's, a regular at this time of the day. There were no customers at the bar, aside from her, but he couldn't see if there were any sitting at the tables likely to keep Ma's attention away from the open door. He turned away and looked across the street.

"Emma! Phoebe!" he shouted. "I've got 'im. 'Ere 'e is."

"You don't 'ave to make it sound like I'm a parcel or sumfink," muttered Sam, crossly. "I'll be bloody glad when I turn seven and go to the boys' school with you. Then, maybe, you'll all stop treatin' me like a baby."

The two girls turned around and ran back across the road towards them.

"We can stop running now and get our breath," said Johnnie.

"Good, 'cos I got the stitch, ain't I?"

Sam bent over, trying ease the cramp, as Emma and Phoebe ran up to them.

"'Ow many times d'you 'ave to be told, Sam Walkerston?" said Phoebe. "You wait in the playground for me and Emma to get there." She turned to Johnnie. "An' you, Johnnie Kentson, wot d'you fink you're up to?"

"Ain't nuffink to do with Johnnie," said Sam, straightening up. "Leastways not wot 'e could 'elp. 'E just made me run all the way 'ere so you wouldn't get into trouble."

"You know Johnnie would never do anything to get you into trouble, Phoebe," put in Emma. "That wasn't fair of you."

"Sorry, Johnnie," Phoebe said. "Thanks for gettin' 'im for us before I 'ad to go 'ome without 'im. Emma was coming with me so's Ma'd just tell us to go and look for 'im 'stead of giving me a clip round the ear. I'm glad you two are me friends."

"That's okay, Phoebe," Johnnie said, giving a short wave to Mrs. Wiggins, who had come out of the beer-shop carrying her jug of stout porter, something she told people she drank for her health, and turned towards her husband's shoe shop a few doors along. "Me an' Em 'ad better get in before our ma comes out after us. She must know we're out 'ere with the door being open."

"Yes, I think we'd better. Ma said I could go but, if she knows Sam's found, she'll want me to get the tea ready," Emma said. "I'll be round later, Phoebe."

"'Bye, Em. Thanks, Johnnie," Phoebe said, shoving Sam ahead of her. "Come on, Sam, before we both really cop it."

"'Bye, Phoebe. 'Bye, Sam."

"'Bye," Johnnie shouted, turning to follow Emma into the beer-shop. You had to go through the shop to get to the back room if you came in from the street. Johnnie usually went through the door in the fence from the alley into the backyard and used the scullery door. Ma was sitting on the stool behind the bar. She had her sewing basket beside her and was working on an old dress of her own from which she had cut out the good parts to make a dress for Emma. It was already nearly half past five according to the clock on the shelf behind the bar, the time of day when most men were still at work and women were busy getting their children's tea, so there were only a couple of customers at a table in the far corner; a young man reading a newspaper to an older man. Once Johnnie had heard Mr. Rolfe, the newsagent, tell Pa that he should pay more than the going price for newspapers because so many people chose to save their money for beer by reading them in his beer-shop instead of buying their own and it was doing him out of the money. Pa said they'd not likely spend their money on a newspaper anyway and, more often than not, came in here as much to find out what was going on in the world as they did for a pot of beer, and he gave Mr. Rolfe a drink on the house.

"Okay, Johnnie," Ma said, looking up. "How come you found Sam when you had no business anywhere near the infants' school? Emma, you go up and put on your old pinafore. Close the door for me first."

Emma turned back and pushed the doorstop aside, letting the door swing shut, then went through to the back room.

Ma continued, "Well, Johnnie?"

Johnnie hung his head. "I didn't," he said. "I mean he found me. You know 'ow 'e 'angs round me..."

"Yes, but you're supposed to come straight home from school and put your old shirt and trousers on and do any jobs I need done and have your tea before you go out to play – not go sneaking off up to the Artillery to watch soldiers and horses marching around."

"'Ow...?"

"Johnnie, Sam Walkerston doesn't just hang around you. He tells his little brother Will all about how the two of you are going for a soldier when you grow up and that you go up the barracks and watch them drill. Then Will tells his ma. So, when Sam's not in the infants' school playground when Phoebe and Emma get there, it's most likely he's up the Artillery with you, don't you think?"

"I made 'im run all the way down to try to catch up with them, Ma. Soon as I saw 'im, I did."

"I believe you, Johnnie, but you shouldn't've been up there in the first place, should you?"

"No, Ma. I'm sorry. I won't do it again."

"You'd better not. Now, get upstairs and change into your old clothes, then sponge the grass stains off those trousers – I won't have you shaming us going to school looking like a ragamuffin."

* * * * *

Two elderly men came in and sat at the bar drinking their beer after Rebecca sent Johnnie off to change. They were busy discussing whether there'd be more casual work for the young loafers hanging around the streets and taverns with nothing to do, now that the prison hulks were being done away with and there'd be no more convict labour to work on draining the marshes out past the Arsenal. They were regulars who finished their twelve hour day at the gasworks at five and just stopped in, on their way home to supper, for a mug of ale and probably wouldn't be ordering more. However, knowing that there'd be women coming in to get jugs filled with ale in preparation for their men finishing the day's work in the Arsenal and coming home for supper, she folded up the dress she was making and pulled out stockings to darn instead – better to do something you couldn't make mistakes with when you were picking it up and putting it down all the time.

Rebecca didn't really like having to be at the bar all day. In the winter John mostly rented his lighter out and hired someone else to do his regular jobs because, with his bad chest, he couldn't be out in the fog on the water getting unwell, so he was able to serve beer duringboth the day and evening, and she didn't even need to work in the shop unless she wanted to. The rest of the year, especially when he had cargoes of fruit and vegetables, and the hops, to take up to town, he wasn't around so much and she had to get the upstairs housekeeping finished, washing done and hung out in the yard and get potatoes and vegetables ready for dinner before she opened up in the morning. After that, she had to be in the shop or where she could hear the bell ring, which meant no further away than the back room with the door open, because you couldn't trust even your best friends and neighbours when you lived near the wharves. At least, that's what John said and he should know – he'd been born and brought up right around the London wharfs where his father operated the family lighterage business. Rebecca was from a family of farm labourers and had spent her own childhood in the Essex countryside, where nobody was better off than anybody else and your best friends and neighbours wouldn't find anything worth stealing anyway, if they did walk into your house when you weren't there. The neighbourhood alongside the river at Woolwich was as rough as any of the areas around the wharves and docks along the Thames and there were thieves and worse around.

Fortunately, they didn't often get strangers in the beer-shop. In the daytime, it was mostly frequented by the older people in the neighbourhood, living off annuities or pensions, or working as night watchmen, whose one extravagance was having a chat over a pot of beer after shopping in the High Street or in the market and, maybe, having a game of bagatelle or shove ha'penny or, mostly, just buying jugs of beer, ale or porter to drink at home with their meals. Young women would often come in after taking their children up to the infants' school but, more to exchange gossip than for a drink. There were plenty of taverns around for serious drinkers. Evening customers were mostly mates of John's from the wharf or lightermen acquaintances from London, or other riverside towns, waiting for tides to change and John, himself, was usually around to take care of things then, whether it was winter or summer. Even the men who played in the skittles tournaments were people with whom they were well acquainted. Still, she knew her husband was right when he insisted that she trust nobody and she abided by his judgement.

"Here's your tea, Ma."

Emma came in from the back room, carefully carrying a cup of tea and a plate with a slice of bread and jam and a rock cake on it.

"Thanks, love. I'm dying for a drink of tea."

She took the cup and saucer from her daughter, blew on the tea and took a small sip.

"Better let it cool off a bit, Ma," said Emma, putting the plate on the bar. She glanced towards the customers and lowered her voice, "D'you need to go out to the privy? I'll shout out to you if someone comes in."

Rebecca laughed. "No, I'm all right just at the moment. You and Johnnie have your tea. I'll give you a shout if I need any help, but it's not like there's a lot going on of a Monday, so you can probably go out and play for a while, if you like, after tea – as long as you come in and get your night lessons done before bedtime."

"Johnnie, too?"

"I s'pose so. I should really punish him for going up the Artillery after school but I think he learned his lesson with Sam being so much trouble."

"It was nice of him to get Sam back here before Phoebe had to go home without him, wasn't it?"

"Yes, it was. And it was nice of you to offer to go home with her so she wouldn't get into so much trouble. The two of them are lucky to have friends like you and Johnnie."

"But that's what friends are for – to help you in times of trouble. That's what my teacher says."

"Well, yes… That's right, love…" Rebecca found it rather irksome when her daughter quoted her teacher, which she did often. "You go and have your tea now."

Emma ran off just as a young woman, who Rebecca hadn't seen before, came into the shop. She was probably one of the women hired for the new paper cartridge factory in the Arsenal come to live in one of the many lodging houses in this part of the town. They'd hired a number of women to make the cartridges because their smaller fingers were better for the job than men's and this had attracted young women from all over. You could hardly blame them jumping at an opportunity to work at something other than domestic service, slop tailoring or the laundry. Rebecca hoped she was working at the factory. Some of the lodging houses around were little better than brothels. The girl handed over her jug and asked for *'just a half fill'* of stout.

"New around here?" Rebecca asked, pulling up the tap on the barrel of stout.

"I got a job at the cartridge factory – start tomorrer, and me and me sister've moved into the flat over the shoe shop – well, it's just the one room, really. Me landlady – Mrs. Wiggins, that is – said to come in 'ere. She said you was respectable."

Rebecca laughed. "I should hope so. Where are you from?"

"Up London way. Spitalfields. We thought it'd be 'ealthier away from the city a bit. Me sister's 'usband was stationed 'ere, but they moved them down to the new barracks at Aldershot when the cavalry battalions come back from Crimea. 'E only enlisted last November, see, and 'e told us about the factory opening in the Arsenal and them wanting women and suggested for me to apply, so me and Lizzie could move down 'ere but, as luck would 'ave it, 'e got moved on before it even opened. She's going to 'ave 'er first baby, see, is Lizzie. That's what the stout's for – build 'er up, Mrs. Wiggins says. 'Ope yer wasn't thinking I was no better than I ought to be?"

"'Course not," said Rebecca, putting the filled jug on the bar. "We used to live in Wapping – Great Hermitage Street. Kentson Lighterage, near the coal wharf, is my father-in-law's business. Me 'usband, John, got his lungs scarred up in a barge fire. Not his own boat – he went to help a bargeman who'd hit his head and knocked himself out trying to get over the side. Anyway, we came down here to be out of the city smoke and he handles cargoes from the market gardens and the hops farms up to the city. We

took on the beer-shop so's we'd have enough for the extras –
school pennies and clothes and shoes and things like that. And
to get us through the winter when it's too dangerous for John to
be out in the damp and fog on the river. It was hard just making
enough to pay the rent at first, but word soon got round the lightermen driving up and down the river and it became their place
of an evening and, of course, the neighbours soon came to like it
in 'ere, so we do all right."

The girl took a sixpence from her pocket and put it on the bar
beside the jug .

Rebecca handed over her change. "There you go. Tell your sister to come in for a chat during the day if she gets lonely. She
doesn't need to buy anything. Neighbours often drop in for a chat
in the morning or early afternoon. Can't always afford a drink,
though – 'less it's payday."

"Thanks. I'll tell 'er. Me name's Jenny."

"I'm Rebecca."

"I know. Mrs. Wiggins told me. Pleased to meet you, Rebecca.
I'll tell Lizzie to come in and introduce 'erself. It's important for
us to know respectable people, bein' on our own, like." Jenny
slipped the change into her pocket and picked up her jug. "See
you again, then. G'bye for now."

"G'bye."

Two more young women came in as Jenny reached the door.
"Wait a minute, Jenny," Rebecca called. "Edna, Kitty – this is Jenny.
She's just moved in at Mrs. Wiggins's with her sister. Jenny, this is
Edna and Kitty. They live over at Taylor's Buildings in Globe Lane.
Kitty's expecting her first, too, in a few months, so you tell Lizzie
to come in here and meet 'er tomorrow morning. You're not work-
ing at the laundry this week, are you, Kitty?"

"No, Ma got called in, but 'Arry says there ain't enough to 'ave the rest of us in this week," Kitty told her. "Pleased to meet you, Jenny. You tell your sister to meet us 'ere tomorrow morning. I'll bring me mate, Vera, oo's 'aving a baby, too, and we'll all 'ave a chat about things, okay?"

"That's really nice of you. I'll tell 'er. It'll be lovely for 'er to 'ave you and Vera to talk to. We're on our own, see, so it's a bit lonely for 'er 'til we get to know people. Me, I'll get to meet people at work, but she's on 'er own all day. I better run – she'll be wondering what's 'appened to me. G'bye all."

Jenny left and Rebecca told Edna and Kitty about her and her sister as she filled their jugs.

"Sounds like their parents must be gone to their reward, so to speak, if they're on their own," said Edna. "Wouldn't be much fun 'avin' a baby with no ma around and yer 'usband off fer a soldier like that, would it? Leastways they don't sound like they're 'ard up, though. Wish I could've got one of them jobs at the Arsenal, but they wouldn't even look at you 'less you could read and write proper."

Edna, Rebecca knew, had never had the opportunity to go to school. She'd been set to looking after her younger brothers and sisters, from an early age, so that her mother could work at the laundry to ensure the family had the few pence a week needed for the boys to go to school so that they'd be able to 'get on' when the time came. Rebecca, coming from a family of agricultural labourers, whose main objective in life was to find the means to put food on the table which meant children, too, must work, could sympathize with her. She'd been lucky herself – she hadn't thought so at the time, of course, but being loaned the fare money, an address and a character reference, by the rector's housekeeper, after her father refused to house a spinster daughter any longer, after she had rejected what he saw as her last possible chance of marriage, had been a blessing in disguise. Ellen, the nursery maid in the city banker's house where she'd been engaged as a scullery maid on the strength of the precious 'character', had taken her along to the room in the basement of nearby Waterman's Hall where a lighterman's wife had set up a schoolroom and was teaching uneducated young women like themselves to read, write and improve their rudimentary arithmetic. Her teacher, who had eventually become her mother-in-law, was the kind of person who could really awaken a desire to learn in her pupils and Rebecca – despite the late hour, for she was a scullery maid and the evening wasn't her own until she'd finished cleaning up – quickly progressed beyond just reading, to appreciating what she read.

"Well, Edna, you'd get more education if you'd remember to come round here Tuesday evenings 'stead of walking out," Rebecca said, referring to the informal lessons she gave the girls.

Her teaching efforts had come about when she had been writing a note to her sister-in-law for John to take up the river with him and a young neighbour, who had come into the beer-shop, had remarked on how she'd like to be able to write to her ma in Ireland. The priest would read it to her, she'd said. Following the example of her mother-in-law, Rebecca had immediately offered to help the young woman write to her mother. After that, she had taught any of the neighbourhood women who asked her to and, at the request of some of the young girls who had to work all day, had set aside Tuesday evenings for lessons. The evening lessons were more formal, despite taking place at a corner table in the beer-shop with men discussing the way the country should be run nearby, or playing shove ha'penny. These were young, unmarried girls who truly wanted to improve themselves and their prospects, unlike the young mothers, who came in during the daytime, with the objective of being able to write letters and to read the cheap penny novels and serials they'd buy in the market and pass around.

"I wish I was walking out," retorted Edna. "My Fred complains he never sees me. If it ain't the mistress keeping me late – even today, which is me afternoon off, I 'ad trouble getting away – and, if it ain't 'er, it's me ma expecting me to be 'ome with the little two while she's off out."

"I was just teasing, love. Try and make it tomorrow, if you can. Is it porter you need?"

"Yes," Edna said, handing over her jug. "Thanks, Rebecca. Not for the porter – thanks for keeping on with me, I mean. You're a saint."

"Here you go." Then, as Edna went to pick up the filled jug, Rebecca added, "Saints that run beer-shops got to get paid, you know."

"What? Ooh, sorry." Edna put the jug back down and pulled some coins from her pocket. They all three laughed.

"Good try, Edna," said Kitty and they renewed their laughter as they left. "Come on, let's get back. I've got to go next door and buy some of 'is leftover bread cheap for supper. 'Bye, Rebecca. See you later. Ooh, 'ere's your evening paper–" she interrupted herself, taking the newspaper from the boy at the door and handing it to Rebecca who came out from behind the bar to take it.

"Thanks, Kittty. G'bye girls. Enjoy the evening."

"Ma?" Emma came in from the back room. "We've tidied up the tea things and Johnnie's playing cricket down the alley. Can I go over to Phoebe's house now?"

"Just don't talk to anybody you don't know along there," Rebecca told her, moving back behind the bar and putting the evening paper at the end where they placed the newspapers for customers to read. "If she's not allowed out, you come straight back or go down and see if they've finished loading your pa's boat and come back with him. I don't want you hanging about down there by yourself."

"Yes, Ma. Their cousin, Mary Ann, is at Phoebe's house. They're looking after her while her ma's having a baby. She's the same age as Sam but she's not used to boys, so it's better for her to play with me and Phoebe. Phoebe's other auntie is having a baby, too, but she doesn't have any other children. I told Phoebe that we have a new cousin, as well, but that James William's turned twelve and wouldn't want anybody looking after him."

"No, he certainly wouldn't," Rebecca agreed, thinking how young James William's nose was going to be out of joint after being his parents' only child all these years. "You make sure you get back here in time to do your night lessons before bedtime. And, walk round by the road – don't go through that alley."

"I know. And I can do my spelling with Phoebe – she's not very good at it because of having to miss so much school, so I can help her." The door opened and the bell jingled. Emma slipped through as the customer came in. "'Evening, Mrs. Barlow. I won't be long, Ma."

"She's growin' up, ain't she, young Emma?" said Mrs. Barlow. "'Member when you first took over the beer- shop? The two of them in the corner there with their toys and that fence wot your John made so you could 'ave them under your eye when you was in 'ere and 'im gorn up the river, like? Wot's she now, then – eight? Nine?"

"Nine. Johnnie's eight," Rebecca said, taking Mrs. Barlow's jug and filling it with porter. Funny how these older people clung to their porter and would never dream of trying anything else. Well, she thought, I'm glad there's so many of them around here, even if they are renting rooms to street women. Gives us a regular income, it does. "There you are, Mrs. Barlow," she said. "I'll put it on your bill. How's Mr. Barlow keeping?"

"Oh, not so good, is 'e now. But a few more nice days like today, sittin' out in the back there, and 'e should be getting over it. Give me a scare 'e did this time – thought we was goin' to lose him, I did."

"'E's a tough one, is Bert Barlow," one of the elderly men at the bar observed. "'E'll be around for a while yet, see if I'm not right?"

"I s'pose so. Annie know you're in 'ere with that Sid Jones, Arthur?"

"No, and don't you go letting on, neither. Tell Bert I was asking after 'im."

Rebecca carried the jug across the shop to the door before handing it to the old lady.

"Well, thank you, ducks." Mrs. Barlow took the jug while Rebecca opened the door for her. "'E should be well enough to come round and settle up the bill in a day or so."

"Not to worry. We trust 'im."

Rebecca watched her totter round the corner into the alley where she lived. She didn't really trust the old bugger, in the least, and John had said that, if he didn't get up off his posterior by the end of this week, he was going round to collect the money himself.

"'E'll be over 'is malingering tomorrer, you'll see."

She turned back and saw Will Parker, the bread baker, standing at the door of his shop.

"Cut them off, did you?" she asked.

"'Ad to, didn't I? Hetty told 'er this morning that this was 'er last loaf of bread 'til the bill was paid 'cos we 'ain't a big enough enterprise to carry that much money owed us for so long. Old miser's got 'undreds stuffed under 'is mattress, no doubt about it, but 'e won't trust 'is wife with the shoppin' money, will 'e?"

"John said he was going to go round there if they hadn't paid up by the end of the week, but I'll tell him you've cut them off so we'll probably all be getting paid tomorrow."

"You don't want your good 'ubby round there with all them loose women around."

Rebecca laughed. "He sees plenty of loose women around the wharfs of a Saturday night when the men get paid, believe you me."

"'S'pose 'e would," said Will, reflectively.

"Don't you get any ideas, Will Parker, or I'll tell Hetty about this conversation word for word."

The Parkers were a devoutly religious family, but Will wasn't above a saucy remark now and again.

"Just me little joke. Hetty'd never let me out on a Saturday night, anyway. Me crusty baps is nearly all gone, by the way, if you was wantin' them for your supper and John's dinner tomorrer."

"Oh yes, Will. If you don't mind bringing 'alf a dozen out for me, I'll get the money and a basket."

After the transaction with Will, the men who'd been sitting in the far corner, sipping on one drink each and reading the morning paper for more than an hour and a half, finally stood up, stretched and said good night. Rebecca served more jug customers, then one of the two men sitting at the bar left to go home for supper and the other one ordered another pint and settled himself to read the evening newspaper. Locking the cash drawer, she took the bowlful of dirty beer pots through to the wash house, where they would light the boiler and wash them all thoroughly in the big tub in the morning, and put her head around the door in the fence to call Johnnie in. Back in the shop, she put the bowl under the bar ready for the evening's dirty pots, then served two more jug customers while listening for Johnnie to let himself in at the scullery door.

"I was just comin' anyway," he said when he came through from the back room. "Philip's ma called 'im in and 'Arry's pa come through the alley, so 'im and 'Erb went 'ome with 'im. Where's Emma?"

"She went over to Phoebe's house. She's doing her night lesson with Phoebe, so you get on with yours before your pa gets in, wanting his supper. It's past seven o'clock already. What d'you have to do tonight?"

"Sums, but I can do them all. They ain't 'ard ones."

"Good. You get your satchel and sit down in here and get on with them before we get customers in, needing all the tables. We can be company for each other when Mr. Jones takes himself home to his supper."

Johnnie glanced at Mr. Jones, who gave no sign of having heard, and grinned because Mr. Jones tended to make a habit of forgetting to go home. Then he ran off to get his school satchel.

"D'you know Willie Parker next door's the monitor for my group, now?" he asked, when he came back and settled himself at the table nearest the bar.

"He is? But he's only just ten – a few months older than Emma."

"I know. That's pretty young to be a monitor, isn't it?"

"Bit too young, I would've thought, but I s'pose the schoolmaster knows what he's doing. Willie always was very clever, I must admit. Wonder why his pa didn't mention it when I was talking to him earlier on."

"'E probably doesn't know yet. Willie only got chosen today and 'e 'as to go and do 'is gran's garden on Mondays, straight from school and 'e wouldn't've been able to tell 'im at dinner time because 'is ma leaves their dinner ready for 'im and Jackie and the girls 'fore she takes the loaves over to the almshouses. She's usually not back 'fore it's time to get back to afternoon school and Mr. Parker and the 'prentice are busy in the bakehouse."

"I see. Well, you just get on with your sums. You don't want Willie to be thinking you're stupid when he checks them in the morning."

Johnnie busied himself with his night lesson. Rebecca, continuing with her darning, gave Sid Jones a few more hints to the effect that he'd be in plenty of trouble at home if he didn't get a move on, and he eventually finished his beer, stood up and said he'd better be on his way.

He'd no sooner left than John came in, followed by Emma.

"I stopped by the Walkerstons' in case the children were there," he said, shutting the door behind him and turning the sign to the "Closed" side, "and I brought Emma home with me. Look, lovey, I got a message from Jim, a bit earlier on, sent down with a fellow driving down to Chatham. Pa's likely not going to last the night, so I've left Eddie supervising the jobber and they've nearly finished loading and we're going up on this evening's tide instead of in the morning. I'm getting my coat – in case it gets chilly." He stopped as he realized the two children were staring at him in bewilderment. "Look, you explain to them. I 'ave to get a move on – tide's already flowing and I want to make the best time I can while it's still light."

Rebecca followed him into the back room. "Let me just get you some bread and the bacon I was going to fry up for your supper." She quickly went through to the scullery and got the knuckle of bacon and a piece of cheese from the pantry and put them in a sack with some of the fresh baps. "There's enough there for Eddie, too. You want me to go round to tell Sarah? Save you the time..."

"That'd be a big 'elp, love." John draped the pea-coat and muffler that he had taken from one of the hooks by the scullery door over a chair, and hugged her. "'Ope I make it in time. We'll tie up at Pa's wharf for the rest of the night and I'll find someone to take the boat on with Eddie in the morning. I'll be back on the ebb tide tomorrow evening because there's Docherty's new spuds and turnips to load the next day, so the lighter's got to be back 'ere. So you see if Sarah can't mind the pub Thursday and see the children get their dinner and tea, and you come up with us then, righto?"

Rebecca pulled away from him and held out the sack. "Don't worry. I'll look after everything. You just get on your way and make sure you put the scarf around your throat." She kissed him, pointed him towards the door to the shop and picked up the coat and scarf.

They made their way to the shop door, John stopping to kiss the children, who were both sitting silently at the table where Johnnie had been doing his night lesson. Rebecca handed over the coat and muffler and opened the door.

"You lock up, now," John said, leaning over to kiss her again. "Don't need to stay open any longer tonight. Any jug regulars'll know to knock and anyone intending to sit in will just 'ave to go somewhere else, an' they're out of luck if they want to play skittles." He nodded towards the children. "Spend the time with them."

"Don't worry. Go on, now." She closed the door behind him and drew the top bolt across, then turned to the children. "Come along, put your book and pencil case in your satchel ready for tomorrow, Johnnie, and we'll all have a drink of cocoa before you go to bed." She shepherded the two of them through to the back room, leaving the door ajar so that she'd hear anybody knocking on the beer-shop door. "First, I have to run round and tell Sarah that Eddie and Pa have gone up the river early, so you two go upstairs and get yourselves washed and into your nightshirts while I do that. And you don't answer the door. Anyone who wants a jug filled can come back later, although I can't think of any regulars that haven't been in already to fill their jugs for supper."

She waited for them to start up the stairs, then picked up her shawl and went out through to the scullery door.

* * * * *

"Is Grandad going to die?" asked Johnnie, as he and Emma reached their bedroom.

"I s'pose so," she answered. "He's been unwell since March and that's three months now. I don't think you can go any longer being unwell without dying."

"Mr. Barlow's always unwell," Johnnie pointed out.

"That's called malingering – 'least that's what Willie Parker says his pa calls it. It means not really being unwell, but just getting people to feel sorry for you."

"Why would someone want to do that?"

"I don't know," said Emma. "Anyway, we'd better get ready for bed. Let me use the washbowl first."

Emma always said she didn't want to wash her face in water he'd put his grubby fists in, but he didn't feel like arguing about it tonight. He sat on the bed and began to unlace his boots. "Pa's not s'posed to go on night trips 'cos he gets wheezy. So, why don't 'e wait 'til the morning? Because Grandad *is* going to die."

Emma was standing at the washstand in her chemise, washing her hands and face. She pulled the towel from the hook on the wall and dried herself. "Look, Johnnie," she said, pulling her nightgown out from under her pillow. "Ma will be back from Sarah's house in a minute, so get your clothes off and put your nightshirt on and wash your face and neck. I'll wait for you, then we'll go down and Ma will tell us.

"All right," replied Johnnie, pulling his boots off. He hurriedly took off his clothes, throwing them over the bottom rail of the bedstead, pulled on his nightshirt and hastily dabbed at his face with the wet flannel.

"Back of your neck and behind your ears," said Emma, watching him while she brushed her hair.

"You're not my ma," he retorted. "I think I heard the scullery door." He rubbed his wet face with the towel, put it down and made for the door. "Come along."

They ran down the stairs to the back room where Ma was putting a saucepan of milk mixed with water on the stove to warm. She opened the damper and stirred up the coals which had been banked up and left to smoulder after Emma had boiled the kettle at teatime. They did this so that the stove would be ready for getting Pa's supper – which wouldn't be needed tonight, Johnnie thought, because Pa would already be back at the wharf by now, preparing to drive the lighter up the river. Emma gave him a push in the direction of the table and they both sat in silence while Ma placed three cups on the table and spooned cocoa and sugar into them.

"D'you want a ginger nut to eat with it?" she asked, as she picked up the jug and poured a little milk into each cup. The children, carefully stirring the cocoa and sugar into the milk, shook their heads. Ma went back to the stove and peered into the saucepan, decided the milk was hot enough and brought it to the table. Johnnie watched as she filled each cup and then put the saucepan down on the table instead of taking it out to the sink in the scullery as she normally would.

"Is Grandad going to die?" he asked. Emma gave him a kick under the table, but he ignored her. "'E is, isn't 'e?"

"Yes, Johnnie, he is," Ma said, sitting down and putting her hand over his. "Uncle Jim wrote a message to Pa and sent it down by one of the lighters to tell him that the end is very near. You know he's been unwell – he was in his bed when you saw him at Easter, remember? Then, he was up again when you were there last month but he wasn't the way he used to be, was he?" They both shook their heads and she reached out her other hand and took Emma's. "No, he was very thin and weak – not the big, strong grandfather he used to be. You're both old enough to understand that none of us lives for ever, aren't you?" They both nodded. "And... well, it's Grandad's time to die – just like your Grandfather and Grandmother Lynch died when you were both still litl'uns." She let go of their hands and stirred floating cocoa into the milk in her own cup.

"'As 'e 'ad 'is three score years and ten, then?" Johnnie asked.

"Pretty nearly. He's lucky, isn't he? Some people have accidents and illnesses and don't get their three score years and ten."

"Or, they get killed in battle," added Johnnie.

"Yes, some do." Rebecca nodded.

"We're talking about Grandad," said Emma, crossly, "not stupid soldiers killing each other. My teacher says that the war in the Crimea was a waste of lives and differences should be settled by neg – neg-something... It means talking about it."

"Soldiers defend our country..."

"It wasn't *our* country they were fighting about."

"Drink your cocoa," Ma interrupted them and Johnnie, who wasn't sure what the war was really all about, didn't respond to his sister and, instead, slurped his cocoa.

"You've got no manners," muttered Emma, sipping from her own cup with the ladylike air she sometimes adopted.

"Why does Pa want you to go up with 'im Thursday and leave us?" Johnnie asked Ma. "I 'eard 'im saying that to you."

"Well, families must gather together when people die and see what they can do to help, and it's a school day, anyway."

"We're the family, too. Me and Em are."

"I meant the grown-ups. We'll all go up on Sunday for the funeral."

That's why Pa had taken them up there so often lately, Johnnie thought. He wondered why he hadn't realized that Grandad was ill enough to be dying. Emma seemed to have known, but hadn't said anything about it. Maybe she hadn't actually known and was just acting like she had because it had just all made sense to her a bit quicker than it had to him, like when she'd said that about not being able to be unwell so long without dying, maybe. He thought about the last time they had gone up on the lighter. Pa had docked and taken them across the High Street, a much busier High Street than the one they lived on in Woolwich because it was lined with wharves on one side and commercial chambers on the other and was, consequently, always full of carmen, cabs, porters and, often, a constable would be needed to sort out the carmen, cabs and porters and everybody else. From there, you walked through another quite busy road and around a corner to Grandad's house.

Leaving them with their grandparents, Pa and Eddie had taken the cargo on up to the wharf at the Hungerford Pier where it was unloaded for the market there, although some things had to be taken by carmen to another place. Johnnie couldn't remember the name of it, but Pa had told him that the market gardeners all wanted their crops to go there now that Hungerford had become better known as a fish market than a vegetable market. Now there was talk of turning the suspension bridge into a bridge to take trains across the river, Pa said, and the market might be torn down altogether. Anyway, he and Emma had stayed at Gran's and Grandad's house for dinner and then they'd gone around to Uncle Thomas's house for the afternoon and played toy theatre with Janie and Ruth because it had been raining and they couldn't play outside and they'd had their tea there and, later in the evening, Pa and Eddie, Uncle Jim, Uncle Thomas and Tommy had all come in from the wharf and Auntie Sarah had sent Mary Anne to the nearby beer-shop to get a jug of ale for them to drink with their supper. Then, she and the children had all walked back to Gran and Grandad's house, leaving the men to eat their supper which she'd served up for them before leaving. It had stopped raining so the girls decided to play shuttlecock in the court behind the house. Johnnie hadn't minded playing toy theatre with them but wasn't going to play a girls' game outside so he went and sat beside Grandad who said it was about time they had a man-to-man talk. That's when he said the thing about him and Tommy being his most important grandchildren because Uncle William and Uncle Thomas had all girls except for Tommy, and Uncle Jim didn't look as if he was going to ever get married, so they would be the ones to carry the Kentson name on to the next generation of lightermen and something told Johnnie it was not the right time to say that he wanted to be a soldier in the cavalry when he grew up, not drive a lighter up and down and across the river. He felt guilty, though, despite telling himself that Grandad already had Tommy apprenticed and James William was set to be apprenticed in a couple of years as soon as he was fourteen but, of course, he wasn't a Kentson. It was his mother that was. But, then there were Great Uncle Joseph's boys – they were Kentsons and lightermen – apprentices, anyway, like Tommy. But he still felt guilty. Then Grandad had asked him about what he was learning at school and Johnnie got busy telling him about the schoolmaster and the pupil teachers and the hard spelling and difficult sums they had to do now and forgot about Grandad wanting him to be a lighterman, not a soldier... until now.

"You all right, Johnnie?"

He realized that he had been so deep in thought that he hadn't noticed Ma go out into the shop to attend to a customer who must have knocked on the door. Emma must have gone with her because she was just behind Ma in the doorway.

"I was thinking 'bout the last time I was talking to Grandad."

"That's just what I was telling Emma," Ma said, coming to stand beside him and patting his shoulders, "it's much better for you to remember Grandad the way he was the last time you saw him–" Johnnie wasn't so sure about that "–and that's why children are best away from the house when people are coming by to pay their respects."

"It'll be very sad for Gran, won't it?" said Emma, sitting down again. "Being left on her own, 'though Uncle Jim still lives there so she won't actually be on her own. Why doesn't Uncle Jim get married and have a wife and children? He's awfully old not to be married, isn't he?"

"Well, I s'pose he just never met the right woman," said Ma, picking up their empty cups and the saucepan and taking them out to the scullery. As she returned to put the kettle on the stove to warm some water for the washing up, she added, "And you don't get married just for the sake of it. You have to–"

"–be in love, I know. But you'd think he would have met someone to be in love with by now. But, it's lucky for Gran that he hasn't or she'd be all alone."

"Not really. They always have one or two of your cousins staying because they can go to school from there just as well as from home. Both Uncle William and Uncle Thomas live nearby and have houses full of girls, remember."

"Overflowin' with 'em, Tommy says," put in Johnnie. He liked to say things that his almost grown-up cousin, Tommy, said. "I wouldn't want to have all them sisters. One's bad enough."

"Well, I'd rather have some sisters than a grubby little brother," retorted Emma.

"That's enough," said Ma. "I think you're both tired and had better get to bed. Off you go now. I'll come up and kiss you good night as soon as I've seen who's at the door this time." She moved the kettle to the side of the stove and turned to go into the beer-shop. "And, no, Emma," she added, as Emma started to say something, "you don't need a candle – it's June and still light out. I haven't even lit the lamps down here yet. Johnnie, you run out to the privy first."

After going out to the privy, Johnnie went up the stairs while Emma, after her trip out to the privy and Ma's return from serving the customer who'd knocked on the door, continued to try to get Ma to change her mind about the candle, saying that she needed to read a bit of her book before she went to sleep or she'd have bad dreams about people dying. She'd insisted on reading some of it aloud to him, so he knew that she was reading Captain Marryat's book, *Children of the New Forest*, which was about some children whose Cavalier parents die and whose house is burnt down by Roundheads. He thought the book was more likely to give her bad dreams than Grandad dying was. Thinking about Captain Marryat made him remember one of his own books, *Jacob Faithful*, which Gran and Grandad had given him for his last birthday, about a boy who was an apprentice lighterman. Grandad had said it was a good book for him to read, even though the Captain was not a river man, himself, and had got some of his facts wrong. That was in December – before he'd discovered he wanted to be a soldier. Johnnie sighed. Maybe he should have asked Grandad, that day, if he'd mind a lot if he went for a soldier, instead of being a lighterman. Perhaps he should have talked about it instead of being afraid of disappointing him. No, it was better not to say anything – all his sons were lightermen so, of course he expected his grandsons to go on the river, too. He picked up the Russian button that the soldier had given him, from the little shelf over the bed, and rubbed it against his nightshirt to shine it, then pulled back the counterpane and got into bed.

He was almost asleep, with the button still clutched in his hand, by the time Emma came into the room. She must have kept on about the candle until Ma gave in because she brought one in and put it on the table beside the bed. Johnnie turned away from the light and sleepily remembered Grandad patting him on the head, saying, *"There's a good lad"*, the way he'd always say it when Johnnie had done something he'd asked him to do. Then he must have fallen asleep because the next thing he was aware of was Ma straightening the blankets around him and kissing him on the forehead and saying good night, then telling Emma it was time to go to sleep and she was taking the candle and not to argue because she had to get back downstairs to the shop where somebody else was knocking on the door.

AUGUST 2006

"So, how are you getting on with the family history research?" Julie asked Holly.

"I'm actually pretty pleased with myself," Holly said. "I've found all four of my great, great, great, great grandparents on Mom's side, alive and well and living in Woolwich, Kent in 1851. They lived on neighbouring streets – they're still there, the streets, I mean, not the people."

"Ri-ight..."

"I found them on the Streetmap.co.uk site. The boy from one family married the girl from the other and begat my great, great grandfather. How's that?"

"Sounds romantic."

"Not really. They were only eighteen and seem to have disappeared after that. The little boy – my great, great, grandfather – lived with his maternal grandparents according to the 1871 census. I have to do some more searches – with the names getting misspelled either on the original census records or by the transcribers or both, it's not always easy to find people–" She broke off as Julie's dog, Arthur – a rather scruffy, but lovable, collie-lab cross, started to bark outside.

"Are they okay?" she said, referring to the children, as she went over to the window, at the other end of the cottage's big living room from the breakfast nook, where they were sitting with their coffee.

"You worry about them too much. They're all old enough to play by themselves and they know the lake's out of bounds when there's no adult out there. And Arthur barks at everything, anyway," said Julie, pouring herself the rest of the coffee. "Hope you didn't want any more," she added as Holly came back to the table.

"It's the Coulson kids coming over to play."

"That's good. Now you won't have to worry about the boys being mean to Carolyn. She'll have Shelley to play with. Have they been up all the week?"

The Coulson family had bought the neighbouring cottage at the beginning of the previous summer and had three children of similar ages to their own children. Both Holly and Julie found them all a little overpowering but agreed that there was something to be said for neighbours being contemporaries, the previous owners having been a childless older couple who were good friends of Julie's parents.

"No, the whole family came up yesterday morning. Joan was over and said Doug decided to take the rest of the week off. She said he'd arranged to get a lift back with Paul on Monday morning so she could keep the van up here next week. Didn't Paul tell you?"

"Never mentioned it. I never like to trust these guys with the cars myself. If I'm staying up without Paul, I drive myself. I don't take the risk of being stranded here without a car."

"I don't blame you," Holly laughed, but her mind flashed back to a row she and Justin had had about exactly the same thing and she flinched at the sudden pain. She drank the rest of her coffee and began collecting the breakfast dishes together to take to the sink. "I'll wash. You dry," she said lightly, but Julie had noticed.

"Sorry," she said. "It happens to me, too. Let's get back to the family history and your great, great grandfather."

Holly sometimes almost resented Julie having been Justin's twin. Her grief felt like an intrusion on Holly's own. She knew that was silly and selfish, even, but it didn't help. Julie's nine months with Justin in their mother's womb somehow seemed to nullify Holly's ten years of marriage to him and the years they had been together before marriage and parenthood. She had found herself alternating between resenting all her in-laws and feeling guilty about resenting them. Yet they had been her salvation. Julie's husband, Paul, had looked after everything when Justin died and had been a great help with Jamie, continuing to include him on outings with Ryan and himself, just as they had before... only now, Justin was missing. Julie's parents had been wonderful, too. And Julie... well, Julie had been her best friend long before they had become sisters-in-law.

"Too late," Julie continued, peering in the direction of the open kitchen door. "We have a visitor. Come on in, Joan."

She jumped up as she spoke and collected the rest of the break-fast things, putting the dirty dishes into the sink which Holly had started to fill with water, while Holly quickly rinsed and rang out the dish-cloth and wiped the top of the table, replacing the creamer and sugar bowl. Joan Coulson came in, leaving the screen door to swing shut behind her.

"Hi Joan," Holly said. "Come and join us. I'm just putting on some fresh coffee."

"I thought you said Julie was coming up at the weekend," Joan said, looking at Holly.

"Well, Julie didn't know herself as it turns out," Julie replied be-fore Holly could answer. "I only decided last evening when Ryan did a complaining about having nothing to do act. I don't have much work to do just now – brought my trusty laptop with me just in case, much to Holly's disgust. She thinks a vacation should be a true vacation, but you'll note that she doesn't mind borrowing it to check her own email." She sat down at the table again, motioning Joan to do so. "Paul has a meeting Saturday morning, so the plan was for Ryan and I to come up on Friday morning – well, you probably know all that. Holly says Doug's going back to the city with Paul on Monday morning?"

"Ah-ha. Did he not mention it?"

"No. Forgot, I suppose. It's nice for the kids to all be up here together for a few days. They'll have a great time."

"It's good for Shelley to have Carolyn to play with."

"That's what I was saying to Holly when we saw them come over. Once Jamie's got Ryan to play with, poor Carolyn gets left to her own devices."

"Coffee's up," said Holly, bringing two mugs over to the table and then going back for her own. "Doug wasn't following you over, was he?"

"No," laughed Joan. "He's taken the boat over to Pete's – there's something wrong with the motor – it's missing or something. That's part of the reason he figured he may as well come up with the rest of us. I was originally going to bring the kids up on Monday..."

Holly felt rather thankful that their plans had been changed. It had, at least, allowed her to have two days peace, she thought. Shouldn't be selfish, though, it was better for the children to have other kids around – they had probably been getting bored with each other, anyway, by the time the Coulsons arrived yesterday morning. She sat down at the table with the others and sipped her too hot coffee, aware that she hadn't heard the rest of Joan's sentence, but it didn't matter because she seemed to have progressed to telling Julie that her sister would be bringing her ten-year-old twin boys up next week for a few days. Holly was glad she was leaving on Sunday and had the children enrolled in a local horseback riding camp for the last two weeks of the summer, so couldn't be persuaded to leave them with Julie. The Coulson boys were usually fine playing with Jamie and Ryan, but when their cousins were around as well, rivalries tended to develop and, somehow, Jamie was the one who ended up out in the cold. The scrutiny of other children had been difficult enough for both Jamie and Carolyn since their father's death and these twins were not boys who were sensitive to other children's feelings. The screen door opened and Carolyn came in, followed by Shelley Coulson.

"They're playing Lord of the Rings and want me to be Gollum," said Carolyn.

"And they want me to be Wormtongue," chimed in Shelley.

"So, we're not playing," Carolyn said, firmly. "We're going to play Barbies in the tree house, but can we have a drink first?"

"There's orange juice in the fridge," Holly nodded. "Be careful pouring it."

"Can't we have red pop and take it with us?"

"If you do, you'll have to take some out to the boys, too."

"We'll have to go looking for them all over the place," said Carolyn. "O-okay. We'll have orange juice for now and the cream soda later." She stood on a stool to reach two plastic beakers. "Can you go and get my Barbies, Shelley. They're on the window seat. Put yours down here for a minute. We already went over to get Shelley's Barbies," she added for the benefit of any interested adult.

The two little girls drank their orange juice, collected their bulging Barbie cases and ran off to climb the ladder to the tree house which was in a large maple tree near the cottage. Julie and Justin's father had built the original tree house years before, and Paul and Justin had renovated it for Jamie and Ryan when they became old enough to safely climb up into it. Carolyn was the one making the most use of it this year. She liked to take books to read or her markers and drawing pads or colouring books up there. Holly had been a bit concerned in case it indicated symptoms of withdrawal but told herself not to anticipate problems.

"Shelley got the new Ken for her birthday," Joan explained. "That's the real reason they want to play by themselves, I think, although it's a bit mean of the boys to want them to be the bad guys. We'll likely have Joel in here next complaining that they said he had to be Gollum because he's the youngest."

"Oh, I don't think so," said Julie. "They'll make do with imaginary sources of evil. Six-year-olds don't make good Gollums. They'd better not extend Middle Earth to the other side of the road again or they'll be in trouble. Agreed?"

"Definitely," agreed Holly. "I told Jamie the last time that he'd have to stay where I can see what he's up to, for the rest of the summer, if he went over there again. Not that there's a heck of a lot of the rest of the summer left."

"It's gone quickly, hasn't it?" said Joan. "I did all the back to school shopping last week because we're staying up until Labour Day now. But, then, I'm luckier than you two that way, being home full time. Not luckier in other ways, though, believe me. I sometimes find myself crying out for adult conversation."

"You should think about doing something part time this year with them all being at school all day at last," Holly suggested. "Or, even some kind of volunteer thing. You could even do a career change and take a course, like I did. That gets the grey cells working again."

"I'd been thinking of following your example, to tell the truth," Joan replied. "A real estate course isn't terribly hard, is it?"

Holly wasn't quite sure about whether to take this as 'any fool should be able to do it, if you did' or that Joan really was worried about not making it.

"What did you do before Josh was born?" Julie interrupted, probably wondering the same thing since you never could tell with Joan. Holly always tried to be patient with people who acted superior because she knew that their real problem was insecurity, but they sometimes made it very hard.

"I didn't," said Joan. "We got married when I graduated, then I started doing a master's but had to drop out because of Josh. I know, I know," she said, facing their raised eyebrows. "Who's stupid enough to get pregnant at twenty-three these days? Well, I was."

"We weren't judging you," Julie said quickly. "We're just surprised. Anyway, if you were doing post-graduate courses, you shouldn't have any trouble with the real estate course, should she, Holly?"

"Shouldn't think so. I only ever did a graphic arts diploma course, myself. My mother wasn't very encouraging about university and the graphics course would have me fully self-supporting faster. Anyway, if you're really thinking about getting a real estate licence, I still have all the material, so you could look through it before you make up your mind. We'll be coming up for Labour Day weekend for our usual big family get-together, so I'll bring it with me then."

As soon as she said it, Holly thought, it'll be the first Labour Day weekend without Justin, and felt the familiar pang, the kick in the stomach that accompanied such thoughts.

"That'll be great, Holly. Thanks. I didn't know you were a graphic artist, too."

Holly took a deep breath and steadied herself. "That's where Julie and I met," she said. "At Sheridan..."

"Oh. I had assumed you just knew each other as sisters-in-law. How come you didn't freelance like Julie after Jamie came along?"

"I just got lucky," Julie put in, before Holly could reply. "My boss talked me into it instead of taking maternity leave and going back as an employee, which I wasn't really intending to do anyway because I think you should stay home with your children until they go to school, at least. So I was doing it all along – once Ryan got into a regular routine as a baby and I had enough time and energy to do something besides sleep, that is."

"I wasn't so lucky and graphic art isn't something you can stop and start," Holly said. "Things progress so fast that you've got to relearn all the software once you've been out of the industry for any time at all. When I decided to work again, I wanted to do something which I could do around the children rather than co-ordinate childcare with meeting deadlines, and thought selling real estate might fit the bill. I'm not brilliant at it but I make a living and I have couple of dependable baby-sitters for when I have evening appointments and Julie and all the grandparents come to my rescue at weekends if I get stuck. It works out–" she broke off, looking out across the lawn. "I think the hobbits and elves are on their way back for a morning snack. And, here we are with the breakfast dishes still in the sink."

"My fault," said Joan. "I interrupted you. Tell you what? Why don't you let me make amends by having you all come over to our place for lunch? I picked up a couple of roast chickens on the way up yesterday to have cold."

Julie agreed and volunteered to look after morning snacks for all the children while Joan went back to tidy her cottage and prepare for lunch.

The next four days went by in a blur of child-oriented activity and Holly was glad to get home on Sunday evening – early Sunday evening because they'd left the cottage after lunch to avoid the worst of the traffic. She and Julie had not got back to their conversation about Holly's latest family history findings, but she had, from time to time, found herself thinking about the 1858 death record she had found for John Joseph Kentson, a death which would have left Rebecca, like Holly herself, to raise two children alone.

March 1858

Phoebe Walkerston stared at her mother. It couldn't be true. Grandparents died, like Granny Walkerston had died when Phoebe was still a baby, and children sometimes died of fever like Pa's little sister, but mothers and fathers shouldn't die. She shivered.

"'E can't 've died," said Sam. "'E was right there in the beer-shop day before yesterday when I went 'ome with Johnnie after school so's 'e could 'elp me do them sums I can't do. 'Ad a bit of a cough, 'e did though, and was wheezing like 'e does sometimes, but 'e was there be'ind the bar like always."

"It must've been 'is bad chest," Ma replied. "Your pa only knows what Eddie Jones said – that Mrs. Kentson sent him down to the stairs, to find your pa and see if 'e could take the children up to their gran's. 'E's gone to fetch them – tell 'er 'e can take them but needs to get at least the best part of the way 'fore the tide starts to ebb, with it being so cold."

"And 'e's bringing them round 'ere on the way back to the boat?" asked Phoebe.

"That's what 'e said. 'E thought you and Emma would want to see each other. Look, I got to see to the baby. Phoebe, get Georgie out of my sewing – they ain't goin' to pay me if 'e gets 'is sticky fingers all over everything."

Phoebe rescued her mother's slop work from three-year-old Georgie. She led him over to the window where Sam and Will were kneeling on the window seat looking down at the street.

"They won't be coming yet," she told them. "Pa only left five minutes ago."

"What will they do, Phoebe?" asked Will. "Emma and Johnnie? Without a pa?"

"I don't know, Will." Phoebe helped Georgie onto the old rocking horse and set it rocking; he was too young to get it going by himself. What *would* they do? Johnnie had turned ten the week after her own tenth birthday, just before Christmas, and Emma was only eleven. They were too young not to have a pa. Maybe they wouldn't have enough money to go to school any more. No, their gran would give them money for school if that happened – she was a stickler for education, Emma said. But, then, they might go and live with her. Their grandfather had died the summer before last, she remembered, and there was only Emma's Uncle Jim that lived with her, so there'd be plenty of room for Emma and Johnnie and their ma. Pa always said that the Kentsons had lots of business up there in Wapping and, when Pa said lots of business, he meant they made lots of money, so the house must be big, maybe not big like the toff's houses up the hill, but big compared to this. She looked around their own crowded quarters – a kitchen with a sleeping alcove for Ma and Pa and a bedroom for the children, with a privy and wash house in the yard, shared with the other families in the building. 'Course that would be another problem – Mr. Kentson often hired Pa during the summer for loading, when all the steam packet runs cut the watermen's upriver customers down to next to nothing, and sometimes even to go up the river with Eddie, if he wasn't going himself for some reason. Pa knew how to handle the long oars on a lighter. She'd heard Ma telling Auntie Mary, who was her sister, that it saved their bacon and provided the school pennies when he got hired for lighterage work even if he found it less to his liking than taking passengers about.

"Wot d'you fink, then, Phoebe?"

Phoebe started.

"Didn't you 'ear anyfink I said?" Sam asked.

"Sorry. I was looking after Georgie."

"Georgie's 'appy as long as you keep rocking the 'orse. Wot I said was, d'you fink Ma'll let us go with them up to Wapping?"

"I'm s'posed to look after Georgie and keep you two happy while she finishes the shirts."

"Will swears 'e'll play with Georgie."

"He's only six."

"*You* used to 'ave to look after me *and* Will when you was only six and she was sewing the shirts."

"Yeah, but I'm a girl."

"Oh. That really makes all the difference, dunnit? Well, I'm going to ask anyway soon as she's finished feeding the baby–" he broke off. "You keeping watch, Will?"

"Said I would, didn't I?"

"You really think you can keep Georgie happy all day, Will?" asked Phoebe. "Best part of it, anyway?"

"Well, 'e'll 'ave 'is sleep after dinner. That'll take up some of the time."

"What about the tide?" she asked Sam. "Pa's not going to want us with 'im if the tide's against him coming back. He'll want to have a rest first. Maybe he'll even get a fare up there."

"Not unless it was a private customer – the reg'lars chase you off if you ply where you ain't s'posed to. 'E already told Ma that if 'e got going now, water'd still be 'igh up there and 'e'd be able to come straight back on the ebb so it won't take so long which is as good as anyfink Johnnie Kentson could 'ave ordered for drivin' a lighter. 'E meant Mr. Kentson – 'e's Johnnie, too. I mean – 'e was…" Sam faltered, which was unusual for him.

"It's okay, Sam. It's going to be hard to get used to. I still can't believe it, really. It must be awful for Emma–"

"And Johnnie."

Just then, Will shouted, "I see them. I see them."

"Okay. You watch Georgie, Sam, and I'll go and ask," Phoebe said. Ma wouldn't want Sam dashing into the bedroom where she was nursing baby Charlie, especially if he was falling asleep.

To Phoebe's surprise, Ma agreed straight away. She had just put the sleeping baby in the cradle and was straightening herself up, when Phoebe cautiously peeked in at the door, and immediately agreed that it would be company for Emma and Johnnie to have her and Sam go up the river with them. They'd probably find a waterman's wherry pretty frightening on a cold March morning, she said, since they were used to making the journey in their father's larger and heavier boat. Phoebe, herself, had never made a long journey in the winter before, but decided not to remind Ma of that.

She'd only ever gone up the river, past Greenwich, once in her life and that was when Pa had taken her and Sam and Will up to London Bridge last summer. She wasn't quite sure why he had taken time off to do so – maybe he just decided not to ply for hire that day or maybe there were just no vessels out in midstream needing sailors taken to shore and back. Like he kept saying, there were too many watermen after not enough jobs in Woolwich and, likely, that day he thought he'd take the children out instead. Ma must have agreed to let her off from looking after Georgie because, usually, on such rare occasions, it was just Sam and Will that went out with Pa, not Phoebe. They'd gone past the Execution Dock, where pirates were hanged in olden times, and the big Hermitage wharves, which were, she knew, near to where you went to get to Emma's gran's house. After they had passed the Tower of London, where traitors used to get beheaded, and princes and kings, even, were held prisoner, they had docked on the south side of the river. London Bridge was just ahead of them, Pa had said, but they wouldn't go any further because he was sculling alone, and under the bridge was no place for taking children when the tide was on the turn creating treacherous currents. They would leave the wherry here at the Battle Bridge Stairs, he said, where there was a waterman he knew who'd make sure the other men kept an eye onit for him. The men, playing cards while they waited their turn to take a fare, gave them hostile looks until the one Pa knew recognized him. They left the wherry and walked through to a street, which took them along to the bridge, and looked at the fiercely eddying water, which Pa said was nothing to what it was like in the old days – not that he'd ever seen the old bridge himself, but he'd heard all the watermen's stories about shooting through the narrow arches. After, even Sam, was suitably impressed by the dangers involved in being a Thames waterman, they went on to a tavern where Pa met some mates and they all had bread and cheese and ale. She remembered Sam, a few days later, questioning Emma's and Johnnie's pa about working upriver in the old days and finding out that he had learned to shoot the old London Bridge as a young apprentice.

"Are you listening, Phoebe?" Ma was saying. "You won't be much use to Emma and Johnnie with yer 'ead in the clouds now, will you? I said you was to make sure you wrapped up warm. Sam, too. I don't 'ave time to look after ailing children, so you'd better not catch cold."

"Yes, Ma," she said, going to the chest of drawers. "I'll get our woollies to put on and, with coats and mufflers on top, we should be warm."

"Your pa's got blankets in the boat for passengers. You wrap them over your laps."

Ma went back into the kitchen and Sam came into the room.

"They're just coming up the stairs," he said. "Will's gone to open the door. I 'ad to say 'e could come up the Artillery with me and Johnnie, next time we go, to get 'im to agree to keep Georgie out of Ma's way. I 'ope Johnnie'll understand."

Phoebe wondered if Sam had considered the possibility of Johnnie and Emma and their ma going to live in Wapping but decided not to mention it. "Here," she said, handing him his jersey. "Put this on. Ma doesn't want us catching cold."

When they came out of the bedroom, Ma had already told Pa that they were coming up the river, too, and Emma said she thought that it was very nice of them to come and keep them company on such a nasty day. Ma had put an oatcake each and some cheese for their dinner in Sam's satchel and held it while he struggled into the too-big great coat which had last been Alfie's – Pa's youngest brother, who was too young to be called Uncle – after being passed down from his older brothers.

Phoebe wasn't sure about what you should say when your friends' pa had died. "I'm really sorry, Emma, Johnnie..." she said, and found her eyes filling with tears. "So's Sam."

"It's all right, Phoebe," Emma replied, putting her arm around her. "He was coughing and coughing and could hardly breathe, and now he's at peace."

"Why didn't you tell me? You said he was poorly when I went to the beer-shop, on the way 'ome to dinner, to see why you weren't at school. Then next thing I know Eddie Jones comes round after breakfast, this morning, on his way to the wharf, and says your pa's died... I should've known it was a serious matter, what with Sarah looking after the shop..."

"Come on. Get your cloak and muffler. Your pa said we have to get on our way. Tide's way up and he wants to get going so's he makes good time."

They didn't talk much as they hurried down to the wharf where Pa had left the wherry with his apprentice, Barney who'd rowed Eddie Jones along to Emma's Uncle Jim's lighter which Emma told Phoebe he was taking down to Gravesend because Uncle Jim was helping her ma. Pa set a fast pace walking along the narrow street and the four children had to run to keep up with him.

Once they were in the boat, wrapped in blankets, and Pa and Barney were pulling away from the dock, Emma explained that her ma had decided to send them up to their gran's house while she looked after things. Her pa had run a fever Thursday night and she and Johnnie had been sent to get the doctor instead of going to school yesterday, then they'd had to mind Eddie and Sarah's babies while Sarah managed the beer-shop, so that their ma could look after their pa, keeping him cool, wiping him down with cloths soaked in cold water. Then, Johnnie had been sent down to the docks to find someone to take a message up to their relations. Luckily her Uncle Jim was bringing down a cargo, anyway, and had arrived in the afternoon and Eddie Jones had agreed to take it down to Gravesend with the apprentice, when the tide turned later today and they'd taken off some of the cargo that was being carted down to Plumstead. Uncle Jim had asked Eddie to see if Phoebe's pa could take them up to Wapping, before he went down to the wharf to meet up with the carman, who was taking the goods that had to go to Plumstead, and the apprentice, who'd slept onboard to keep watch on the cargo and must have been frozen, despite the brazier, Emma thought. Uncle Jim said the other two uncles would be down this morning – Uncle William's lighter was being loaded, when he left, with a cargo for Greenwich, so Uncle Thomas would come with him and they'd leave it at the wharf, with the jobber, to be unloaded and get somebody to row them up Deptford Creek so's they could go over to New Cross to get the train to Woolwich because that would be the quickest way. They might be there by now. They hadn't been when she and Johnnie left. Of course, they were too late now, anyhow, but they didn't know that. Emma sniffed and a tear rolled down her cheek. It was Phoebe's turn to comfort which made her feel better because she'd been a bit ashamed when Emma had comforted her earlier when Emma was the one whose pa had died.

"I wish you could have stayed at our house instead of going to your gran's," she said, putting her arm around Emma's shoulders, after extricating her cloak from the blanket. "I mean if we had a bigger house or less children, so that there was more room."

Emma smiled through her tears.

"That's nice of you," she said, "but I think the idea is as much for us to be a comfort for Gran as it is for her to look after us."

"She won't want you to stay there, will she?" Phoebe asked. "I mean for good."

"What?"

Emma looked at her, startled. Johnnie, on Phoebe's other side, turned away from Sam who, not knowing quite how to behave, had been telling him about how they had played 'Battle of Balaclava' in the playground when he was away from school yesterday, and stared at her.

"I thought she might want you to live at her house…" Phoebe faltered.

"No, of course not," said Emma. "They just think it's better for children not to be around when there's a funeral to arrange." She shook her head. "No, no, Ma wouldn't make us live in Wapping. Before I was born, they lived in the city and had a baby – her name was Rebecca Jane, after Ma, whose name is Rebecca and Gran, whose name is Jane, and she died of the fever. That's why Ma and Pa came to live in Woolwich, so that me and Johnnie could be born where there wasn't so much fever, and because of Pa's bad chest… they wanted to live where he wouldn't get fever or croup and such, either." She sniffed and Phoebe squeezed her shoulders. "But he did…"

"Ma says it might not be Shellow Bowells," put in Johnnie, "but it's not as bad as Wapping and Rotherhithe for fever killing babies and children. Both of our Uncle William's boys died of fever. 'E's only got girls now."

"What's Shellow Bowells?" asked Sam.

"It's a place, not a thing, where me ma was born – where we go to see our cousins on her side." Johnnie told him. "Remember when we went last summer? I s'pose Ma'll have to write a letter to her relations about – about… about what's 'appened," he stopped and miserably looked out over the river.

"With my pa's relations, you can always get messages through the lightermen, but Ma has to post letters to her brothers and sisters but they can't read much so mostly they have to find some-one to read them and write back what they want to say, 'though my younger cousins are going to school now and can write some things." Emma explained. "They're farm workers, you see, and never had enough pennies for the children to go to school when Ma was growing up. She learnt to read and write when she was already grown up. She says they're the most important things to know how to do, and doing sums, of course. That's why she's always helping people to learn and she always tells me to work hard at school because she doesn't want me to be a scullery maid like she had to be."

"Everybody 'old on steady now!" shouted Pa. "It gets pretty rough around the point 'ere."

"We're making good time, ain't we, Pa!" Sam yelled back. "We're at Blackwall, already," he told the others.

"We ain't lost our eyesight, Sam," said Johnnie.

Even Phoebe, the least experienced river traveller, knew the route as far as Greenwich well enough to recognize where they were. "He's still young," she said quietly, in an attempt to apologise for Sam acting so know-it-all. Sam, himself, was busy leaning over to study the rough water and getting his face sprayed in the process.

"Sit up straight, Sam," shouted Pa. "Steam packet's coming and it's going to get bumpy.

All four children concentrated on keeping their seats as the small boat tossed in the wash created by the passing passenger steamer.

"Be a lot faster to go up on the steam packet, or–" Sam said, jerking his head towards the other side of the river "–you can get on a train over there, you know, what goes to the Docks."

"Steam packet ain't going to stop at me grandad's wharf, is it? And 'ow we going to know where to get off the train and where to go when we do?" asked Johnnie. "Besides, me ma needed to know we'd get there safely and she trusted your pa to get us there."

Phoebe was beginning to wish Sam had stayed at home.

"It's Gran's wharf," corrected Emma. "Grandad bequeathed everything to Gran so she's the owner of all the boats and everything," she explained, then leaned closer to Phoebe and whispered. "Your pa wouldn't take the fare money so Ma told me to slip it to you to give to your ma. She says you can't afford for him to lose fares for what might end up being most of the day although she won't insult your ma with the full amount because she knows they both want to do a kindness. I'll pass it to you under the blanket. Tell her it's our secret." She continued in a louder voice, while Phoebe took the coins and slid them into the pocket of her dress, "But, of course, our Uncle William and Uncle Thomas are the real bosses."

Phoebe couldn't help but feel a thrill of pleasure at the thought of handing the money over to Ma and having a secret – just the girls and their mothers. Ma had only had enough money to get the little jug filled this morning when the milklady came round and she knew the cheese in Sam's satchel was stale – bought late last market day when the stalls were closing. She was probably counting on Pa making some money today which, together with her own wages from the slop tailor, would make enough to buy meat for Sunday dinner, when the prices went down in the market tonight, and potatoes, vegetables, cheese and oatmeal for the week. Phoebe spaced the coins out in the folds of her handkerchief so that they wouldn't chink together. The handkerchief was one that she'd sewed herself at school. She'd have to remember not to pull it out to wipe her nose…

* * * * *

"Ahoy there, Johnnie! Want to come and 'elp me and Tommy?"

Johnnie started and looked up to see his cousin, James William, coming towards him from the far end of the wharf where casks of spirits were being unloaded.

After dinner at Gran's house, his Auntie Sarah, who'd come in from her own house along the road, had suggested he come down – keeping to the road, as Gran always told them, out of the way of drunken sailors in the courts and allies between Great Hermitage Street and the river – to the wharf to find his cousin Bill who would give him some work to do. But Bill was no longer around. Maybe he'd gone home or to a pie shop or tavern to get his dinner. He hadn't seen him among the men working along the wharf and felt a bit shy about going over to ask them, since the customs men were there and he didn't think he knew any of the men moving the casks. It was definitely a Kentson lighter but he couldn't see who was driving it. He'd decided the best thing to do was to sit on the bench outside the counting house and wait for Bill to come back. The counting house was built up against the wall of a warehouse – the owners rented this end part of their wharf to the Kentsons in exchange for having first call on their services which was why it was easy to recognize the lighter along there as one of theirs. Johnnie sat watching the traffic on the water, amid the din of the busy riverside – mostly noise from the coal-whippers at the coal wharf up river – not really seeing or hearing anything, but thinking about his pa. Emma and two of their cousins, Ruth and Becky, were helping Gran and Auntie Sarah bake buns and biscuits which, together with the huge pot of stew that was simmering on the hob, would be taken down to Woolwich tomorrow. James William's mother, Johnnie's Auntie Jane, had gone back with Mr. Walkerston, saying that a woman's hand was needed to make sure her brothers were a help and not a hindrance to Ma. Johnnie had heard her say to Gran that Ma would have no stock left with the three of them drowning their sorrows and likely giving drinks away to the neighbours and attracting ne'er-do-wells, but he didn't think Ma really needed Auntie Jane to keep order in the beer-shop. She'd had lots of practice at refusing to serve people who drank too much – if she had any trouble, she sent somebody to get the constable who lived just along the road, anyway. Not that they often had rowdy customers – Ma and Pa were well respected, although Uncle Jim did sometimes attract what he thought Auntie Jane might mean by ne'er-do-wells. Anyhow, when he'd swept and washed the beer-shop floor this morning, Uncle Jim had said not to worry about putting down fresh sawdust because they wouldn't be open for business for the next little while.

"We 'ave to ballast Uncle Thomas's lighter for Tommy and Joe to take the grown-ups down to your house tomorrow before dawn to be on the ebb," James William said when he reached him. "Not rightly built for carrying people is a lighter – even with Auntie Sarah in the 'old, there ain't enough weight to keep it balanced."

Johnnie giggled. Then sobered as he remembered the cargos of soldiers the lighters in Woolwich had taken from ship to shore, the day the regiment came home from Crimea, and Pa telling the soldiers that he'd brought Johnnie along because he wanted his son to always remember that he'd played this small part in the Crimean War.

"You all right, Johnnie?" James William asked.

Johnnie nodded and sniffed hard. "I can 'elp," he said. "I know 'ow to do it and I'm pretty strong, you know, for ten."

"'Course you are. You're a Kentson, ain't you? Best lighterage family on the river, right you are!" James William didn't wait for a reply. "We're over at me pa's wharf. Uncle Thomas left Tommy in charge of 'is lighter and 'e told 'im that if the worst 'appened, 'im and Joe was to fit it up with seating accommodation and take the grown-ups down river tomorrer at first light before the tide turns. So, when 'e got word the worst 'ad 'appened from Bill, who come over to say you and Emma was 'ere, 'e said for you and me to 'elp him load the ballast, soon as the jobbers had finished unloading the tea they was transporting, 'fore we bring it round 'ere. You ain't been to me pa's wharf before, 'ave you?" Johnnie shook his head. "Come on, then – won't take long."

Johnnie wished James William wouldn't keep talking about the *'worst'* happening but understood that the older boy was uncomfortable and didn't really know what to say. He followed as James William started back across the wharf, and was conscious of the men working there looking at him as they went past – looked like they knew who he was even if he didn't know them. "Where were you?" he asked, catching up with his cousin.

"Missed me, did you? Got stuck with all them girls for dinner, didn't you?" James William seemed more comfortable now that he could make a joke.

"There was only Becky and Kate," Johnnie said. "And me sister, of course."

"They're always there – unless they're over at Uncle Thomas's with Janie and Ruth. Thick as thieves, them four. Me ma left me little sister at Auntie Sarah's but I expect Janie'll 'ave to mind 'er and Lyddie, so's her Ma can 'elp Gran with the cooking. I think cooking stuff stops women from feeling so bad or something. They always do it when the worst 'appens."

"I s'pose so," Johnnie agreed, hoping James William hadn't seen him flinch at his last sentence.

"I work with me pa Sat'day, see," James William continued. "Counting stuff. 'Opefully, when I get bound to Uncle William in May, I won't 'ave to anymore. Anyway, Uncle Thomas's cargo was being unloaded and, like I said, 'e left Tommy in charge and went down to Woolwich with Uncle William. Tommy'll 'ave 'is freedom soon, but Cousin Joe'll be going with 'im tomorrer. 'E's a freeman, see? 'Is brother Bill's bound to Uncle William, but he's done four years and 'e works on 'is pa's boat mostly with his brother now, since their pa's been poorly. But that was their lighter bringing rum up from the West India Dock back there, and you need to be a freeman to pick up from bond, so Bill 'ad the job of cleaning up around the wharf – regular Saturday job that is for apprentices – and come over to tell us you and Emma'd come up and to tell me pa that Ma'd gone back with the waterman and that Emily was at Auntie Sarah's 'ouse."

Joe and Bill were Great Uncle – Grandad's younger brother – Joseph's sons. Johnnie didn't know them well, but he'd seen Bill in the counting house when they'd left Phoebe and Sam with Barney in the wherry, and he and Emma had crossed the wharf with Mr. Walkerston on the way to Gran's house.

"I was wondering where Bill'd gone," Johnnie said, and told him how Auntie Sarah had told him to find Bill, who'd give him some work to do.

"We'll 'ave to 'elp 'im finish cleaning up when we get back 'cos 'e stayed round with Tommy to 'elp with the ballast. Right old sergeant-major, ain't she, Auntie Sarah?"

"Well, I didn't want to stay, anyway. So she did me a favour, but I'm s'posed to be being a comfort to Gran."

"Gran'll be all right all the while she's busy. Your pa was her favourite child, though, according to me ma, so she'll take it hard."

Johnnie felt the tears start to come back again at the mention of Pa, so he blinked and looked hard at the ground as he hop-skipped to keep up with his cousin.

"Thanks, anyway, James William," he said, when he felt he could safely speak again, "for coming to get me. I'd rather be working on the river than sieving flour and such."

"'S okay, chum. We blokes've got to stick together. You call me JW – all me mates do."

"Right, JW."

Johnnie felt a thrill at being accepted as a mate by JW, who was almost fourteen. It made him feel taller and it seemed as if he could walk faster. The term *blokes*, he supposed, meant fellows around here. He'd have to remember to say it when he got home. They cut around the coal wharf, past the dock-gates and through a number of lanes and alleys to, eventually, arrive at the provisions wharf which Uncle Jamie, James William's father, managed.

"Come on, you two," shouted Tommy, from the lighter, "what took you so long. Never mind, get down in 'ere with me and I'll pass to you, then Bill won't 'ave to wait for me to carry a sack over each time before passing down the next one."

The two boys jumped down into the boat and took the sacks of river rocks Tommy passed on to them and laid them end to end until most of the hold was filled.

"Okay, Bill. We can switch to bales now," shouted Tommy. "You two boys get up and 'elp 'im bring 'em over."

Johnnie and JW clambered up on the wharf again and followed Bill towards the corner of the warehouse where straw bales were stacked. They were squared off and tied so you could sit on them.

"'Ope there ain't no mice in them," giggled JW. "Can't 'ave that with all the ladies on board."

"Right card, ain't 'e?" Bill said to Johnnie. "So 'ow's things going, Johnnie? You all right, then? I saw you there this morning, when you tied up on the pier, but you and your sister were busy talking to the waterman and I didn't think I should interfere under the circumstances. I went over and talked to the apprentice and 'e told me 'bout your pa." He put his arm around Johnnie's shoulders. "They your chums, are they? The girl and boy in the boat with 'im?"

"The waterman's their father. Their ma let them come even though Phoebe – she's the eldest – was s'posed to look after 'er brothers while 'er ma did the shirts. She sews shirts, see? You know, slop tailor work. They ain't so well off, are they? Sam? I s'pose you'd call 'im me chum now that 'e's older. 'E used to be a nuisance, but 'e's eight now and not so bad."

"That's 'ow I used to feel about JW, 'ere," Bill said, cuffing James William. "That was when I was your age. But 'e got better as 'e got older." The two sparred for a bit until they reached the straw bales. "The father should get into lighterage," he continued. "Not so much call for watermen these days, not for long trips, 'less you go way upriver. Too many steamers down 'ere and now there's the trains, too, cutting journeys in 'alf where the river loops – even talking about the trains going through the tunnel, eventually–" here, Bill jerked his head in the approximate direction of the Thames Tunnel "–they are. Lighterage, 'course is changing with trains taking a lot of the kinds of cargos we always carried up from the country, but it can only get busier over the long run. Steamers are getting built so big now – got to carry coal as well as cargo, ain't they? So they can't get into the docks no more, and, now, there's more lighters on the river than ever round the Pool 'ere, ain't there?"

"'E works for me pa, sometimes, Mr. Walkerston does," Johnnie said, then corrected himself. "Well, 'e did..." He blinked hard and looked at the ground.

"Come along, old chap," said Bill, patting him on the shoulder. "'Ere, you and JW take an end each of that," he pulled a bale of straw off the pile, "and keep tight 'old of the twine – keep some straw between the twine and your fingers, so it don't cut you. Then I'll top you up with another one... and another one... and off you go 'fore ol' Tommy gets on the warpath with us all. 'E's the boss, see, in the absence of your uncles and me brother."

The two boys staggered back to the boat, Bill following them with another bale carried across his shoulders. Johnnie flexed his hands and rubbed them where the twine had cut into them despite the straw, while the others threw the bales down to Tommy in the boat.

"Okay," said Tommy. "Now – there's your pa for sure, JW. Then, my ma and Gran. Your pa," he nodded towards Bill, while counting on his fingers, "and your ma. Your brother, of course, but 'e'll be driving. Any of your sisters?"

Bill shrugged. "Dunno. Only know about Joe for sure, since you and 'im are driving."

"Yeah – well, your brother for sure or we can't, none of us, go – not with Gran in the barge, 'though you could come and drive with me, s'long as your pa's along." Tommy went on. "I think there'll be two of my sisters, Eliza and Mary Ann. Dunno about Sadie or about Uncle William's Jane, 'though our Janie can likely take care of the young'uns with Kate to 'elp 'er. Elizabeth'll be able to come, I should think. So let's say at least ten in all. So, with the two of us in the back on the sweeps, we need seating for, leastways, eight and whatever they're taking down there. We'd better throw in a couple more bales to be on the safe side. You jump down and 'elp me organize these, Johnnie, and you two nip back for them. And, get a move on. Looks like one of them lighters, unloading the grain ship out there, is going to be needing this slip in a minute."

Johnnie looked upriver to where the lighter, Tommy had indicated, was just leaving a coaster out at midstream, then jumped down into the boat and began tugging the bales into position towards the stern of the lighter.

"You're a good worker, young Johnnie," said Tommy. "I'm really sorry about your Pa. 'E was a good bloke. Brave, too, Johnnie. You 'ave to be proud of 'aving a pa like 'im. I was just a little tyke when he got that burning man out of the canal barge, but it's a day I'll always remember, long as I live. Just up there, it was." Tommy nodded in an upstream direction. "Risked 'is life to save a dolt who didn't know enough not to turn 'is back on a frying pan on the 'ob of 'is brazier – leastways, that's what they said was the cause. Should be made to learn about the river proper, like we do, 'fore they're allowed on the Thames them canal men should. Boards the barge and throws 'im overboard into the skiff, your pa does, then can't get clear of the black smoke from the burning tar, 'cos the deck's gone up by then, ain't it? 'Is lungs are just filled with it. Took weeks afore 'e could breathe proper again, your ma nursing 'im the while." Tommy shook his head. "Bargeman ended up with pretty bad scars but that was better than not being able to breathe proper for the rest of your life like your pa. Don't seem fair, it don't."

"'T ain't fair," said Johnnie, but he wasn't going to cry this time. He was too angry at the unknown bargeman. He kicked the bale of straw in front of him and decided he would always hate bargemen. Tommy had turned away to take the other two bales from Bill and JW, who both jumped down into the boat. Johnnie looked out at the coaster surrounded by the lighters that were unloading grain while Tommy and Bill used the lighter's long oars to steer the boat away from the wharf and out into the river. In no time at all, the ebbing tide brought them back down to their own wharf.

* * * * *

Rebecca had tried hard to sleep but was finding it impossible. She was so tired, couldn't keep her eyes open, in fact, but the jumbled thoughts spinning around in her head seemed to be driving sleep away. Her sister-in-law, Jane, snuggled in the fresh sheets and blankets, was snoring softly beside her. Jane's brothers were soundly sleeping in the other two rooms, William and Thomas in the children's bedroom and Jim in the small chamber they kept for anyone in the family, or driving for the family, who was waiting for a tide to accommodate his lighter's journey up or down the river. Johnnie had taken to sleeping there lately when it wasn't being used. They'd been going to let him make it his own bedroom permanently, now that both children were getting older, and see about getting a bedstead or couch to fit in the alcove downstairs for visitors or, in the case of one of John's brothers, she could always sleep with Emma and put him in here with John. Now it would be more likely a case of Emma coming in here to sleep with her so that they could rent the larger room to a lodger – one of the girls who worked at the cartridge factory or at one of the other places in the Arsenal that employed women or, maybe, the young wife of a soldier stationed at the Artillery. Definitely have to be one with some education and a head on her shoulders. As a widow, running a beer-shop, she couldn't risk her own reputation renting a room to a girl who turned out to be making her living on the streets.

Why was her mind running on about that, now? There was plenty of time to think about what she was going to do later. There was money in the strongbox and in the savings bank. John had always insisted on having money put by for a rainy day, so they weren't going to suddenly become poor. The funeral was going to be expensive but John's mother had money with a burial society for all her sons, according to Jane. That was the way in the lighter-age business, so she wouldn't have to contribute a lot herself. Many people spent years climbing out of debt after the expense of a funeral. She remembered how she and John didn't have a lot put by when their first child, little Rebecca Jane, died. But that was before the barge fire when John was healthy and there was no problem at all paying back the money his father had lent them. She had always suspected that the reason John was so cautious about spending money outside of the necessary expenditures, always insisting on there being a substantial sum in the strongbox, was for this very reason – the possibility of an illness that he would not survive. Oh, John, John... Pneumonia, the doctor had said. He hadn't stood a chance of fighting it with his bad chest. It wasn't fair. The empty feeling that had been in her stomach all day – as if somebody had kicked her and there was nothing there anymore, seemed to well up into her throat, making her feel hollow inside and she knew she was going to cry if she lay there any longer unable to sleep. She supposed she must have been in shock, too shocked to cry since it happened.

Carefully, so as not to awaken Jane, she slid out of bed, found her slippers and shawl in the dark, crept across the room, quietly opened, then closed the door, and felt her way down the staircase in the dark. It was warm in the kitchen. The fire in the stove had been banked up for the night but was still sending out some heat. She glanced, falteringly, towards the little candle flickering in the alcove where the coffin rested on the writing table there, then sat down on the rocking chair near the stove. Rocking soothed you, she thought, perhaps it would help her find a little peace. She should be tired. She'd had no sleep last night and little the night before. Jim, who'd left her, at her own request, to sit with John's body, had gone to bed for a couple of hours early this morning but had been awake again when the children got up. He'd looked after breaking the news to them, but she had finally stirred herself because she knew it was their mother they needed. She'd quickly washed her face and tidied her hair and brought them in to say a prayer together and they'd talked about dying and going to heaven. In the meantime, Jim had been so good with taking the ashes out, kindling the embers to get the stove going, lighting the boiler in the wash-house and putting the beer pots to soak and even going to get the milk.

It was when Johnnie had started asking what would happen next, when they were all sitting down trying to eat their breakfast and ending up just drinking tea, that she had realized it would be over a week before they could have the funeral and that the doctor had arranged to be here this morning, that the death had to be registered and the coffin bought and mourning clothes aired out... The children would be a lot better off out of the house. It appeared that her in-laws had already discussed this when her message telling them that John had the pneumonia had reached them yesterday, because Jim had answered Johnnie and told him that he'd look after things as soon as they'd arranged for the two of them to be taken up to their grandmother's house. Then Emma had asked if her friend Phoebe's father could be hired to take them so Jim had run through the alley to catch Eddie Jones, on his way to look after Jim's cargo which was still waiting at the wharf, and asked him to see if he could find Sam Walkerston and tell him they wanted to hire him to take the children up to their grand-mother's house. The children, meanwhile, had insisted on starting their usual Saturday morning tasks – Johnnie sweeping the saw-dust, then scrubbing down the beer-shop floor and Emma washing the beer pots in the wash-house and polishing them. Rebecca started to tell them to leave it but, then, realised that they would probably cope better by doing normal things.

It was hard parting from them, but she knew it was best for them to be away from here. She'd told Sam Walkerston that Emma and Johnnie would show him where to tie up and asked him to take them up to the house and break the news to her mother-in-law, although she'd know as soon as she saw the children there.

Since they'd normally have opened the shop by that time, the first thing she'd done after the children had gone was to find a square of paper and make a sign for the door, inking in a black border which even the people who couldn't read the words, 'Closed due to death in the family', would understand. The neighbours would respect her privacy, she knew, for a couple of days, but she left space to add something to the effect that personal callers were welcome to join the family and pay their respects, when she was ready for them on Monday. The doctor had arrived just as she was putting it up and had said he was truly sorry not to have been able to do any more for John, and said for her not to trouble to come upstairs with him. When he came back down, he'd asked about the children and whether her brother-in-law would be staying to help her take care of things and she'd explained about the children having been sent to their grandmother's house and said that all the Kentsons would probably be back and forth during the next few days, but that she didn't know about her own sisters and brothers as they lived out in the country and she'd have to post a letter to them. He'd gone over to the writing table in the alcove where he'd written out the death certificate which he'd given to Jim, then advised her to get some sleep and left a sleeping draught, then had gone on his way, giving Jackie Parker from next door a penny for holding his horse. Jackie must have gone in and told his mother about the doctor coming and the black-bordered notice on the door because Hetty Parker had come, through the yard, to the scullery door just after that with a basket of fresh baps. She'd said that she didn't want to intrude on Rebecca's grief but wanted her to know she was there if needed and would send Jackie up to let them know at the church. Rebecca wondered if Will knew that his wife was giving away so much bread, but she couldn't refuse what was Hetty's offer of comfort, so she'd thanked her and told her that the family would be here tomorrow, but that she'd be happy for others to come and pay their respects during the week.

Thinking about it now, she wondered how on earth she was going to get through the week. Jane had said she was staying with her since it was hardly likely either of her own sisters would be able to get here and, after all these years, she was probably closer to her than they were anyway, which was true. Her husband, Jamie, would be down tomorrow, she said, with Tommy and young Joe who would be driving her mother down, together with Sarah and some of the older girls, at least that's what she and her mother had hurriedly decided before she left herself. She didn't know if

Uncle Joseph would be coming – his health was not very good, but Auntie Mary would want to. However, she shouldn't worry as, travelling by lighter, they'd all be coming down early and going back up on the evening tide. Thomas would probably go back with them, and William had to get back to his boat, too. The brothers would need to organize the jobs and hire on some jobbers and ensure that family members were transported back and forth between Wapping and Woolwich. They'd also be giving out the funeral cards she and Jane had started writing out this evening and would finish in the morning. Rebecca hoped they wouldn't have to hire too many extra carriages for the old people who couldn't be expected to walk the three miles from the river to the new cemetery and back. It was when she'd mentioned this to Jane that her sister-in-law had said not to worry about it – her mother had kept up penny policies on all her sons because she said good funerals were expected for respected families in a business and the Kentsons were well known on the river, look at the number of people who had attended her father's funeral the year before last. Her mother might be nearly seventy but she still insisted on having her say in where the money went, Jane had laughed, and why not when none of them seemed to have inherited her brains, except for poor John and William's Elizabeth?

Jim and Thomas had gone to the registry office, and then on to the funeral undertaker, to purchase the coffin and make the arrangements. They'd ordered carriages for the family and said they'd get back to him with the final number needed during the week. That had been before Jane arrived, and she'd had a long chat with William about widowhood while they were gone. William's wife, Ann, had died in childbirth, leaving him with five daughters, including the newborn. The youngest two, Kate and her own namesake who was usually called Becky, had mostly lived with their grandparents as young children and the second daughter, Jane, after her older sister's marriage, had been her father's housekeeper for years, although she had recently become engaged to be married at last. Elizabeth, the middle daughter, was a schoolmistress, and the pride and joy of her grandmother. Having experienced the heartbreak of burying his wife, William was a helpful person for her to have to talk to. He said he'd found the worst part of being widowed to be people trying to get him married again despite him saying that nobody could ever replace Ann in his affections, although he must be honest – he had recently become friends again with a woman who he'd known as a child and had to admit he was enjoying her companionship, a different kind of affection, of course, but then he was a grandfather now, wasn't he? Rebecca smiled thinking about their conversation. William had a reputation in the family for being a bit pompous, but she had seen a very human side to him this afternoon.

Jim and Thomas had come back from the funeral undertaker with the cards and black crepe and ribbons and that was when Jane had arrived with her mourning dress bundled up in her basket because she hadn't had time to air it and wouldn't want to arrive in black, anyway, in case Rebecca had not yet had time to ready her mourning dress which, of course, was the case. Jim had cut some bread and cheese for his sister, because she had missed having dinner, and Thomas drew them all a mug of beer each. During what was left of the afternoon, she and Jane had made the bows for the doors, then pressed their black dresses and laid them over the clothes horse near the stove to air. The funeral undertaker's men and their laying out assistant arrived with the coffin at teatime, or what should have been teatime. William told the men to take the coffin upstairs and said they'd bring it down them-selves once his brother's body was laid out, so the men did so and left, leaving the elderly lady, who used to be the local midwife but now mostly worked for the undertakers now, to go on with her work. The finality of John's body being laid out and placed in the coffin suddenly made Rebecca's head spin and she found herself being helped to the couch with Jane holding smelling salts under her nose, and Jim handing her a glass of brandy which he wouldn't release until she'd swallowed most of it. They made her lie down there until the one-time midwife had left and Jane took her out into the yard for some fresh air while her brothers brought the coffin downstairs and set it on the writing table in the alcove. The curate arrived after that and Jane and her brothers went into the beer-shop, closing the door, and Rebecca was left standing beside the coffin with the curate, doing her best not to breathe brandy fumes all over him. He led her back to the chairs near the stove where they seated themselves and he spoke reassuringly about death and dying and God's will, while she tried to concentrate but could only think of John's fever and his failing struggle to keep breathing last night. Then the curate had brought the others back in and they had stood around the coffin while he prayed, then stayed for a cup of tea, talking to the Kentsons about their own church. Jim saw him to the door and she could hear the sounds from the market stalls across the road when the shop door was opened and wondered at the people over there carrying on with Saturday evening activities when it seemed to her as if the world had ended.

Jane began cutting some lengths of the black ribbon and they had sat and sewn armbands, Jane talking softly about the chil-dren and how James William would most likely ask Johnnie over to their house and her mother would probably have one of William's girls stay with Emma for the night to make it less lonely, most likely Elizabeth who had been just about Emma's age when her own mother died. Rebecca imagined Johnnie spending the evening with James William and his father, and Emma telling Elizabeth and their grandmother about how she was a monitor at school now and the teacher saying she'd make a good pupil-teacher in a few years, something that Emma was very proud of. Yes, it was better for them to be up there rather than here, in the house, with their father's coffin.

Except for going out over to the market to buy some pies for their supper, the men had lit the stove in the beer-shop and spent the rest of the evening sitting around one of the tables there, with the shutters closed as they would remain all week, discussing arrangements for the funeral and for tomorrow when the rest of the immediate family would be down, who they'd get to drive which cargoes during the upcoming week and, ultimately after several pots of beer, of the boyhood days of William, Thomas and John, Jim being several years younger and not involved in most of the escapades, until their one-time little sister ordered them all to bed.

Jane had warmed a cup of milk each for herself and Rebecca to help them sleep. It seemed to have worked for her, Rebecca thought, and wished she could just blot everything out for a few hours, and sleep. Perhaps she should take the sleeping draught the doctor had left but, no – the only time she'd ever taken one, she had felt groggy for days afterwards. She kept the chair rocking gently thinking about how John had come to walk home with his mother that first evening when she'd gone with Ellen to the night school, and Ellen telling her how either Mrs. Kentson's husband or one of her sons always came to walk home with her. Ellen had also said that John had seemed struck by her which Rebecca had said was silly because how could he possibly have noticed her in the passageway with all the other girls. But she hadn't been able to stop thinking about the good-looking young lighterman as she lay in the tiny attic servants' bedchamber she shared with Ellen. Later, when they came to know each other better, she'd found that Ellen was right. John had not only noticed her, but had fallen in love with her, that night.

Their courtship had been slow to begin. The night school was open two nights a week, but Rebecca could not always go. The cook was quite happy for her to have the time off but there were often dinner parties when she was not able to get away in time. One evening, when she finally was able to attend after not being able to go for two weeks, Mrs. Kentson had asked her what she usually did on her afternoon off. Rebecca had no family in London to visit, except a cousin, with six children, who was mostly only interested in whatever small treats for the children she brought with her, often just went for a walk or, since starting to go to the night school, had been taking the tattered old novels she'd bought from a market stall, to the park where she would sit and try to read them. So she replied that she did have free time on her afternoon off, and was invited to come to the Kentsons' house for tea the next Tuesday afternoon and they'd have a chat about what she was learning. Rebecca hadn't realised how much she had missed her family until she came to know the Kentsons. Their house was large for a working class family that wasn't taking in lodgers and, while the oldest two sons were married with young families of their own, the other two and their sisters still lived there. John was a freeman, working one of his father's boats, and had just about saved enough to purchase a lighter of his own, and

Jim was apprenticed to William, the oldest brother. The girls, Jane and Beth, were still attending school when Rebecca first knew them and she found it a little intimidating that, at eleven and thirteen, they knew so much more than she did. Jane, however, soon made Rebecca her confidant, enlisting her help in convincing her parents that she should be allowed to leave school and apprentice to be a wharfinger's lady clerk instead of becoming a pupil teacher. Rebecca received most of her education in the workings of the docks from Jane, in addition to this new knowledge of the job opportunities available to women of the working classes who had been to school and knew where to look for them. And, it was Jane who informed her that her brother was in love with her, but was unlikely to mention it until he had saved enough money to set up a household of his own when he married her.

Oh, John, thought Rebecca, we were so happy. You and me, and the children... Why did this happen to us? She hugged herself tightly as a pang of what seemed like physical pain knifed through her and, at last, the tears began to flow.

OCTOBER 2006

"So what happened to the young couple who left their little boy with his grandparents?" asked Julie when Holly finished telling her how she'd found all her watermen ancestors on an index of watermen and lightermen apprenticeship bindings, transcribed and put on a CD, which she'd discovered and purchased on the internet. "Or, have you still not found out?"

"Not so far," said Holly. "I found the girl, eventually, on the 1871 census, with the name misspelled. She was working as a machinist – sewing machine, I imagine – and lodging not far from her parents' home... so, I guess it was more a question of having a bed to sleep in than of abandoning the child. I still don't know whether the father died or left them or what, though. I haven't really had much time to..."

"Guess not when you're busy selling million dollar houses."

Holly grinned. "You know it's the first time I've ever sold anything that high end. If you want to know the truth, I'm still pinching myself to make sure it's not all a dream."

She really did have difficulty believing that the offer on the rather ostentatious property aspired to by her newly successful stockbroker clients, had actually been accepted, financing arranged and a completion date set in time for her to collect the biggest commission cheque of her relatively short real estate career before Christmas. It had been a busy and exciting few weeks and she was still on a bit of a high. The buyers were young and, at first, she had doubted that they really had the resources to purchase the property. They both worked for a brokerage that specialized in promoting investment in high profile leverage acquisitions that could be swiftly turned around and flipped. Obviously it was lucrative for investors and brokers alike.

"Well, it's not a dream, and you deserve it," Julie said, staunchly, as the two crossed the patio behind the house and made their way to her father's workshop at the back of his garage.

"Hey, Mommy, see my Jack o' Lantern!" cried Carolyn, as they entered the workshop where, under the supervision of their grandfather, the three children were carving pumpkins for Hallowe'en. "Don't you just love his expression?"

"Jamie's and mine have scary faces," said Ryan.

"Which is how it's supposed to be," added Jamie. "Jack o' Lanterns aren't meant to have happy faces."

"Well, I like happy faces," Carolyn said, glaring at her brother. "Come on, Mommy, look at him properly. Grandpa's just cutting the bits I couldn't get out properly."

Holly allowed herself to be led to the end of the workbench where her father-in-law was putting the finishing touches to her daughter's pumpkin. The two boys ignored their mothers and continued to carefully carve out crooked teeth.

"We brought the cookie trays out for you," Julie said, placing the trays they'd brought on the bench beside the pile of pumpkin seeds that had been dug out of the pumpkins. "But don't ask me to spread the yucky stuff in them."

"I'll do it," yelled Carolyn, "I'm already slimy, anyway."

The children all wore old shirts of their grandfather's. He kept them in the workshop for them to wear back-to-front when they worked on messy projects there. The sleeves had been cut back and finished with elastic threaded through narrow hems, by their grandmother, so that the children's clothes were completely covered.

"Go for it," said Julie, wrinkling her nose.

"Come off it, Julie," said her father. "It's not so many years ago that you were doing it, and enjoying every minute of it."

"I guess," said Julie, laughing.

Ryan looked up with interest. "Did Mom make scary Jack o' Lanterns, Grandpa? Or wimpy ones like Carolyn's."

"Oh, I guess it depended on what the fashion was. Some years they made good-looking guys. Other times, you had your Darth Vader and Gremlin look-alikes."

"I bet Uncle Justin made really good, scary ones like me and Jamie."

"Jamie and I," corrected Julie, automatically. "Yes, he did."

She glanced at Holly who gave a little nod and smiled tightly.

"Dad was good at making things," said Jamie, still intent on shaping his Jack o' Lantern's teeth.

Holly envied the objective way the children were able to talk about their dead father. Nine months, of course, was a far larger proportion of their lives than it was of hers so, naturally, it was easier for them. They had already reached the stage where thoughts of him were happy memories rather than the sharp pangs of loss they were for her. She thought of her ancestor, Rebecca, who'd also lost her husband when her children were still young. How had Rebecca coped? She wouldn't have had the advantages Holly, herself, had... She was probably illiterate or semi-literate – it would have been unlikely that a child brought up in a farming community in the early nineteenth century, as she had discovered Rebecca's origins to have been from the 1851 census, would have gone to school. Perhaps she had learned enough about running the beer-shop, she and her husband appeared to have owned, to carry it on alone. But, then, if she couldn't read and write... though, of course, the children must have gone to school – the boy, at least, since watermen's apprentices were expected to be able to read and write and they'd have to be able to calculate, and he'd definitely been bound to his uncle at age fourteen – she'd found evidence of that. Rebecca, like Holly, must have had the love and support of her in-laws in bringing up the children...

"Mo–o–m..."

Jamie's voice broke through her thoughts.

"Sorry Jamie. I was thinking about something..."

"Like what to do with all that new wealth?" teased her father-in-law.

"No, of course not."

"Well, I would be."

"What's he mean?" asked Carolyn.

"He means the money that Mom'll get for selling that house that looks like a castle up on the Sixth Line," her brother told her.

"Will we really get a lot of money, Mommy?"

"Yes, but it has to go into the bank. I might not be lucky enough to sell another house for a while. You never know."

"But we can still have a little treat each, can't we? To celebrate?"

"I expect so," said Holly. "We'll see." Then, she surprised herself. "Perhaps we'll go to England for Christmas."

There was silence. Both children and grownups stared at her.

Julie recovered first. "Hardly little – I'd call that a pretty big treat," she said.

Holly wondered what on earth had made possessed her to come out with such an impulsive suggestion, but recovered quickly.

"Aunt Julie's right," she said to the children, "it would be a big treat for all of us instead of a little one each, so what d'you think?"

"You mean be there on Christmas?" asked Carolyn. "What about Santa?"

Jamie rolled his eyes. "You know there's no such thing," he said. "It's just a story for little kids – the presents are really put there by our mothers and–" he broke off, then looked directly at his mother. "Yes, Mom, I think it would be cool."

"But, where would we be?" asked Carolyn. "I mean, how can we celebrate Christmas if we're in a strange place? We'd miss all the specials on television and the carol service and the Sunday School party."

"We'd go the week before Christmas, so we'd miss the carol service but not much else," Holly said. "But, maybe you're right. Perhaps we should be home for Christmas."

"No, I think we should go," said Jamie.

"Me, too." Carolyn suddenly changed tack and joined her brother, then added anxiously, "they do celebrate Christmas in England, don't they?"

"Duh..." It was Ryan who rolled his eyes this time. "They only started it."

"Well, not exactly," Julie told them then, obviously, decided it was hardly the time to launch into a theological lecture. "So... well, we'll miss you, but you'll be able to meet some of your other aunts and uncles and cousins..."

It was Holly's turn to stare.

"Is that right, Mommy?" asked Carolyn. "Do we really have some cousins there? I thought Ryan was our only cousin."

"Not first cousins like Ryan. Aunt Julie means Nana's brothers' and sister's children and grandchildren."

"Nana has brothers and sisters? Nobody ever told me that," Jamie said. "Are they old people, too?"

"Hey, not so much of the 'old' people, my lad," said his grandfather, joining the discussion for the first time. "Or this 'old' person might just get too 'old' be able to help you finish these pumpkins, then where would you be?" He looked at Holly while he continued to address the children. "How about the two mothers going in to give Grandma a hand with the supper, while we get finished up in here?"

Knowing she should have thought the idea through before saying anything, Holly felt grateful for the interruption. She really wasn't ready for any further discussion on unknown cousins.

"Good idea," said Julie. "Come on, Hol. You want us to take the slime in, Dad?"

"No," Carolyn answered for her grandfather, applying herself to the pumpkin seeds again. "I haven't finished spreading it out yet – and it's seeds, not slime."

"Okay," Julie told her, "but let Grandpa help you. We don't need them getting spilled – especially indoors." She gave Holly a slight shove in the direction of the door and followed her outside.

"What on earth brought that on?" she asked, closing the door.

"It just suddenly seemed like a good idea – not that the idea included visiting unknown relatives. Why did you tell them that?"

"Well, Holly, with two kids suddenly confronted with the idea of spending Christmas far from home for the first time, it was, also, something that suddenly seemed like a good idea." Julie paused and stopped walking. "Anyway, you'd have to look them up – your relatives. You told me yourself, that your mother seemed to be getting interested in the family history stuff you've found..."

"That doesn't mean she's going to want me to make contact with her brothers and sister after all these years."

"When you say 'brothers and sister', do you mean real brothers and sister or her mother's brothers and sister?" asked Julie.

"What?"

"You said she grew up being told her mother was her sister…"

"Oh. Her mother married and had two boys and a girl, but Mom stayed on living with her grandmother who she still thought was her mother. Grace's husband never knew about Mom being her daughter and not her little sister. She used to baby-sit the children until she found out the truth and, after that, wanted nothing to do with her real mother. Later, after their father died, the children – who were grown up by then – were told the truth and the eldest boy, who remembered Mom best, tried to mend fences, aided and abetted by his grandmother. He and his wife would send Christmas cards and that sort of newsletter thing some people do at Christmas time, telling everybody what's been happening in their family since last Christmas, you know the sort of thing… but Mom never reciprocated."

"Is he still alive? Your uncle?"

"My uncle? Funny, I always thought of him as my mother's brother but, of course, he is my uncle. Sure he's alive. He's several years younger than my mother – I told you, she was old enough to baby-sit them by the time she reached her teens. The three of them would be in their fifties, I would think. Mom still gets the newsletter and pretends to forget to throw it out, so that I can read it, without having to admit that she wants me to, can you believe? The brother who does the newsletter writing – well, I expect it's his wife who actually does it – has a son and a daughter, and the girl is married with a couple of children. The other brother has twin boys, neither married as far as I know, and the sister never married but seems to live with somebody called Mark, although whether he's her boyfriend or her son, I don't know. That's all as of last Christmas, next instalment in two months."

"Except you'll have it live this year."

"I don't think Mom would like it if we went there."

"So take her with you? Tell her it's her Christmas present – you can afford it. Does she know about your sale?"

"Yes, I called her last night. I don't think she was really listening, though. She was full of her own news. They're giving her a big retirement party..."

"So it's a Christmas present and a retirement gift–"

"What is?"

"Her trip to England with you and the kids."

Holly looked at her, then shook her head. "I don't know," she said. "Mom always said she'd never go back. She's made no effort to keep in touch with her family – not after her grandmother died, anyway, and, even then, it was just Christmas cards and things like that and she occasionally sent pictures of me when I was little, at my father's prodding. They only know where to write to her because she's always lived in the same house."

"People change, though, especially at turning points in their lives. She's retiring. She'll need new interests. Maybe it's time to take a fresh look at her family. You never know – could be your giving her a push in the right direction is the excuse she needs to get to know her brothers and sister again. You said yourself that she just pretends she forgot to throw your uncle's Christmas newsletter out..."

Holly had wondered about that, herself. Julie was right. Perhaps it did indicate her mother's desire to be involved with her family again. She'd get on the internet this evening and take a look at hotel options and see what attractions were available at Christmas time for the children. They could definitely go to a pantomime. Mom would like *that... she remembered her parents taking her to a real English pantomime once when she was a child. Lionel Blair – that was the name of the actor. It had been at the Hummingbird Centre back when it was called the O'Keefe and which Mom said wasn't very much like an English theatre, but it had been a lot of fun. Yes, Mom would love to go to a pantomime with her grandchildren and take them to the changing of the guard and the Tower of London and Madame Tussauds. All she needed was the excuse and Holly's unexpected windfall right at Christmas time was just the right excuse... The right excuse for me, too, Holly thought, truth be known – what better way to face the first Christmas without Justin?*

That's what Jamie's sudden wave of enthusiasm had been about. Maybe he wasn't really getting as objective as she had thought he was when he talked of his father. Doing the things in which Justin had once played a large part had been hard for her son, she knew. He'd dropped out of hockey last year, but she was glad to see him back on his team again this year, accepting somebody else as coach in place of his father.

"I don't think it's just me that needs to be somewhere else for Christmas," she said. "I'm not sure about Carolyn, but the way Jamie got all enthusiastic when he made the connection with Justin not being with us ... well, I don't think he really wants to do the usual things without his father being here, does he?"

"I think it'll be good for all of you" Julie told her. "Fate dropped the money in your lap – I think you should go for it and, I suspect your mother will see the point when you talk to her about it."

November 1859

"Makes it easier if you 'ave some help, don't it?"

Johnnie wasn't so sure about that. The last time Sam had helped him fetch sawdust from the mill he'd pushed the handcart so enthusiastically that it had tipped. They'd managed to get most of the sawdust that fell out back into the cart again but couldn't avoid it being mixed up with dirt from the road.

"If you didn't act like you thought you was the strong man at the fair, it might be..."

"I promise I'll keep level with you and it won't get spilled. Cut me froat and 'ope to die," Sam said, wetting his finger and slashing it across his throat.

"Even if you do 'elp me," Johnnie said, "I'll still 'ave to ask me ma if you can use it after and, if she says you can, she'll want me to go with you to make sure you don't act stupid."

"Well, that's okay, innit? We won't act daft and we'll give you a share."

Not really okay, Johnnie thought. His ma would kill him if he took a share. She said asking for a penny for the guy was begging, and he and Emma had never been allowed to do it. Their guy always sat on the end of the bar like an ornament until Bonfire Night and the customers would tell them he was a fine fellow but knew better than to give them money. He looked at Sam's guy propped in the cart their father had made years ago for Phoebe and Sam to ride in. Since then it had served three more Walkerstons and was much the worse for wear. Not that the weary-looking cart presented Sam with a problem. No, Georgie and Charlie were the problem. Sam had to look after all his little brothers and it was the Saturday before Guy Fawkes Night – his last opportunity to trundle the guy, he and Will had made, around town collecting pennies and halfpennies on a market day. At four and two, Georgie and Charlie needed to ride and there wasn't room in their cart for the two little boys as well as the guy. Sam had already had to give Georgie a piggy-back most of the way from his house, through Market Hill and across the High Street to Johnnie's house, while Will pulled the cart with Charlie sitting on the guys legs and hiding the 'Penny for the Guy' sign which Sam had carefully lettered with the precious paint from his ancient watercolour set. If they could use the beer-shop handcart, they could put a box inside or, even leave some of the sawdust in it seeing as he was getting it anyway, and sit the guy on top with the sign hanging around its neck and he could push it while Will pulled the younger boys in their cart – well, he'd have to let Will have a turn pushing the guy, too. That was only fair.

Sam explained all this in the alley, where the Walkerston boys had appeared just as Johnnie was pushing the handcart through the door in the palings, between his backyard and the alley, ready to start out for the sawmill.

"We'll come to the sawmill with you," suggested Sam, "and see 'ow it goes. Then you can decide when we get back 'ere."

"I can't 'ave a box in there for 'im to sit on when I've got to get the sawdust, can I?"

"We can put 'im on top of the sawdust," said Sam. "I only said a box when I didn't know about you going to get sawdust. Sawdust'll be better."

Johnnie ignored him. "Well, I've got to get on me way, so please yourselves," he said and started along the alley. "Where's Phoebe?" he asked when Sam, grabbing Georgie by the hand, caught up with him. Will trundled the cart, containing Charlie and the guy, along behind them.

"Got to 'elp me Ma with the slop," Sam said. "Glad I'm not a girl. Wouldn't want to 'ave to sew them things, would you?"

"Emma likes it. She wants Ma to apprentice her to a dress-maker."

"Yeah, but that's not like slop sewing, is it? Them girls learn 'bout makin' frocks and petticoats and such, not shirts for sol-diers and sailors."

"I s'pose so. Em's good at copying 'ow to make nice things. Don't tell Phoebe, but... Promise?" Johnnie watched Sam solemnly nod his head, wet his finger and draw it across his throat again. "She's making Phoebe a pinafore like hers for her birthday next month – with all the frills and the flowers sewed with that col-oured thread our auntie give 'er."

"Phoebe's done that flower sewing, too, on an 'andkerchief for *Emma's* birfday tomorrer. Emma give 'er some of that yellow and the green thread and she sewed a primrose on the corner – don't you tell 'er, now." He waited while Johnnie took one hand off the handle of the handcart to wet his finger and mime cutting his throat, then continued. "She'll like that, Phoebe will. The pina-fore. She thinks she's the worst dressed girl in the school 'cos she says it don't matter 'ow much she irons 'er pinafore, it's too wore out to look nice. Dunno why girls get so worried about what their clothes look like–" he broke off "–'ere, Georgie, you keep up. You're pulling me arm off dragging along like that."

"Arms can't come off," said Georgie. "I could ride in Johnnie's cart, you know."

"You wouldn't be able to see over the top. We could put the guy in, though, and you can ride with Charlie. "'Ow about that, Johnnie?"

Johnnie sighed and stopped walking.

"Okay put it in, but get a move on. I don't want to spend the 'ole morning fetching sawdust."

Sam and Will wrestled the guy, which was quite large, into an upright position in the handcart, with its arms hanging over the sides, and Georgie got into the smaller cart with Charlie.

"See," Sam said, hanging the sign over the guy's head, "if you put the sign round 'is neck and 'old onto the rope, you'll make sure 'e stays up. It's not as good as it would be if we 'ad a box or something inside to prop 'im up, but it'll do."

"Well, you're going to push it, not me," Johnnie told him.

"I want a turn, too," said Will from behind him.

"You can change over when we get to the corner but, for now, you pull them two. Now get movin' the lot of you."

Pleased with his innovation, Sam, after adjusting the satchel containing bread and cheese for their dinner, which was slung across his shoulders, set the pace and their progress was a little faster for a while. They reached the end of the alley and crossed Gough Yard to get to Union Street.

Passing two women with shopping baskets on their arms, Sam said, "Remember, remember the fifth of November!"

His little brothers joined in as he had taught them to.

"Sorry, son," said one of the women, "I need all me 'alfpennies for the market."

"That's okay, missus," Sam said, smiling the special smile he had perfected for when he wanted people to think what a nice boy he was. "What d'yer fink of me guy? And me best 'andwriting on that sign?"

"That's a nice guy you got there. You should take 'im over on Powis Street where there's people about what've got the odd penny to spare."

"That's wot I was thinkin' meself. 'E's a guy they'll want to give a penny for, ain't 'e? I just have to persuade me mate 'ere to lend us 'is cart..."

The woman turned to Johnnie. "Why ain't you letting your friend use the cart, then?" she asked.

Johnnie glared at Sam.

"Stop coddling them, Meg," said the other lady. "That's the Kentson boy from the New Packet. 'E's likely got work to do with that cart and them little devils is interferin' with wot 'e's s'posed to be doin'. There ain't no Guy Fawkes this year, anyway. Just as well, if you ask me. It's an excuse for drunkenness and vandalism, that's wot the Fifth is. Always 'as been."

"There's still Guy Fawkes," Will said, indignantly. "It's just the gover'ment stopped it from bein' an 'oliday. There's still bonfires and fireworks. My teacher says so."

"Not so much of the lip, you."

"Wot's she mean there ain't no Guy Fawkes?" asked Georgie, looking as if he was going to cry.

"We 'ave to go. Now!" Johnnie said, very decidedly. "Come on the lot of you. I've got the sawdust to fetch."

He gave Sam a shove and began to walk quickly towards the corner where he'd told Will it would be his turn to push the handcart. Will pulled his little brothers around Sam and the handcart and hurried to catch up with Johnnie, reassuring Georgie that it definitely would be Guy Fawkes Night on Thursday, as he did so.

"Ta ta," Sam said to the ladies. "Glad you like me guy. Got to run along now."

He pushed the cart as fast as he could to catch up.

"'Ere, Johnnie," he said as they all reached the corner. "I didn't know she'd take on so. I was only bein' polite-like, talkin' to 'er."

"'S okay, it wasn't your fault. But me ma's goin' to wonder where the 'ell I've got to, so let Will have 'is turn with the 'andcart and you look after the litl'ns. You'll 'ave to let me 'elp you, Will. You're too small to manage it by yourself."

"Yeah, 'e's right, Will," Sam agreed. "It's a lot 'eavier than our cart and there's a bit of an 'ill before we get there." He took the handle of the small cart from his brother and continued along the road towards the lane, that led to the sawmill, at the next corner.

"You take that side, Will, and you can 'old the rope," Johnnie said. "Okay? We gotta work together now, ready?"

Will nodded and they pushed together.

"She didn't oughter 'ave said that in front of Georgie and Charlie, did she, Johnnie?"

"Maybe she thought Georgie was younger – 'e is small for 'is age – and 'e wouldn't understand. It was all Sam's fault anyway. 'E shouldn't 've asked them for a penny for the guy."

"'E shouldn't 've made them think you was being mean to us, either, should 'e? Not when you was really goin' to do us a favour. You *are* goin' to let us use this cart, ain't you?"

"I s'pose so. Long as you all co-operate. This is the 'ard bit comin' up. You up to it?"

"'Course. I am nearly eight, you know."

They reached the lane where Sam and his little brothers were waiting for them.

"You'd better wait 'ere with them, Sam," Johnnie said. "They won't want little kids around in there. Will can come with me, if 'e wants to – that all right with you?"

"Yeah. 'Ere, let go the rope, Will, and 'elp me get 'im out," Sam instructed Will and the two of them manhandled the guy out of the handcart. "Georgie, you 'elp Charlie out of there. Okay, Will, I got 'im, so you grab the legs and in we go. There, off you go then. You come back 'ere, Georgie and 'old Charlie's 'and until I get it straightened up for 'im to get back in 'ere."

Sam's instructions faded as Johnnie pushed the handcart on along the lane towards the timber yard with Will hurrying behind him. He'd only suggested that Will come with him because he'd been afraid of Sam coming instead, leaving Will in charge of the others and the three of them ending up under horses' hooves in the lane. Sam, luckily, must have recognized the danger, having been here with Johnnie before and seen that the lane was used by the heavy carts bearing timber in and out of the yard. Johnnie had actually expected Will to elect to stay with his brothers, and even had hopeful visions of them all getting fed up with waiting for him and going on their way. Much as he'd rather not have to, it looked as if he'd have to spend the afternoon carting the guy around with them.

"Get over to the side, Will," he told the younger boy as a cart turned out of the yard ahead of them and into the lane. "And make sure you stay right beside me out of the way of carts and 'orses and there's 'oists and things there, too. The sawpit's on the left when you go in, but you stay beside the sawdust piles. Don't go near the men and the saws..."

* * * * *

At a frown from her mother, Phoebe put the thimble back on her finger and finished the seam. She didn't actually remember taking it off. She must have done it while she was thinking about how she was going to manage to smarten up the better one of the two dresses she owned for Emma's birthday party tomorrow. If the boys stayed out collecting for their guy until after she and Ma had got all the shirts finished, she would have time tomend the tear and press it while Ma went up to the slop tailor's shop to get paid, and to the market on the way back. She'd decided to embroider little yellow flowers around the neck – there was enough of the yellow embroidery silk that Emma had given her left over after making the pocket handkerchief she was going to give her for her birthday. Then she'd check it, carefully, all over for stains and sponge them out and press both the dress and her good petticoat with the hoop which she had starched this morning, before they started work on the shirts, in the hope that it would rustle when she walked. They hadn't stopped for dinner, the boys having taken bread and cheese with them, but Ma had let her stoke up the fire to boil some water to make tea to drink with their own bread and cheese while they worked, the stove being needed to heat the flatiron to press the completed shirts. It should stay hot enough to heat the iron again after it was banked up when they'd finished and Ma went out. She applied herself to doing the hem before passing the shirt to Ma to do the buttonholes which she could not do neatly enough herself.

Sewing buttons on the second to last shirt, Phoebe began thinking about the party again. She half wished Emma's cousins weren't coming. She didn't know them very well and they were older than she was and lived in the city and had nicer clothes than she did. It wouldn't be so bad if it was just the girls from school. She was used to them and some of them had worn-out dresses, too. Although, truth to tell, most of those going to the party would be girls in the upper class who, like Emma, were finishing their education in readiness to begin apprenticeships. Most of the girls from the poorer families were working all day now or minding baby brothers and sisters and helping out with washing, mangling or slop tailoring, just as she would be after Christmas. Ma said that, with another mouth to feed when the new baby arrived in March, she'd be needed at home all day, especially since she could now sew well enough to help her with the slop and they could get more done between them. As it was, half the time Ma made her stay home to look after Georgie and Charlie and sew on buttons and press the shirts while they had their afternoon sleep. A future of pulling Charlie and the new baby in the cart four times a day to take Georgie back and forth to the infants' school, when he started going after Easter, getting dinner and tea for the boys and sewing seams compared dully to the future plans of the girls in the upper class.

She finished sewing on the last button and stood up, stretched and splashed a little water on the shirt which she then rolled tightly and put down on the table.

"Want me to put the kettle on and warm up the tea in the pot for a drink before you take them up, Ma?" she asked, picking up the flatiron which needed heating up again.

"That'll be nice, love."

Phoebe put the iron on the stove top and picked up the kettle to pump a little more water into it at the sink.

"I've just got two more button'oles to go," her mother continued, "so you can press that one and then do the buttons on this one and press it while I tidy meself up to go out. I 'ope them boys is be'avin' theirselves and not getting into any mischief. We should've kept Charlie 'ome 'ere really. Maybe you'd better go out and look for them and bring the litl'uns 'ome."

Phoebe's heart sank but she surreptitiously slipped a small lump of coal into the stove when she opened the damper to stir up the smouldering embers to heat both kettle and flat iron, ensuring that it would stay hot enough to heat the flatiron again after Ma had gone. She was counting on having the next hour or so to get her dress ready, while Ma was getting paid for the shirts then spending the money at the market. She pictured herself struggling home carrying Charlie, with Georgie grizzling beside her...

"They'll make a fuss and I'll 'ave to carry Charlie. Sam and Will need the cart for the guy. And, that's if I find them – they could be anywhere. It'll take hours..."

"All right but, if they're not back by the time I get back, you're going to have to go out and find them," Ma decided. "It'll be getting dark by then. I'll keep a lookout meself, of course, but they're not likely to be between 'ere an' Warren Lane, and the stalls on the 'ill won't be good enough for Sam – it's Beresford Square Market 'e'll be goin' to if 'e's after what 'alfpence people 'ave left over from their shoppin'."

Phoebe breathed a sigh of relief. "I expect they'll be back by then," she said. "Sam's not likely to let them spend any of the money and they'll be 'ungry for their tea. Besides, you agreed that Sam and Will could go out after tea for a while if they looked after the litl'uns today." She came back to the table, picked up the teapot and took it over to the stove where she waited for the kettle to boil to pour over the tea leaves which had already been brewed several times.

While her mother worked on the buttonholes, Phoebe pressed the shirt, which she'd finished and dampened down, on the end of the table where a blanket was folded to soften the surface, and then hung it over a chair by the stove to air. She put the plates from their bread and cheese dinner into the sink and poured the warmed up weak tea into their cups, stirring in the shared out tiny bit of honey that remained at the bottom of the pot.

"I 'ope I'll be in time to get another pot of that 'unny before they're all sold out," Ma said as she finished the last buttonhole and stabbed her needle into the pin cushion. Phoebe passed her cup across the table to her and took the shirt which her ma was holding out to her. "There, that's all done. I'll give meself a breather while I drink me tea, then we'll fold them all up in the basket ready to be off as soon as you've done the buttons on that one and pressed it."

Phoebe took a sip of her tea, then threaded her needle to begin sewing the buttons on.

"Ma," she asked, cautiously, concentrating on her sewing. "D'you think, if you see – only if you 'appen to see – any yellow ribbon at the market that would match the embroidery silk that Emma's Auntie Jane gave her, that she gave to me, that I used to make the pocket 'andkerchief for her birthday..."

"Well, spit it out, girl."

Phoebe picked up the next button. "If you see some, d'you think you could buy me a bit? Just about a foot long..." She put the shirt down and demonstrated the length between her hands.

"Well, I 'ave to go to the draper's stall to get me dozen skeins of cotton for next week – this time of the day, they'll be a lot cheaper there than getting them at the shop, but they'll not likely sell ribbon at less than 'alf a yard. I'll see what I can do – you've been a good girl 'elping with all them shirts all day and deserve a penny or two in wages."

"Thanks, Ma, I'd go meself but it'll be tea time by the time you get back, and the boys'll be 'ome and..." Phoebe tried to think of a polite way of saying that she wouldn't have an opportunity to go up to the market because Ma would have too many things for her to do this evening.

"I said I'd see what I can do, didn't I?" Ma stood up, stretched and then started folding today's shirts, which Phoebe had pressed and hung over chairs and stools as well as on the clothes horse to air. She piled them into the basket on top of the ones from yesterday. "Now, soon as you've finished and pressed that one, I'll let you fold these last two while I'm getting meself tidied up. Make sure you do it right and don't damp it too much as there ain't time for it to air. I'll get some of them sausages, you kids like, for tea. Them boys'll be 'ungry, out all day. There's enough spuds in the bin, so you can peel them ready to boil when I get back. Smartening up your dress for Emma's birthday party ain't goin' to take you as long as all that."

"No, Ma. I mean, yes, Ma, I'll do the potatoes."

They always had a cooked meal at teatime on Saturdays, instead of at dinnertime. Pa would let Barney, who used to be his apprentice, use the boat to ply on his own account, taking sailors back and forth to the ships out at midstream, and he'd go to the bathhouse, then have tea with them and take Ma out for the evening – usually up to the New Packet. He said it was a *'genteel'* pub and a fit place for his wife to have a mug of beer and meet up with friends and relations who also went there. Saturday night was also the children's bath night which, of course, meant that Phoebe had to get her brothers bathed and to bed, except Sam who helped Johnnie Kentson in the skittle alley on condition he handed the tips over to Ma. Then, once the boys were asleep, she could add a little more hot water and have her own bath, leaving the water in the iron bathtub so that it could be heated up yet again with water from the kettle, kept warm on the banked up stove, for Sam when he came in. They were all supposed to be in bed and asleep by the time Ma and Pa came back. Sam said that was because they liked to have what he called a cuddle of a Saturday night – you could tell because the curtains were always drawn across the alcove on Sunday mornings. Sam was always saying things like that.

Finishing the last of the buttons, Phoebe pressed the shirt and folded the last two shirts loosely – because they were both still a little damp and Ma wouldn't want them to get too creased, and put them into the basket. She put the button box and remaining thread into the workbasket and picked up the cups and saucers and took them to the sink. Ma finished tidying her hair and putting on her bonnet in front of the little mirror by the door, took her shawl off the hook and wrapped it around her.

"If any of them boys 'as wet clothes when they come in, you make sure they take 'em off and put them on the 'orse by the stove to dry out," she said, picking up the basket, "And you'd better get down and get that petticoat off the line – it's spitting again outside. You'll probably 'ave to finish drying it by the stove. Well, I'm just going down to the privy, then I'm off."

"'Bye, Ma," Phoebe said. "I'll look after everything.

As soon as the door closed behind Ma, Phoebe ran into the bedroom to get her dress and the embroidery silk. There'd only be enough to do two flowers, so it wouldn't take her long. Maybe she should run down and get the petticoat off the line first, though, or it might get too wet to iron it if it rained a lot, and a glance out the window told her that this could happen. She fleetingly thought about what a mess her brothers would come home in if it did, and laid the dress over the back of a chair. Taking the key from the keyhole, she locked the door from the outside, removed the key and ran down the stairs. Ma must have already gone along the alley from the yard to the street, so Phoebe quickly used the privy while she was there and then unpegged her petticoat from the washing line.

Back upstairs, she hung it over the clothes horse in front of the stove, thinking that, at any rate, it wouldn't need to be damped down before she ironed it, but it was still pretty wet and should dry out a bit more. She'd sponge and press the dress first.

She brought the dress and workbasket over to the settle by the stove where it would be more comfortable to embroider. The girls in the upper class learned how to embroider at school. A special needlework teacher came on Wednesdays to teach them. Ma thought it was a waste of time and said she couldn't afford to pay out the extra for Phoebe to go to the upper class and learn such things. She said it was all right for girls whose families could afford to apprentice them to dressmakers and milliners and suchlike, but what good would they be to Phoebe when she could be helping out with the slop-tailor's work and looking after her little brothers? No, as soon as that regular class teacher had taught her to do blind seams more neatly and button holes properly, Phoebe could stay home and help her sew shirts and drawers. Emma had shown her what she had been taught and given her some embroidery silks to use and a proper needle. Emma also said she was good at it and it was a shame she wasn't allowed to come to the upper class after Christmas when she'd be old enough. She sighed and wondered if Ma would ever stop having babies…

* * * * *

Business had been brisk in the New Packet all afternoon. Rebecca told Emma to light the boiler in the wash house so that Johnnie could wash all the pots and mugs as soon as he came in, because there wouldn't be enough clean ones to last the evening. Johnnie had been told to stay with the Walkerston boys while they used the handcart and was to come home when it started to get dark. Rebecca didn't trust young Sam Walkerston by himself, least of all when there was a likelihood of him showing off to his younger brothers, and wasn't going to risk damage to the handcart by entrusting it to him. However, while he was not likely to admit it himself, she knew that Johnnie's approval, coming from an older boy, was important to him and, also, the Walkerston children were unlikely to have any fireworks of their own unless they earned a few pennies with their guy. She remembered the days when she watched other children's fireworks on the village green with her brothers and sisters, wishing they had some of their own. Even when they did get a few halfpennies for their ragged-looking guy, their pa said that the money was better spent on food and tea and they had to hand it over.

These last few years, on Guy Fawkes Night, they would buy homemade sparkling torches – there were a lot of homemade fireworks sold in Woolwich, although people said there should be a law against it – to hand out to the children as they brought their guys to put on the bonfire across the road on Market Hill. John had always lit them and given them out while she served their fathers, or even some mothers, who'd rather be inside drinking beer than out on the street with their children. You could see the fireworks well enough through the open door, they said. Last year Johnnie had been in charge of lighting the little torches for the first time. As they'd grown older, both he and Emma had helped their father, making sure that the children held the torches properly and that those without parents or older siblings to watch them, stayed nearby until their sparkling torches were burnt out. The two of them would wait until they were all distributed and finished, then take the guy over to the bonfire. Last year Johnnie had let young Will Walkerston take their guy over to be burned and neither he nor Emma had gone over themselves.

Rebecca drew the two pewter pots of beer requested by the stranger who had just come in. She'd been making the change to glass pots for several months now but many people refused to drink their beer from the glass ones which were, of course, much quicker and easier to wash. The children, who had been polishing pewter pots ever since they were old enough to do so, were enthusiastic about the change but she knew it would be years before all the customers would be agreeable to drinking beer from glass mugs. She gave the stranger change from his shilling and watched him carry the beer over to the table where his mate was sitting, already in conversation with a couple of men at the next table who, she knew, were dock labourers. Maybe the strangers were just looking for work. She hoped that was the case and that they weren't looking for trouble. She was glad Ben, the brawny young bartender she employed to work in the evenings to keep out riffraff as much as to serve beer, was due in shortly.

A couple of jug customers came in just then and she forgot about the strangers.

Emma came back in from lighting the boiler, while she was filling the second jug, and began filling a third customer's jug with cider.

"Johnnie's back," she said. "Pretty cross he is, after having to mind the Walkerstons all afternoon. He's putting the rest of the sawdust in the bin and says he'll spread some in the alley and set up the skittles and everything and then do the pots when he's finished – water should be hot by then." She stopped and looked at the customer. "Oops, you said threepenceworth, didn't you? Well, you've got a bit extra there, but I won't charge you."

"I'd pay the extra, love, but I've only got a threepenny piece on me. Just for our tea this is."

"It was my mistake."

"Better be more careful, 'adn't you? You'll 'ave yourselves in the poor 'ouse, you will," the woman said, then smiled to show she was joking.

"Emma's a good help to me," said Rebecca, after giving change to her own customer. "So's my boy, Johnnie. We all make mistakes sometimes. How's your girl getting on, Mrs. Tidy?"

"Oh, she loves it, but it's darned 'ard work and it's a worry 'bout their backs bent over all the time... I mean, they're still growing girls at fourteen. It's not really good for them."

"Emma's thinking about going in for dressmaking. Thirteen she is tomorrow, so we'll have to start keeping our ears open for a good apprenticeship place for her next year."

"Don't be 'asty, then. You give yourselves the time to find an 'ouse that cares about the girls' 'ealth, is wot I 'ave to say. It'll cost you, but it'll be better for 'er if you can manage it."

Rebecca nodded at Emma who indicated that she'd serve the man who'd come up to the bar from the group playing cribbage in the corner. "Thanks for the advice, Mrs. Tidy," she said. "It's appreciated."

"Only too pleased to 'elp. I'll let you know if I 'ear of anything meself. Better get on me way - they'll be wondering who I run off with, they will."

Rebecca laughed. "We'll see you later on. G'bye." She turned to a young man who'd come to the bar. "What can I do you for, Alfie? Same again?"

"Please, Mrs. Kentson."

"And for your mate?"

"Please."

"How're you managing? Your lodgings okay?"

"Do for now. Me mate thinks 'e can get us both taken on, in a few months, as waiters at the big tavern where 'is uncle works. The fellows 'e's got workin' for 'im now'll be movin' on, 'e says."

"That's good. You're best off learning the trade in a big place, if you really want to get a place of your own eventually. There you go." Rebecca passed over the mugs and took the pennies Alfie had piled on the bar. "Didn't see your nephews around, on your way over, did you?"

"No. Wot they up to, then?

"Sam talked me into letting them use our handcart to take his guy around today. Johnnie was with them and just got in, so they should be on their way home for their tea by now."

"Try to avoid that young Sam as much as I can - always something 'e's tryin' to put over on you that one is," replied Alfie, picking up the mugs and moving off.

"You're right about that, Alfie."

Alfie, who was young Sam and Phoebe Walkerston's uncle, had asked Rebecca for a job a few months ago, after the death of his father. He was five years into an apprenticeship to an ironmoulder but had decided not to finish, partly because there was no longer the money, although his master was willing to wait and take it out of his wages later, and partly because he'd never actually wanted to be an ironmoulder, in the first place. Alfie saw himself as a beer-shop keeper. Years before, he had done the jobs Johnnie now did and had, indeed, shown Johnnie how to polish pewter and strew sawdust. Rebecca had felt badly about not being able to help him, but could only afford one bartender and needed an older more experienced one than Alfie.

She had hired Ben soon after John's death. He was good at his job, popular with the customers and she had come to rely on him. Perhaps, he would want to move on when he got married next summer, to a job where he didn't have to work so many evenings, but she hoped not. He was a waterman and had inherited his father's wherry on a shared basis with his brother but, like most watermen these days, both young men needed other jobs to make ends meet. Jenny, the young girl who had moved into lodgings, with her sister, at the Wiggin's house back in the summer when John's father died, was Ben's fiancée. Her sister had, eventually, joined her husband in Aldershot, but Jenny enjoyed her job and the friends she had made and had stayed in Woolwich. When old Mr. Wiggins passed his business on to his son and the senior Wigginses went to live with their daughter in Broadstairs, the son and his family had moved into the house and needed Jenny's room. She had found other lodgings but, when Rebecca had put the word out that she had a room to rent, Jenny had eagerly asked if she could have it.

Before long Ben, on his way to the New Packet of an evening, was going by way of the Arsenal gates to walk her home and they'd go out for the day on Sunday afternoons – the only time when neither was working. Rebecca had been happy for them when they announced that they were going to get married and had bought them train tickets, as a present, to go down to Aldershot to introduce Ben to Jenny's sister and her husband. She was thinking of clearing out the little box room next to Jenny's room and getting a stove put in there to make a very small private sitting room so that Ben could move in with Jenny after they were married. That way, she'd keep both her lodger and her bartender, at least until they started having children. Perhaps they would prefer to find somewhere with a bit more space and a scullery with a pump and sink, but staying here would give them the opportunity to continue saving a fair bit of money. They might even be wondering how to approach her on the subject...

"Penny for them, Ma," Emma said, coming up beside her.

"Just thinking, dear," Rebecca picked up a cloth and wiped the bar down.

"Why d'you think Becky and Ruth aren't here yet?"

"You know I don't know, Emma. Maybe they decided to wait for Tommy to bring them."

"But they won't be here until the morning if they do that," wailed Emma.

According to the message entrusted to a waterman working on the steam packet and brought into the beer-shop earlier in the week, the plan had been for Tommy to bring the two girls with him to Deptford Creek, where he had a cargo of sacks to deliver to one of the flour mills, and see them on the train at New Cross or Lewisham because Deptford Creek was tricky. Rebecca remembered John explaining once how, coming down river, you had to wait until the tide was on the turn to move a lighter down the creek and out into the river again, and it would be well up by the time Tommy's cargo was unloaded and ballasted or, maybe, he was taking on a load of flour, but, either way, they'd have to wait for morning to carry on down to Woolwich.

"I meant that maybe they're leaving the boat at the mill for the night and they're all coming over here," said Rebecca, laughing off the painful pang which came with thinking of John talking about Deptford Creek. "It would make more sense and would save him the walk all the way over to the station and back again. Anyway, it's all right for Tommy and James William to spend the night on the boat, but I don't think he'd want his sister and cousin sleeping there, so you can rest assured they'll be here." And I'll have to work out where they're all going to sleep, she thought.

"You think Tommy and James William will want to come to my birthday party?" asked Emma.

"No, dear, not really. Can you take Mrs. Clark's jug now? How are you this evening, Mrs. Clark? Emma'll look after you while I see to Stanley here. 'Nother pint, Stanley?"

"Did I hear something about a party?" asked Mrs. Clark.

"It's Emma's birthday tomorrow. Her friends are coming to tea."

"Won't that be nice, dear?"

Rebecca turned away to draw Stanley's pint. Stanley was a young man who came in every Saturday afternoon to have a few drinks before going home to hand his pay packet over to his mother, whose reputation in the neighbourhood was that of a lady who others were not likely to cross. Rebecca felt sorry for the boy. She'd just finished serving him when Johnnie came in with the crate of clean pots and mugs.

"Tommy and everyone's 'ere," he said. "Walked down from the station and come in through the alley. They're all in the back room. I told 'em you and Emma was busy at the bar."

Emma overheard him. "Can I go, Ma?" she said, handing over Mrs. Clark's jug and sliding the customer's correct change along the bar to her mother.

Rebecca nodded, exchanging a smile with Mrs. Clark as Emma ran into the back room.

"Sounds like you've got a 'ouseful," Mrs. Clark said. "I'll wish you luck."

"Oh, we'll manage. Have a nice evening, Mrs. Clark."

"They decided it wasn't a good night for sleeping on the boat and didn't think you'd mind," Johnnie continued, putting the pots on the shelf. "Tommy said 'im and JW would get out the way of the party tomorrow and I could go with them. That's all right, innit? And 'e said 'e'd be setter up for skittles tonight if me and JW wanted to go down the music hall. Can we, Ma? We'll go to the early show before all the drunkards get in there."

"I don't know about that, Johnnie."

"You let me go before with Uncle Jim."

"Well, I don't know about you and James William going by yourselves..."

"We can look after ourselves, Ma. JW's fifteen..."

"We'll talk about it when we're having tea. Ben'll be in–" she broke off as Ben and Jenny came in the door. "–here he is now. You go along. I'll be in to get the tea in a minute."

"Tommy bought us all pies and baked potatoes in the market at Beresford as they come by there. 'E says we'd better pop them all in the oven to warm up again."

"Stoke the stove up a bit, then. I'll be there in a minute."

Johnnie left and Rebecca slid the crate onto the shelf ready for collecting the evening's dirty pots, as Ben hung his coat up and took his place behind the bar for the evening.

"Off you go, Rebecca, and get your tea," he said. "Me and Jenny've just 'ad our tea an' she's stayin' in 'ere with me 'case it gets busy. So you can relax with the kids for a bit."

"There's more than the kids back there. Their cousins just arrived – bought pies on their way in, though, so I won't need extra bread for tea or anything, but there'll be a bit of a houseful tonight... Want me to take your shawl through, Jen?"

"Thanks," Jenny said, shrugging off her shawl and laying it over Rebecca's outstretched arm. "I'll pour you out a jug of ale to take through, shall I?"

"S'pose I'd better," Rebecca said. "There's Tommy and James William as well as the girls down for Emma's party. Tommy's volunteered to set up the skittles, by the way, Ben, so James William and Johnnie can go to the music hall, 'though young Sam'll probably be over later to help. D'you know if what's on there's all right for Johnnie to see?"

"There's not much can corrupt a boy Johnnie's age. You worry too much, Rebecca."

"I s'pose you're right. Wait 'til you have kids, the two of you. Be a different story then, you know – you'll find out how it is worrying about what's right for them and what's not. Whether you're doing the right thing... You'll see."

* * * * *

Johnnie snuggled into his cocoon of blankets. It was nice sleeping on the couch by the stove. He'd given up his bed to his cousins and Ma had given her place to Becky and Ruth. She was already asleep in the bed in the alcove across the room. It was fun having the cousins staying for the night.

He felt pleasantly tired but his mind was too busy to sleep. There'd been all that trundling around with the Walkerstons and their guy this afternoon and the satisfactory feeling of benevolence when Sam and his brothers collected enough pennies, halfpennies and farthings to buy a nice little supply of fireworks, though he hoped Sam wouldn't go bringing crackers to school and getting himself into trouble like the boy who put one in the stove last year. Then, after getting back and washing and polishing pots, there'd been the surprise when Tommy and JW had come over with the girls from Deptford, and Tommy volunteering to look after the skittle alley so that Johnnie and JW could go to the gaff, Tommy's treat for his young cousins. It would have been nice if some of the boys from school had seen him, in the company of his fifteen-year-old cousin, going to the music hall. That was the problem with winter evenings – it was dark and you didn't get noticed unless you stood under a gas lamp. Still, he'd felt older than nearly twelve. JW said the turns at the gaff were tame stuff compared with what you'd see along Ratcliffe Highway but Johnnie noticed he laughed and yelled as much as everybody else. They'd gone to the coffee house near the Royal and bought currant buns and coffee with cream in it. JW had paid and Johnnie said he'd owe him because his ma paid him after he closed up the skittle alley of a Saturday night but JW said Tommy'd given him enough money to buy the coffee and buns, too. Johnnie had been glad to hear that because Ma didn't pay him and Emma very much for helping out in the beer-shop and he couldn't really afford to pay for coffee with cream in it and currant buns in a coffee house, especially with it being Guy Fawkes Night on

Thursday. JW said, jokingly of course, that they'd better make sure to get back before it was time to close up the skittle alley or Tommy'd get paid instead.

When they'd actually got back, the men's tournament was over and he'd set up the skittles while Tommy and JW played, then the girls had come out and played, 'though they weren't very good and giggled a lot, until Ma said she couldn't afford to pay for the gas being on and no customers in there and turned off the jets and chased everybody off to bed. It was nice having his cousins over, Johnnie thought, and wished they could come more often, but then, like JW had said at the coffee house, not much more than a couple more years and Johnnie would be apprenticed to Uncle Jim and living at Gran's house – then, they'd get him educated, JW said. Johnnie wasn't sure what he meant by that but didn't think it had anything to do with the education he got at school. He didn't really want to be a lighterman but, apart from it being expected of him, being bound to his uncle meant that Ma didn't have to find a lot of money for an apprenticeship for him and would be able to afford one for Emma. He didn't really have a choice but to go along with everybody's plans for his future. Like Sam Walkerston, who was also destined for a waterman's apprenticeship, had been known to say, it wasn't like you could go for a soldier when you were only fourteen anyway, so may as well go along with it and pay your way. 'Course he was older than Sam and the cavalry wasn't as appealing as it had been when he was younger. When it came right down to it, he didn't really know what he'd like to do – unless it was to stay and work in the beershop, but Ma said he'd do better for himself as a freeman on the river and all the Kentson men were lightermen and that's what his father and grandfather had wanted for him. JW liked working on the river, 'though his pa viewed his apprenticeship as just part of his training and expected him to learn to be a wharfinger as well, just as he had done himself.

Johnnie decided to stop thinking about leaving Ma and the beer-shop – it was over two years away so there was time enough for that. He thought about what JW had said about the American painter. Mr. Whistler, his name was. He'd been down on the wharves, drawing the river traffic on his sheets of copperplate, in the school holidays last summer when Johnnie had stayed at Gran's and worked on Uncle Jim's boat. The copperplate was used for making something called etchings, they'd been told. Tommy said you put ink where all the grooves from the drawing were and printed it like pictures in books – not the line kind, the smooth ones. Like them, only bigger. They looked a bit like doing a draw-ing on a slate only with thin, thin needles. Johnnie had gone, with Uncle Jim, Tommy and Ed Bates, who was a mate of Tommy's hired to ferry the artist back and forth and up and down the river, to the tavern where Mr. Whistler was staying, and seen two of them. One was of the Black Lion Wharf, just up from the coal wharf, and the other was looking up the river from the tunnel pier. That one included the Kentson's wharf, but you couldn't re-ally see it squashed in between the bigger commercial wharfs. Now he was back making sketches for a proper painting he was going to do. Be nice to make your living drawing pictures, wouldn't it? Doing the etchings would be good because you could sell copies of the same picture and get paid for each one. JW said Mr. Whistler was back at the tavern where he'd put up before and had been out drawing the vessels, including the lighters at work on the river and asking around among the old watermen about when they thought the river would get icy. Must be going to draw a winter picture, then… Johnnie wondered if he'd be around when they went up there at Christmas. He was nice – in the tavern, that night, he'd acted just like he was one of the regulars, not like a toff at all… Funny how he'd left America to come and live in England when usually it was the other way round with English people going off to America…

Johnnie fell into a doze at this point, but awakened again a few minutes later. Disoriented, he sat up and looked around in the darkness then, remembering that Tommy and JW were in his bed and he was sleeping on the couch downstairs by the stove, snuggled back into his blankets. Tomorrow would be a good day. The cousins would be staying until they got up really early on Monday morning, in time to get the first train – the parliamentary, that would be – back over to Deptford to get the lighter out of the creek on the turn of the tide and have Becky and Ruth back home in time for school. He and Emma would walk up to the station with them before they did their morning tasks around the house and went to school themselves…

December 2006

Holly had enlisted the help of her stepfather, Ray, in presenting the Christmas-in-England plan to her mother. Like Pat, he was newly retired, and had thought the trip would a nice break for them before settling into their new lifestyle. His family roots were in Yorkshire so he decided that he and Pat would extend the two week holiday to three or four and take a look at the Dales. He understood Holly's wish to make the trip a Christmas gift to her mother but said he'd look after all the hotel bills. Holly wasn't sure why she hadn't expected Ray to want to come with them, but was grateful for his enthusiasm. She'd always rather resented him for taking her father's place and had never really given the poor man a chance, she knew, despite also knowing that she was hardly being fair since her father had been dead for twelve years before he even came into her mother's life. Funny how having a bit of extra money made you feel so much more benevolent.

Pat had warmed to the idea once the tickets were purchased and the hotel booked, and had given her brother's address to Holly. His name was Eddie and his wife was Janet. Holly had written to them both and introduced herself, explaining that they were all coming to

England for Christmas and would like to visit them. Eddie had re-plied, sending along his email address which, of course, made communications a lot faster than she'd expected, although why she had thought ongoing correspondence would be by mail, she had no idea. Perhaps the family members her mother had left behind were somehow slotted into her mind with those of the nineteenth century, discovered in her research.

Things became a little hairy when Eddie suggested they stay with them over Christmas – saying that there were two empty bedrooms now that their son, Brad, had moved in with his girlfriend. Pat in-sisted that they should return to the hotel after having dinner with them – it was all and fine Holly becoming email friends with them, she said, but they might not get along when it came to meeting face-to-face, and the whole trip would be ruined.

Holly, who was corresponding with Eddie and Janet's daughter, Vicki, the eldest of her cousins, by this time, had to admit that her mother's point was valid. Vicki told her, however, that there was no public transportation on Christmas Day and taxis would be at a premium and, while one of them would be happy to pick them up and drive them back to Central London, it might be more conven-ient to stay over. Since nobody had wanted to offend Janet who, Vicki said, was over the moon at the idea of having such a big fam-ily Christmas dinner, it was eventually agreed that Pat and Ray would stay the night with Eddie and Janet, while Holly and the children would go to Vicki's house which wasn't far away. Eddie would drive up to town, as he put it, on Christmas morning and bring them all down to Purley, where they lived, and Vicki and her husband, who had a mini-van, would drive them back again in the afternoon on Boxing Day in time to take the children, her two little girls included, to a pantomime.

Eddie had also insisted on meeting them at Gatwick Airport when they landed and had taken them to meet Janet and Vicki and her daughters. They wouldn't be able to check into their hotel until after lunch, he said, so they might as well spend the time in comfort getting to know each other instead of getting stressed out carting luggage around with children in tow.

Everything had worked out wonderfully Holly and Vicki agreed when, Christmas Day almost over and the children all in bed, the two of them were sitting in Vicki's living room, before making their own way to bed, with mugs of milky coffee which Vicki called milk and a dash. Vicki's husband, Peter, had already fallen asleep in front of the television set, which they had put on to see the Queen's speech on the news since they had forgotten to watch it earlier in the day.

"I still can't believe that my mother got along so well with your parents," Holly said. "She's spent my entire lifetime determined never to have anything to do with her family. And now she tells me that, since they don't have to be back up to London tomorrow, she and Ray are staying another night. We could have booked those panto-mime tickets for a different afternoon if she'd gone along with your father's suggestion in the first place."

"I'm really happy for my dad," Vicki told her. "There he was ex-tending the olive branch, so to speak, all those years and never hearing anything back. It's a pity you didn't start researching the family his-tory earlier – that's what got her thinking about us and how it might be nice to see her family again, isn't it?"

"I think so. It's funny – when my friend, Julie, first got into gene-alogy last summer and suggested I see what I could find out about my family, too, the first thing I thought was, 'Better not; Mom wouldn't like it'. I didn't even mention my discoveries to her for months be-cause I knew she'd disapprove and I didn't want to any ill feelings about it – you know how people are about family history, thinking you're only interested in all the skeletons hidden away in the closet and not being able to see beyond that. Then, after I owned up and showed her the chart I'd printed out of our ancestors, she seemed to really get interested."

"Julie's your sister-in-law, isn't she?"

"Yes, but she was my friend before she became my sister-in-law."

"I just wasn't sure – thought there might be two Julies."

"As far as this reunion goes, I think Mom did it more for me and the kids than for herself. We needed to be somewhere new for this Christmas and she wasn't about to let us flail around over here on our own."

"It must be very hard for you getting through Christmas at all. I don't know what I'd do if I lost Peter. It must have been so difficult to keep going with the children..." Vicki broke off. "I'm sorry. I don't suppose you really want to talk about it to a comparative stranger..."

"Not really. But don't worry. I don't want you to feel like you're walking on eggshells. I can handle it being mentioned now, but it is very hard to live with. What I meant was that Mom didn't really expect to find that she actually liked her brothers and sister after all these years. She just went along with my extravagant family Christmas present... for me, not for herself. And, hey – you're not a comparative stranger. I thought we'd come to know each other pretty well during the last few weeks over the internet. Our daughters seem to be getting along fine, too. I don't think they'd see themselves as comparative strangers."

Carolyn was a little older than her cousins and enjoyed the role of being the eldest after having been Jamie's younger sister all her life. The three little girls had become instant friends when Vicki brought Kate and Claire to her parents' house the first morning.

"They're having a great time, aren't they? It's a shame we don't have a playmate for Jamie."

"Peter filled in pretty well this afternoon, playing soccer with him in your father's backyard."

"I'm sure Peter enjoyed that as much as Jamie did. Took him back to the days when he was captain of the first eleven at primary school – isn't that right, love?" Vicki raised her voice, but Peter did not stir from his sleep. "Seems to have knocked him out, yeah?"

"It does," Holly laughed.

"Well, he'll be needing the sleep, anyway, because he's going to have to look after the lot of them while you and I go over the family tree in the morning, and decide where we're going to go next week to see what remains of the places our ancestors lived in, okay?"

"Sure. I told you we walked along the river a bit – just past the Tower of London. It was rather like going down to Harbourfront in Toronto – all the old docks turned into upscale living and leisure."

"I know what you mean. It's nice to see derelict areas becoming people places, again, but hard to lose our history at the same time. Of course, in London all the dockland areas were badly bombed in the war, so rebuilding really started way back then – although that was more of a matter of re-housing all the people who had lost their homes than the gentrification of more recent years. Dad says the Pool was still very busy when he was a boy – before container ships changed everything and cargoes were unloaded straight onto trains and juggernauts further down the river, I suppose. And before factories and warehouses were purpose-built out in the new towns to create jobs, so the London docks and wharfs weren't needed any longer."

Holly nodded.

"The Thames seems to be used mostly for moving rubbish these days, apart from pleasure boating and tourist traffic, I mean." Vicki added. *"Anyway, I also want you to show me on the internet how to go about finding ancestors so's I can see what I can trace of Peter's family. I can't believe you found out so much about ours. You did bring it all with you – didn't leave it in the hotel room?"*

"No, it's all in my duffel bag," Holly told her. *"You said you wanted to see everything that was printable so I'm not going to let you off lightly. And I have the gedcom of everything on a CD, so we'll get you set up with a program – I brought the one I use with me, but you can download something else if you prefer – then, we'll import the gedcom and you'll have everything that I've got."* She finished her drink and yawned. *"I think it's time for me to hit the sack or I'll end up zonked out like Peter, there."*

"Jamie won't wake up when you go in, will he?" Vicki asked. Carolyn was sleeping in her cousins' room and Jamie and Holly were in the guest room.

"Shouldn't think so," said Holly, standing up. She picked up Vicki's empty mug and started to take it, along with her own, to the kitchen.

"Hey," said Vicki. *"You're the guest. I'll do that."*

"There you go." Holly handed over the mugs. *"Goodnight. Sleep tight. Say goodnight to Peter for me if he wakes up. And thanks for the lovely day."*

"I think I'll just leave him there. Good night... and you don't need to thank me. It's lovely to have you here and to get to know you all."

After quietly fetching her wash bag and nightdress, and getting ready for bed in the bathroom so as not to wake Jamie, Holly placed her belongings on a chair in the corner of the guestroom and went to the window. She pulled the curtain back a little and stood looking out at the street. Most of the houses were in darkness. With a pang, she thought of her own house on the other side of the Atlantic and all that it had meant to her until this last year. She would have sold it, had the children been a little older, and moved somewhere new. It might have made the bitter sweet memories easier to bear, but the children needed continuity. She couldn't jeopardize their adjustment to the loss of their father by removing them from the familiarity of the only community they had ever known. So they had stayed and she awoke every morning to the unbridgeable chasm that Justin's death had left in her life.

She had been right about the children needing to be somewhere else for Christmas as much as she did herself. They'd all had a wonderful time so far. After lunch on the first day, Eddie had insisted on driving them to the Fulham hotel which they had booked at his suggestion because it gave them easy access to the Underground and, at the same time, was a relatively convenient drive to and from Purley. They had all capitulated to jet lag after checking in and had a nap, but had gone out in the evening to see the Christmas lights. She and the children had eaten a room service supper, on their return, and Jamie and Carolyn explored English television, but she'd insisted Pat and Ray go and have a proper meal in the hotel restaurant on the promise that she would have a drink with them, in their adjoining room, once the children were in bed.

After seeing Buckingham Palace, which Carolyn didn't think looked like a palace at all, watching the Changing of the Guard and walking through St. James's Park, most of Saturday had been spent amid the Christmas splendour of Regent Street's famous Hamleys and at Selfridges, where the children lined up to go on the giant slide which was called a helter skelter here. They'd conspired among themselves to buy each other small Christmas gifts without being overlooked and, weighed down with packages and afraid they'd be certain to lose something along the way, they'd taken a taxi back to the hotel. After a certain amount of subterfuge, everybody had managed to wrap the presents before going back out to visit Trafalgar Square to see the lights and the great Christmas tree and to sing carols.

On their return to the hotel, Ray had sent Holly and Pat off to have dinner together, settling for room service chicken and chips with the children, himself. He'd bought crayons and re-usable adhesive and set Jamie and Carolyn to work crayoning a Christmas tree on a large, slit open Selfridges bag to stick on the wall, then helped them pile the gifts at the foot of it to surprise Pat and Holly when they came back.

Yesterday they'd taken a tourist bus trip and learned a lot about London that even Pat, who'd grown up here, hadn't known and, after lunch at a McDonald's, had visited the Tower, then walked through the 'gentrified' St. Katherine's Dock, along the river path towards Wapping. This was where their ancestors had once lived and worked. It was hard to imagine how it would have been, Holly thought. Tower Bridge would not have been built yet, and the river would have been full of ships, lighters, barges and early steamers when John Joseph and his father and brothers were busily moving cargoes to and from the wharfs and docks on the Thames. Now there were only marinas and upscale apartments, bars and boutiques to be seen along the river. It wasn't that she'd expected everything to be as she imagined it once had been – after all, regenerating docklands was the trend in most major cities. It was... that was it – she'd become so involved with what she imagined the lives of her ancestors to have been that the modern day version was disappointing. Silly, really, to have become so caught up in perceptions of a past that she knew so little about.

"Mom, what's wrong? Why are you standing there staring out of the window?"

Holly started and turned to see Jamie sitting up in his bed peering sleepily at her in the dim light. She dropped the curtain and hurried over to sit down beside him.

"Did I wake you? I'm so sorry – I shouldn't have let the light in like that. Come on, you lie down and get back to sleep."

He laid back on his pillow. "You didn't wake me up. I just did. It's been a nice Christmas, hasn't it Mommy?"

"I'm glad you think so, honey."

"It's amazing here, isn't it? I'm glad we came – I didn't really want to be at home for Christmas without Dad…"

"Yes, I know, dear."

"It's hard – learning to live without him, isn't it, Mom?"

"Yes, it's hard, Jamie, but we're getting there. We'll always miss him, but we have to go on with our lives. That's what he would want us to do."

"I know. I wish he was here though to see all the neat stuff we're getting to see and to meet Nana's relatives."

Holly wondered why he perceived the cousins as Nana's relatives and not his own.

"They're our relatives, too. Yours and mine, not just Nana's."

"I suppose they seem like they're just hers because she kept them secret all this time."

"Not secret exactly. I told you – something happened a long time ago that caused a rift. Now, how about you getting back to sleep? I'm going to get into my bed now, and we'll both go to sleep."

"Okay" Jamie replied, then said. "They say 'relations' instead of relatives, don't they?"

"There are lots of things they say differently from us. All the English-speaking countries have different words for some things. Expressions, too."

"Like 'a proper Charlie'? That's one I like. I can't wait to see what Ryan does when I say that when we get home. Maybe, I'll even have an English accent by then." He was starting to sound sleepy again. "'Night, Mom."

Holly smoothed his tousled hair, then bent over and kissed him. "Good night, Jamie."

January 1862

"There's the vessel we'll be starting to unload in the morning," said Jim, pointing to a ship anchored out at midstream. "Tea. We're bringing it into the Colonial Wharf along there. We'll 'ave three lighters on the job – two of our own and one hire. The other three are all working in the Docks just now. Winter, you'll find we do more loading to ship or to wharf than transporting. Your Pa didn't get into a lot of that down there in Woolwich, since 'e was located there more for the 'ops and getting the seasonal cargos up to market. Nice business that was 'til the trains started to take it away from us. Another thing, days when we *are* transporting and the unloading's done, like now, and we're back early, your Gran expects us 'ome for tea. So we'd better look sharp."

Johnnie could just about make out the shape of the vessel through the icy fog that had developed over the river during the late afternoon, in the wake of the pale January sun that had shown itself earlier in the day to, eventually, become hidden by cloud. He finished tying the lighter's mooring ropes to the pier which, attached to the wharf provided moorings for all the Kentson lighters if necessary, then shivered as he stood up. Jim noticed the shiver and laughed.

"Not used to outdoor work in the winter, are you, son?" he said. "Been working in that beer-shop too long. You'll get used to it. We all 'ad to work down 'ere on the wharf after school so we didn't 'ave the problem of getting used to the weather come time to start our apprenticeships proper. 'Course January's not a nice time to start the job. I know your ma wanted us to put it off until the springtime – an' you, too, prob'ly – but with Bill getting 'is freedom next month and James William being 'alfway through and experienced enough to sweep regular, we need to get a new apprentice started now. It was that or me 'aving to hire on a new regular with Steve and Dick driving their pa's boat steady now 'is rheumatism's got the better of 'im. So that's why we insisted on you starting in this icy weather – jus' so's you know. Didn't want to discuss the 'ole business while Steve was with us."

"I'm not cold," Johnnie said defensively, then grinned. "Just somebody walking over me grave, that's all." All the same, he wished he'd been able to suppress the shiver. He'd been proud of his performance helping to manoeuvre the lighter around other vessels, during the short trip down from Irongate after Steve left to go home from there, and wanted to impress his apprentice master that he would be as useful as if he'd grown up in Wapping like the rest of the family. "You got anything you need me to do down 'ere, Uncle Jim? Or shall I get me box out?"

"Nah, too chilly out 'ere tonight and your Gran's expecting you. I'll lock up the sweeps and you can jump down and throw up your bundles, then pull the tarp over – no sense in risking a barge full of snow to dig out in the morning. And," he paused, "no need for the 'Uncle', son. You're me apprentice now. Jim's fine."

Johnnie grinned and touched his cap in a sketchy salute then jumped down and clambered over to the stern, retrieved his luggage and the small keg of porter his mother had sent with him. Jim took the oars up and locked them away in the counting house, then came back along the pier, shouldered the keg of porter and began to make his way home. Johnnie, meanwhile, pulled a tarp over the length of the barge and tied it down, wondering if it really would snow. Jim was good at foretelling weather conditions, he'd always been told. He climbed back up onto the pier, picked up the small wooden trunk containing his belongings and the bundled quilt his mother had insisted he take with him and looked back at the river. The vessel Jim had pointed out was no longer visible in the gloom, but he could hear low voices and the distinctive splash of a lighter's long oars above the fog-muted din of the adjoining wharves.

"That you there, young Johnnie?"

It was his Uncle Thomas's voice. Johnnie could now see the bow of the lighter and put down the bundle and trunk again.

"It's me," he said, "I just covered Uncle Jim's barge." He stepped forward to catch the rope his cousin Bill, threw up to him, as the boat moved in alongside the pier.

"'Ello there, Johnnie. Nasty day for travelling up the river. You must be chilled to the bone. Pull 'er all the way up – we've got goods to unload. Nobody else coming in 'ere tonight, any'ow."

Bill sprang up onto the pier and caught the rope which Thomas, shipping the oar he'd been using to steer the boat in, threw up to him. "Jim's gone on 'ome, eh?"

Johnnie finished tying his rope and coiled the remainder. "He took the keg of porter that Ma sent for Gran up to the house. I was just about to follow 'im when I 'eard you comin' in."

Bill finished tying his rope and straightened up. "Nice to see you, Johnnie. You run off up to your Gran's now and get warmed up. We need to get someone to help unload from the warehouse there – I'd better get them to bring out some lanterns, too. It's dark early, innit? See you later. Jim's goin' to bring you along to the Prince – make sure everyone knows who you are, and we got to celebrate your binding, ain't we?"

Johnnie was glad to be told to go in. "Be seein' you, then," he said, picking up his things again. He wasn't really cold. In fact, his clothes were quite dry under the heavy waterman's oilskin which had belonged to his pa. He was glad Bill had talked about getting chilled, though, because Jim had made him feel childish for shivering. He did feel hungry, however. Jim had bought pork pies and coffee for their dinner, from a stall near Watermen's Hall, after they'd gone in to sign his indenture, but it seemed like a long time ago now.

It was going to feel strange living here with Gran and Uncle Jim, and the housekeeper who Jim had recently installed to help Gran now that she was getting too old to look after the house alone. His cousins, Kate and Becky, who had spent much of their childhood living at their grandparents' house, now both worked long days as lady clerks in a warehouse and lived with their father and stepmother, where supper was ready for them when they arrived home at night and the only demands made on the short amount of time they had to call their own was that their room be kept clean and tidy. Johnnie had met the housekeeper, whose name was Sally, before Christmas. Ma had taken a day off from the beer-shop and they'd come up, by train, to make the arrangements like the clothes he'd need and where he would sleep when he started his apprenticeship. Regular train and steam packet services made the journey much shorter than it used to be. Ma had said that, while she felt like a bit of a traitor to the Thames watermen, time and tide wait for nobody. He understood what she meant – trains would be the way both goods and people travelled in the future. He had a feeling that Ma disapproved of Sally. She hadn't said anything to him, but JW had nudged him and winked, when he and Jim were staying the night back in October, and Jim had first talked about getting a housekeeper. Johnnie decided that what Jim and Sally did was none of his business and, anyway, it would be nice having someone around who was paid to clean and make meals. Maybe she even cleaned boots... That made he feel a bit ashamed of himself, but he decided it was a natural reaction to no longer having to do all the menial jobs around the beer-shop that had been his responsibility for as long as he could remember, and he shouldn't feel badly. He knew he was going to have to work hard and do his part to maintain the Kentsons' good name on the river. Lighterage jobs depended on reputation and he wouldn't be allowed to slack off. JW had told him their uncles were stern taskmasters, although why they all imagined that working in the beer-shop was a soft job, he couldn't imagine. Thinking about that, he wondered how Will Walkerston was getting on. He'd talked his mother into employing Will and spent the last week showing the boy everything that he had to do. He was only ten but Johnnie, who had once been his monitor at school, was pretty sure he was capable. He also knew that Will worshipped him and wouldn't let him down. The only trouble was that the Walkerstons' pa was working for the steam packet company now and, with the opportunities for more contact with upriver watermen, was on the lookout to get back to wherrying at stairs above bridge where watermen could still make a living, and might well move up to

London if he found an opening. Perhaps, he should have chosen a boy who wasn't likely to move away. On the other hand, according to Phoebe, her pa had been talking about moving upriver for years but never had, although she'd told him that she wouldn't mind moving now that he was off to Wapping and she hardly ever saw Emma anymore. Poor Phoebe, Johnnie thought, we're all moving out into the world and she's stuck at home helping her ma make shirts and look after babies.

Arriving at the bend in the road still deep in thought, he was startled out of his reverie by two small girls running to meet him. They were Lyddie, the youngest of Uncle Thomas's many daughters and JW's little sister, Emily.

"Where've you been, Johnnie? Uncle Jim said you was just be'ind 'im…"

"We're frozen cold from waiting for you."

"Why didn't you put your coats on then?" asked Johnnie.

"We thought you was just be'ind Uncle Jim, I told you," said Lyddie. "'E said 'e didn't know why you 'adn't caught up with 'im."

"All right, all right. I'm sorry. Your pa and Cousin Bill pulled in and I stopped to talk to them. Come on, now, and let's get inside where it's warm," Johnnie said, waving them ahead of him as they reached the door. "What are you doing here, anyway?"

He closed the door behind them.

"Emily goes to the infants' school now, did you know that? And I walk home with her – only her ma works down at her pa's wharf now that she's big enough to go to school, so she comes to my house."

"But, today," little Emily chimed in, "Auntie Sarah made ginger biscuits and currant cakes because of you coming to stay and we're all having tea at Gran's with you."

Johnnie put his luggage down at the bottom of the stairs, took off the oilskin and his pea-coat and hung them on a hook on the wall alongside Jim's, then let his little cousins pull him into the big kitchen at the end of the passage.

"'Ello, Johnnie," Auntie Sarah squeezed his shoulders and offered her cheek to be kissed. "You grow taller every time I see you."

"Where've you been, young man?" demanded Gran who was already ensconced at the head of the table with the teapot in front of her.

"Sorry Gran." Johnnie went forward to kiss her proffered cheek. "I stopped to speak to Uncle Thomas and Bill."

"Well, off you go out to the scullery. Jim's left some hot water out there for you to wash your hands and face. Now, you girls sit down and stop bouncing around. No, Lyddie, Jim and Sally do not need help from you toasting the muffins."

Lyddie, who had been heading for the old fashioned fireplace where the muffins were being toasted, pouted and changed direction. Her mother pointed her finger at her and indicated that she sit at the table. Johnnie crossed to the scullery door and went to wash off the day's grime.

Coming back in, he found everybody seated at the table.

"Come on, Johnnie," said Emily. "We're not allowed to start till you're sitting down."

"Here, in between me an' Emily," Lyddie instructed.

"You're the guest of honour, Johnnie, so they insist you sit with them," said Auntie Sarah. "'Ow's your ma? She's going to miss you, isn't she? Such a shame…"

Johnnie knew that she meant it was a shame that his father wasn't alive to be his apprentice master in Woolwich where they would have continued the old life, splitting time between the river and the beer-shop and ma wouldn't have had to work as hard as she did.

"First Emma, now you... she must feel like 'er 'ole life is ending. 'Course with Eliza and Mary Ann going off to Australia like they've decided, I'll be feeling the same way meself soon enough I don't doubt but, at least, I 'ad them all 'ome all the while they was growing up."

Her middle two daughters were intending to take assisted passages to the state of Victoria in Australia where there were not enough women to go round and the government encouraged young women to embark on new lives – which meant *'find a husband'*, their brother Tommy said.

"Emma was able to come 'ome for Christmas," Johnnie told his aunt. "We 'ad a very nice Christmas dinner and everything. All the regulars went together and 'ad a party for Emma comin' 'ome and me goin' away. Ben and Jenny arranged it all. Ma and me didn't even know. They pretended somebody'd rented the skittle alley for a party – we do that sometimes when there's no tournaments, putting a brazier in the opening to take the chill off if it's winter. I even 'elped put up decorations not knowing it was our party. And, Emma'd only just got in from Lewisham – they didn't let the girls leave until six. Christmas Eve, it was."

"That's nice, Johnnie," his grandmother interrupted when he stopped for breath. "Now, Jim can say grace and we'll get on with our tea..."

After tea, Johnnie took his belongings up to his bedroom, the big attic room that his father and uncles had shared as young boys. He put his clothes in the drawers of the chest and hung his Sunday suit in the big wardrobe where it looked a bit lost all by itself, then put the books he'd brought with him on a shelf, where they, too, looked a little lonely. It was a large room for one person, more than twice the size of his room at home, but he'd be sharing it, he knew, when Eddie, who still drove Pa's lighter, and his assistant, Geordie, the northerner whose name wasn't really Geordie at all, were up this way, waiting for the tide. It had a big bedstead and another trundle bed. He looked out of the back window but it was quite dark now. In the daytime, you could see across the rooftops and between warehouses to the river and over to the Surrey side. Looking down, beyond the back yard, you saw some of the poverty-ridden courts and allies in between here and the river. From the front window, the masts of ships beyond the walls of the great Western Dock, were visible. He pulled the heavy curtains across both windows to keep out the draught. The fire had been lit but he didn't imagine they intended to let him have a fire every day; it was just to rid the room of its chilly dampness from lack of regular use. He could hear somebody coming up the stairs.

"You ready to come along to the Prince with us, Johnnie?" Jim put his head around the half open door. "We'll walk along with Sarah and the girls and pick James William up on the way – 'e should be 'ome by now. Thomas should be in by the time we get to 'im and Sarah's 'ouse, too. Spoiling you, eh?" he added, seeing that the fire was lit. He advanced and went over to the fireplace. "'Ope you're not expecting a warm bedroom every day."

"'Course not. I expect Sally just noticed how damp it was when she was airing it out ready for me."

"She even seems to have left you with enough coal to keep it going for the evening. Better put a couple of bits on before we go or it'll be out by the time we get back."

He moved the fireguard aside and picked up a piece of coal with the tongs hanging beside the little fireplace and threw it on, then followed up with another piece. "Now, let's get on our way," he said, putting the tongs back on the hook and pushing the guard back in place before turning to leave.

Johnnie followed him down the two flights of stairs.

"You better go and say goodnight to your Gran 'fore we go," Jim said when they reached the bottom. "She'll likely be asleep by the time we get back."

Johnnie went through to the kitchen where his little cousins were also saying goodnight to Gran. Sally could be heard doing the washing up in the scullery.

"'Ere's Johnnie come back down, Gran," Lyddie told Gran who was sitting by the fireplace. "'E's goin' to walk along with us, ain't you, Johnnie?"

"Lyddie," said her mother, "you go and get your cloak on ready to go 'ome an' leave Johnnie to talk to Gran. You, too, Emily. Come along, both of you."

Auntie Sarah bustled the children out into the hall.

"Well, Johnnie," said Gran, "it would have been nice to have sat and chatted to you this evening but I understand. It's important you go with Jim. I hope you understand that. It's a Kentson tradition that you celebrate and get introduced to the local lightermen after you're bound. Your uncles and cousins'll all be there. So we'll have our chat tomorrow night."

"Yes, Gran. Emma said to send her love. And Ma, too."

"She's a good girl Emma is. I wish she hadn't got it into her head to be a dressmaker, though... even allowing for it being a good house she's in. I would have much preferred her to have followed Elizabeth into being a school mistress – girls need teachers more than society ladies need dressmakers. Well, you go and enjoy yourself. Sally'll have some soup and bread ready for your supper when you get back. And a brick warmed to take the chill out of your bed. Sally's a good girl, too – does all my work for me now, you know. Come and give your old Gran a kiss goodnight, then."

"Goodnight, Gran," Johnnie said, kissing the wrinkled old cheek offered to him. "See you tomorrow." He turned back to the hall where Jim threw his coat to him, jerking his head in the direction of the open door. Auntie Sarah, pushing the little girls ahead of her, had started off along the street. Johnnie struggled into his pea-coat, buttoning it as he and Jim hurried after them.

* * * * *

Charlie Walkerston kicked his baby brother and laughed when he got the desired response and Harry howled more in indignation than pain, since he could hardly have been hurt with all the blankets wrapped around him.

"You do that again, Charlie, and I'll clout you one," said Phoebe. "All right, Harry, pipe down. He didn't hurt you."

"I ain't a baby and I don't want to be in 'ere wiv a baby."

"Look, just be a good boy for me, Charlie, and put up with it. We're late and you can't walk fast enough for us to get there before they come out and we don't want to have to go lookin' for Georgie again, do we?"

"No, it's too bloody cold…"

"Don't you swear, neither. You're the limit Charlie. I don't know what's goin' to happen when you start school in the summer. You'll be getting the strap every day, you're so cheeky. They won't put up with it, you know, at school."

Phoebe stopped talking to concentrate on pushing the cart up the hill. She seemed to have been doing this all her life on and off

– pushing a cartload of little brothers up this hill to the infants' school to collect yet another little brother. Charlie, mercifully, had stopped complaining and was leaning back, against the side of the cart, looking up into the sky and singing *Twinkle, twinkle little star*. Harry, wrapped in his blanket, watched him. She could see children coming out of the school gates ahead of her.

"Nearly there. You can get out now, Charlie, and run ahead to get Georgie," she paused and Charlie stopped singing and clambered out. "No, not you, Harry. You sit still."

Harry looked as if he was going to start crying as Charlie ran off yelling for Georgie at the top of his lungs.

"It's all right," she said. "He's just gone to get Georgie. They'll both come running back in a minute. You just keep watching, Harry."

"Go 'ome?" asked Harry.

"Yes, Harry. We'll be going home. Are you cold?"

"'Arry cold."

"Well, we'll hurry home as fast as we can," Phoebe told him and turned the cart sideways so that it wouldn't roll down the hill while she tucked the blanket more firmly around him. She couldn't see why her mother couldn't let her leave Harry at home with it being so cold and damp just now. It wasn't like he'd be a nuisance while she was working. Charlie, she could understand – he'd get up to all sorts of things the minute your back was turned, but Harry was a quiet, delicate little thing and he shouldn't be out in the cold every day like this. "Look, Harry, here they come."

Georgie and Charlie came running out of the playground, Georgie with his coat undone. Phoebe bent down and buttoned it up.

"Where's your muffler?" she asked.

"Someone took it," he said.

"Who? We 'ave to get it back. Ma'll kill you – and me, too. Come on, we'll have to go back to the school. Walk where I can see you, you two. Go on, now."

Phoebe turned the cart around and headed for the school gates. Just inside the playground, a pupil teacher was holding the hands of two children still waiting to be fetched.

"'Lo, Nellie. Georgie here has a bit of bother. Tell Miss Nellie who took your muffler, Georgie."

Nellie had attended the girls' school at the same time as Phoebe but, unlike Phoebe, she'd stayed on for the upper class until her fourteenth birthday and was now a pupil teacher at the infants' school. Phoebe privately thought she'd be a much better pupil teacher, with all the experience she had in looking after little brothers, than someone like Nellie who was the youngest child of a grocer. But Nellie had been able to go to school regularly, not being needed to help at home like Phoebe. Some people were just luckier than others.

"I ain't tellin'," said Georgie, keeping his eyes fixed on the ground.

"Georgie, Ma doesn't have money to throw away on lost mufflers. Now, tell us who took it."

Georgie continued to look at the ground.

"It's all right, Georgie," said Nellie, "it's not sneaking when a teacher makes you tell."

"There's me ma," said one of the other children pulling away.

Nellie let go of his hand and he ran off. Georgie still refused to speak.

"'Arry wanna go 'ome," whined Harry.

"Bet I know," said Charlie.

"You shut up, Charlie." Georgie glared at him.

"Don't worry about it, Phoebe," said Nellie. "I think I know where it is. Here's Jack come for Jimmie. He'll get it for us."

She led the remaining little boy towards the older boy who'd just come up the road. He was obviously younger than the two girls, but a lot taller. Nellie ushered him towards the high fence which ran between the school and the row of houses beside it. She beckoned Phoebe to follow. Georgie looked as if he was thinking about running off, so Phoebe quickly took his hand, pushed the cart with the other hand and nodded at Charlie to go ahead of her. The older boy, Jack, was plucking the muffler from the top of the fence as they come up. Nellie took it from him and wrapped it around Georgie. "There you are, Georgie," she said. "Now you won't get into trouble with your ma. You take your little brother's hand and walk along nicely for Phoebe. You can hold Jimmy's hand, too. He and Jack'll be going your way." Surprisingly, Georgie did as he was told. "We've got a new boy," Nellie said in a lower voice. "His family just moved here and he should really be at the Boys' School, but he's not up to it. He's the reason I've been making Jimmie and David wait with me to be picked up. Being older, he's been bullying the little ones, although Georgie's the first of the older boys he's done this to. They're scared to tell because he says he'll beat them up if they do. He's thrown things up on the fence and over it before, so it was an easy guess when Georgie wouldn't tell."

"It's hard trying to make them understand when it's right to tell. Thanks for getting it back. It wouldn't only have been Georgie in trouble," Phoebe confided. "I'm expected to have eyes in the back of me 'ead, looking after these three. Thanks for getting it down, Jack."

The boy nodded shyly.

"You go along, Phoebe," Nellie said. "The little one looks cold. You should get him home. I'll report the problem." They had reached the street again and Phoebe and Jack turned to follow the little boys down the hill.

"Thanks, Nell. 'Bye." Phoebe turned to Jack. "What did he do to your brother?" she asked.

"Same thing. 'E thinks it's funny frowin' their mufflers and caps up there so they can't reach them. Me and me mates 'll teach 'im a lesson soon as we can get 'old of 'im." He pointed in the other direction. "''E lives round the corner along that way, see, so there's not enough time to catch 'im after school, but we'll get 'im one day soon, we will."

As they turned the corner, he told Phoebe that they only lived a few houses along and Jimmy could easily walk home by himself and had done so until he started getting bullied. Their mother had something wrong with her legs and couldn't walk, except for getting around the house, so he had to go back and forth with his little brother when he'd rather walk home with his mates. Phoebe laughed and told him she'd been walking to and from the infants' school with various little brothers since she was seven years old. She was hardly the person to look to for sympathy, but she was very grateful to him for getting Georgie's muffler off the fence. They said goodbye at Jack's gate.

"Can we wait for the train?" Charlie asked as they approached the railway bridge.

"No, not today," Phoebe told him. "Harry's getting cold and we have to get 'im home so he can get warmed up. How about we all hurry as fast as we can and I'll read a bit of *Children of the New Forest* to you before tea." Emma had given her the book, along with several other children's books, when she'd left home to start her dressmaker's apprenticeship, and Phoebe had discovered that stories about other children appealed to her little brothers. Even Will, who was ten now, liked to listen, though he wouldn't have much opportunity now that he was working for Johnnie's ma at the beer-shop after school. "We can all sit round the stove and get warm and be out of Ma's way. What d'you think of that?" One good thing about slop sewing, she thought, was that the stove was always, if not burning, at the least banked up to smoulder against the time it would be needed to heat the flat irons, so the room was never really cold like some people's homes.

"We'd rather see the train," said Georgie, looking down at Harry in the cart, "but you're right about 'Arry. We better get 'im 'ome in the warm."

"Well, if you'd each push on either side of me, we'd all get along a lot faster."

This wasn't strictly true. In fact it slowed her down a bit but it did get them co-operating and progress could be made, especially getting over the bridge without them stopping to see if the train was coming.

"When Johnnie Kentson went to London on the train, did he go second class?" asked Charlie.

"You know that he and his ma paid the extra to go second class so that they could go at their convenience," replied Phoebe.

She didn't think they really understood that there were different kinds of railway carriages, or why that was, but had just picked up the phrase and thought it sounded important. The boys knew all the details but they liked talking about Johnnie going to London on the train because he was the only person they knew who'd been on a train and, like all boys of their age, they were fascinated by trains.

"When you and Sam go up to see him, will you go second class, too?"

"I shouldn't think so," Phoebe said, smiling because of Charlie not really knowing what going second class meant. "The parliamentary's the way to go when you haven't got much money. Penny a mile's all that it costs. Anyway, with Pa working on the steam packet, Sam'll likely go up with him and you know it's not likely I'll ever get time off from looking after you lot to go that far away." Maybe never even as far as Lewisham to visit Emma, she thought to herself.

Sam must have been filling their little brothers' minds with fantasy. It was unlikely she'd ever make the journey to London whether by train or steam packet, the way things were, Phoebe thought, and, if Sam did, it would more likely be working on a boat, not lording it on a train. Johnnie should be down a fair bit, though, when the spring came. He'd said that his uncles would probably let him work on the cargoes coming down river so that he'd be able to come home now and again. She'd stopped by the beer-shop, after taking Georgie to school this morning, to see that he'd got off all right. His ma had looked as if she'd been crying and Phoebe still felt sad for her. First Emma'd gone off to Lewisham and now Johnnie was gone, too. She couldn't understand why it was necessary for them to go at all and leave their ma all alone. 'Course, Ben and Jenny were almost like her family, they'd lived and worked at the beer-shop for such a long time now, so she wasn't actually alone, but it wasn't like her own children being there, was it? But it was the same as with Pa, Johnnie must follow the family tradition and do his waterman's apprenticeship, just as Sam would do a couple of years, although, with Pa working on the steam packet, Phoebe wasn't sure how. Pa hadn't taken on an apprentice since Barney got his freedom because he said there was no future in rowing people on the Thames any more and, with Barney not able to buy a boat of his own, Pa let him use his at a percentage. He used it most of the time now, though Pa still liked to ply when he wasn't working on the steamer. You had to get on the lighters or be taken on as steam packet crew, Pa said, to make enough money to live on. But the only place for apprentices on steam packets was as call boys bound, surely, to the captain and it wasn't likely Pa would become a captain before Sam turned fourteen. Maybe he'd be able to get Sam apprenticed to somebody else or, maybe he really would go back to plying for hire above London Bridge like he was always saying he would.

"Johnnie said it didn't seem like it took much time at all, going on the train," Georgie remarked, probably to show he'd had a conversation with Johnnie by himself.

"That's 'cos the train track's straight but the river's all bendy. Ain't that right, Phoebe?" said Charlie.

"Johnnie's ma didn't want to leave the beer-shop for too long 'cos it was just before Christmas so she couldn't spend a lot of time on the river. It was best to get the ferry over and go on the train and they only paid the extra so they could travel during the day. There ain't no penny-a-mile trains in the day – only early and late – and most other trains only have second and first class carriages. Lots of people go on trains now that they've got them running right and they're reliable. By the time you're my age, you'll probably be going on trains, too. Emma has to get the train from Lewisham and back all the time." This was a bit of an exaggeration since, except for her holiday time at the end of the summer, Emma was only given enough time off to go home on public holidays and there hadn't been very many of them since she started.

A few times, her ma had gone up to see her of a Sunday afternoon and Phoebe was hoping that, one day, she'd ask her to go with her and actually had the fare, safely under the mattress of the bed she shared with Georgie and Charlie, in case that should happen.

"Emma don't come and tell us about the train like Johnnie did," Charlie observed. "I ain't even seen Emma for so long that I forget what she looks like. Anyway, Lewisham ain't far away like London."

"It was Phoebe that Johnnie come to see, not us," giggled Georgie. "He just 'ad to talk to us 'cos she 'as to look after us. We should go and see 'is ma like you did this morning when I was at school." They were in the alley beside the New Packet now and Georgie had been pretty put out at dinner time when he found out about them going to the beer-shop without him.

"We only went there to see that Johnnie got off all right and it was when there weren't too many people. Johnnie's ma won't want little boys in there now with customers in and out. Harry, stop that grizz'ling. We're nearly 'ome. Come on, you two, you're forgetting to push and you want to find out if the children managed to hide from the Roundheads, don't you?"

* * * * *

Nearly all the lightermen in the Wapping triangle seemed to be in the Prince when Johnnie arrived there with his uncles and JW. Many were regulars, working for the various members of his family, or jobbers they sometimes hired, but others were men he didn't know, although he recognized some who had been at his Pa's funeral four years ago. They all cheered as he came in and he felt embarrassed. He knew he was being welcomed, as a Kentson – the last one of his generation – to a select community. Being a lighterman was traditional in families, men apprenticing their sons and nephews to a trade closed to anyone without the right contacts. It was in the blood, they said. He smiled and nodded, wondering whether he was supposed to say something but a big man near the bar said, "Your ale's coming up, gentlemen," and began to pass mugs of ale over to them. Uncle William, who Johnnie hadn't seen, sitting at a table in the corner until then, stood up and raised his mug.

"Ssh," somebody said and everybody stopped talking.

"As the senior Kentson these last few years, since my highly regarded father passed on to his reward, it's been my pleasure, along with my brothers and Uncle Joe, here–" he indicated his elderly uncle who Johnnie was surprised to see sitting at the table "–to guide the younger members of the family through their apprenticeships. We've seen first Young Joe, then Tommy win their freedom and we'll all be back 'ere again, in a few weeks, to celebrate with Bill as 'e, too, becomes a Freeman of the Thames. A bit under four years ago it was my pleasure to become apprentice master to my sister Jane's boy, James William, 'ere and, today, my brother Jim took Johnnie, only son of our sadly missed brother, John, up to Watermen's Hall where they signed his indentures and 'e became an apprentice of The Worshipful Company of Watermen and Lightermen. Johnnie, by the way, has been a right 'and 'elp to his mother in the New Packet in Woolwich, which some of you know so, if he forgets 'imself and starts collecting up your beer mugs, just remind 'im that he's a lighterman now. Hip hoo-ray for Johnnie Kentson!"

"'Oo-ray for Johnnie," the men shouted, raising their mugs and clearing a path for Johnnie and his companions to walk through to William's table. Johnnie clinked his mug against those raised towards him. He felt awkward, unused to being the centre of attention, and had no idea what to say or, even, if he was *supposed* to say something. JW came to his rescue.

"Don't forget to thank Uncle Windbag – Uncle William – for the welcome," he whispered close to Johnnie's ear so that nobody would hear. "Profusely…"

They reached the long table at the other side of the room, at the one of which Uncle William, Bill and Joe and their father were all sitting. Johnnie put down his mug and held out his hand to his uncle. He hoped 'profusely' meant 'a lot'. He was pretty certain it did, but wished JW, who had attended an academy instead of going the upper class at the local National School, because his father thought it was worth paying the extra, wouldn't use big words out of the blue like that.

"Thank you very much for introducing me to the men, Uncle William. I really – I greatly appreciate being welcomed here and I truly hope that I can manage to live up to your expectations and be a good lighterman."

"'Course you will, boy. Image of your father, you are, just like he was the image of our pa – your grandad. You're bound to be one of the best on the river." William stood up and shook Johnnie's hand, putting his other arm around his shoulders in a manly hug. "You'll do," he said.

"All right, Johnnie," said Jim from behind him. "You can sit down now and be a lowly apprentice again. You won't be getting another moment of glory 'til you pass your two year test and you're going to have to work hard to learn all that's necessary for that."

Johnnie grinned and slid down onto the bench beside JW who'd already seated himself. The men immediately got into discussions amongst each other and forgot about him.

"Dunno where me pa got to. 'E said 'e'd be 'ere," said JW.

"Tommy's not come, either. I thought 'e'd be 'ere."

JW grimaced. "Get yourself married and you ain't your own man no more," he said. "If 'e's still in the Docks, 'e'll be in but, if 'e's gone 'ome first, that Betsy'll tell 'im 'e's too good to be frequenting dockside taverns now that 'e's married to 'er. You walked out with a girl yet, Johnnie?"

For a moment Johnnie thought of Phoebe Walkerston sewing shirts for the slop tailor and looking after her little brothers, then shook his head. Walking home from school by way of the infants' playground so that he could help her hardly counted as 'walking out', he decided. "You?" he asked.

"There's been a couple but they don't like it when the summer evenings come around and you're working all the time, there's blokes what are more available, so there you are. Apprentice is the last one finished for the day and, when I'm not working on the barges, me pa's got me down the warehouse learning the business. Look, Tommy got 'ere, after all…"

JW raised his arm and Johnnie turned and saw Tommy in the doorway with a couple of other young men who made for the bar, leaving Tommy to acknowledge JW's signal and come towards them.

"Well, if it ain't me little cousin Johnnie all grown up and ready to start work," he said as he reached the table. He held out his hand and Johnnie stood up to clasp it. "Congratulations, mate. Jim took you to get you all signed up?"

Johnnie nodded as they both sat down. "We went straight up there 'fore we went in to unload," he said. "Steve stayed with the cargo, then we 'ad pork pies for dinner and 'ad to wait a bit for the turn, then come down to St. Katherine's to unload, then ballasted an' come down 'ere. We're unloading sugar tomorrow with your Pa and Bill, an' Jim said an 'ire as well."

"That'd be Giles Warner, I expect – bloke in the felt 'at over there."

"Oh, I know him," Johnnie said looking in the direction Tommy was nodding. "'E's been down to Woolwich a good few times."

"Used to work for us regular 'fore 'e bought 'is own lighter. We put work 'is way whenever we can." Tommy turned to his mates, who'd come over from the bar. One handed him a mug of ale and he held it up. "'Ere's to you, Johnnie." The three toasted Johnnie, then Tommy said, "Thanks, Vic. I'll get you next time. You won't know Vic and Andy 'ere, Johnnie. This is Johnnie, me cousin, as got bound to Jim there, today."

"Nice to meet you, Johnnie," the one named Andy said. "Don't you let young JW, 'ere, lead you astray, now." He punched JW on the shoulder in a friendly way and sat down beside him.

"Can't lead Johnnie astray in 'ere," replied JW. "'E was bought up in a pub. Weaned on ale, 'e was."

"I was not!" cried Johnnie.

"But you was brought up in a pub?" asked Vic.

"Me ma 'as a beer-shop downriver in Woolwich. Me sister an' me used to 'ave to play in the shop when me pa was working on the river and me ma 'ad to tend the bar, but she'd be the last person to give little children ale to drink. Never 'ad none but what we sneaked."

"'E was just jokin'. So your pa was the one who worked the downriver end of Kentson's, then?"

Johnnie nodded. "Eddie Jones 'as been running 'is boat the last few years. 'E worked with me pa regular 'fore 'e died, see? So it was the best plan."

"But the lighter really belongs to you, though. Ain't that right?"

"To me ma until I'm free."

"Same thing. An' you got a beer-shop, too."

"Come and 'elp me get some more drinks, Vic," interrupted Tommy, standing up. "Can't stay too long meself, as I got to get on 'ome, but I owe you a pot."

They moved off towards the bar and Andy followed them.

"Don't let 'im bother you, Johnnie," said JW. "Some blokes get pretty jealous of blokes like us that's got boats and equipment in the family. If 'e comes back, you an' me'll go round there–" he nodded to where Bill and Joe were sitting with their father and Uncle William "–and pretend we got to talk to Bill, right-oh?"

"Sounds like 'e thinks I'm some spoiled toff who don't 'ave to work for a living."

"'E don't know much about the Kentsons, then, does 'e? I don't know who 'e is, even. The other one's Betsy's brother. The Vic bloke must be a friend of 'is. I think Tommy feels pretty embarrassed 'bout 'im talkin' to you like that – and so 'e should be, bringin' a nosy bugger like that in 'ere on your first night."

"Don't worry about it," said Johnnie. "It ain't 'is fault if they're 'is wife's people. What can 'e do?"

But he did feel disappointed in Tommy, the hero of his childhood, and just the fact of being here like this with his father's family, was making him want his pa back more than anything else had done since the terrible night when he died…

* * * * *

Rebecca wasn't really surprised when young Phoebe Walkerston came shyly into the beer-shop although it wasn't usual for her to be out in the evening unless she'd been sent on an errand.

Emma and Johnnie had both at times walked to and from the infants' school with her, during the going on for two years now, since she'd had to leave school to help her mother at home. And, until she had started her apprenticeship, Emma had continued to go over, of an evening, to show her some of the things she'd learned at school. Now, with both the children gone, Phoebe was going to be as lonely for them as Rebecca was herself.

"Will went home a while ago, Phoebe. You weren't sent to walk home with him, were you?"

Rebecca had, at Johnnie's suggestion, hired Will to come in before and after school to do some of the jobs that had been his ever since he'd been old enough to do them. Will was turning ten and would, otherwise, be expected to find odd jobs running errands around the docks, as his brother Sam did. A regular wage, however small it might be, to contribute to the household was preferable to the intermittent jobs Will would get until he proved himself reliable and, here, he could have his tea and do his night lessons as well. His mother had eagerly agreed, when Rebecca suggested the plan to her, and Johnnie, over the last couple of weeks, had shown Will everything he was to do. They'd also arranged for both Will and Sam to look after the skittle alley on Friday and Saturday evenings for tips. They'd both helped Johnnie set up skittles and pick up the cheeses and could be relied upon to keep things running smoothly.

"No, Mrs. Kentson," Phoebe said, advancing towards the bar. "Ma says if he's big enough to work 'ere of an evening, he's big enough to walk home by himself. I 'ad to take some of Harry's old clothes, that're too small for 'im now, over to me Auntie Bet's for the new baby, so I just thought I'd stop by on me way back – see 'ow you was… with Johnnie gone, I mean."

Oh dear, thought Rebecca, the poor child's going to have to get used to both her closest friends being away. At least, Johnnie going wouldn't be as hard on her as Emma going to live in Lewisham had been. Johnnie would be coming down quite often although, as the apprentice, he'd be required to stay on the lighter over night unless, of course, it was ballasted, then Jim would, likely, let him come home for the night. Either way, he'd be home from time to time, whereas Emma only had Sunday afternoons to herself and there wasn't enough time for her to come home.

"You know, Phoebe," Rebecca said, drawing beer for two waiting customers as she spoke. "I've been thinking about asking your ma if she'd mind you coming over to Lewisham with me, on the train, Sunday afternoon to see Emma. Thanks, Alf," she interrupted herself, taking the money for the drinks. "I'll pay your fare – or you can pay what you have and I'll make up the difference."

"I have the fare," Phoebe responded, eagerly, "I do get paid a bit, you know, for the sewing, but mostly I end up having to give it back to Ma when she gets 'ard up and there's none left for buying bread and tea, and you can't do without them, can you? But I've kept aside enough, 'oping you'd ask me to go with you. See, if you ask 'er, Ma won't act like I'm being selfish. If I went by meself, she'd make a fuss about me not being there to take the litl'uns over to the infants' Sunday School for the singing and Bible story. 'Course, I've never been on the train before, either, so it'd be a bit scary, too, goin' by meself. Oops. Sorry, mister."

Phoebe moved aside to let some men get to the bar.

"Come round here, Phoebe," Rebecca said, motioning her around the bar. "Here, you can draw the porter for me. It is porter you're drinking, innit, Joe?" The man called Joe nodded and

Phoebe took his mug and walked round behind the bar to fill it. "And ale for both of you two?"

"Right you are. Where's Ben this evening?"

"Just me tonight. Paying for both? All three? There you go." Rebecca took the man's money and handed over his change. "That's all right, Phoebe, duck, 'e left the money here."

Phoebe slid the mug across the bar. "See Will or Sam get out of doing all the things to do with looking after the litl'uns, 'cause it's s'posed to be a woman's job. Emma used to come to the Sunday School with us, before she went off, and we'd 'elp with keeping the children in order and it was nice. That was when it was just Georgie and Charlie. Harry was still a baby but 'e's old enough to go now – well, he's not really, but Ma says he is. So now, I've got me 'ands full with keeping 'im quiet and, what with running after that Charlie, it's a nightmare in there."

"Who'll take them, then, if you come with me?"

"Ma'll get Esther to fetch them, I expect. Esther takes Ena's girls, but they're quiet little things. Her friend Annie Gill usually goes with her, so she can manage, though I don't s'pose she'll want to take Harry so Ma'll 'ave to look after 'im for a change."

Rebecca smiled as Phoebe finished this speech with a firm nod of her head. Esther was Phoebe's aunt, although she was actually a little younger than Phoebe. She had sometimes played with Emma and Phoebe, when they were younger, and was now attending the upper class, a privilege Phoebe had been denied two years before. Phoebe obviously resented both her mother and Esther for the limitations put on her own education. Rebecca was glad she'd asked the girl to come and visit Emma with her, but it wasn't her place to criticize her parents' decisions. She served another customer before continuing the conversation.

"Do you have some writing paper still, Phoebe?"

Emma had given Phoebe an early birthday present of a little writing box, furnished with writing paper, pen and ink, back when she left to start her apprenticeship in Lewisham so that she could write to her regularly, and Rebecca knew that the two girls still kept up an intermittent correspondence.

"Oh yes, I'll write a letter to Emma and tell her to expect us, shall I?"

"That'll be a good idea. Will you have some time to do it tomorrow?"

"I can do it when I get 'ome. I already got all the lit'luns to bed 'fore I come out and Ma will 'ave packed up for the night – give me a tongue-lashing for taking so long, she will, but Pa and Sam'll be home for their supper any time now. Sam doesn't have tea now 'e's been taken on regular to 'elp the porters at the brewery so 'e 'as supper with Pa instead. And I can pop it in the pillar box when I take Georgie to school tomorrow. I already 'ave a Queen's 'ead – Johnnie give me some yesterday so's I could be sure to write to him, too – so I don't need to go into the post office. Now, I'd better get 'ome. G'night, Mrs. Kentson, and thank you ever so much. They got a sewing machine, Emma said. Did you know? She'll be able to tell us all about it."

Phoebe practically skipped out of the beer-shop.

"You certainly made that little girl very 'appy, Rebecca," Stan Rolfe, who kept the newsagent shop down the road, said from the table beside the shove ha'penny board, where he'd remained to finish his pint of ale after his playing partners had left to go home. "What d'you do to 'er. Come in 'ere lookin' like the Queen in mourning down there on the Isle of Wight, then skipped out 'appy as a sandboy, she did."

"S'pose it shows you how just a little thing can mean so much to some," Rebecca said. "Poor Phoebe's been missing my Emma these last – what, thirteen, fourteen months now? – they were always the best of friends. I asked her if she'd like to come with me to visit Emma on Sunday as I could see she was taking it hard, what with losing Johnnie, too, now. He went off this morning, bound to his uncle, you know – Jim..."

"Young Johnnie told me 'e was going up there to Wapping to work. Didn't realize it was today he was off, though. So the little Walkerston girl's left all on 'er own..."

"Hardly on her own with five brothers." Rebecca stopped momentarily to pull some ale for a customer who withdrew to the end of the bar to read the newspaper. "But it's them that's caused her troubles. She's not the only one, of course. Lots of girls have to stay home from school to look after their little brothers and sisters so their mothers can work, and it makes it hard for them to have friends outside of their families, 'though Phoebe was lucky having Emma to help her make up what she'd miss when she was kept home from school. I only had the two children so I really shouldn't judge but it seems unfair for that girl to have no prospects but the same kind of life as her mother – work for a pittance all 'er life and bring an 'ouseful of children into the world. Oh lor', I sound like one of them – you know, the lady reformers you read about in the newspaper."

"Nothin' wrong with that. They're women, just like you, 'elping working class young women with their reading and such, advocating for better schooling for the children..."

"Oh, I agree with them. There should be a law for children to go to school until they're at least fourteen 'stead of being kept home to look after their younger brothers and sisters. And it should be free. I just meant that I shouldn't be carrying on like I was getting above myself."

"You couldn't do that, Rebecca. Around 'ere you're known to be an admirable woman. There ain't nobody wouldn't agree to that." He downed his beer, stood up and took the two steps needed to put his mug on the bar. "Other way round, if you ask me. Them lady radicals just talk about academies for working class girls and better jobs for women. You do something for them, you do." He put the empty mug down. "There you are, m'dear. I'd better get on 'ome. Morning comes only too soon in my business, not to mention the fact that my good woman will be creatin' if I stay in 'ere much longer."

"Good night, Stan."

Rebecca picked up the mug and put it in the bowl under the bar, then took the damp cloth she kept there and went to fetch the dirty pots and wipe the empty table and the ends of the shove ha'penny board where the men had slopped beer. She thought about what Stan Rolfe had said. While, when you thought about it, her *doing*, by helping local women and girls with reading and writing, was just as important as the *talking* that the wealthy ladies did with their pieces in expensive periodicals about the need for proper education for girls and jobs that paid them decent wages when they grew up, she didn't think people really found her so admirable. Many – mostly men, of course – said working class women being able to read and write made them dissatisfied and caused marriage troubles. She'd read in a newspaper article that some of those wealthy ladies held the same view and were really only interested in proper schools for the girls of their own class and even wanted universities for them. That was all very well, of course, but they were only paying lip service to the needs of working class women, weren't they? And just writing about starving slop workers so they'd look good for caring about the poor.

Although, she must admit, Rebecca thought, there did seem to be some acknowledgement, just now, that better education for women and opportunities for decent jobs would do a lot more good than charity and kind words. They were reducing and cutting out school pence for a lot of families which might help more boys to go but it wasn't going to make much difference to girls kept home because they were needed there to watch the babies while their mother's sewed slop, went out to laundries to wash and press or hired themselves out to char. And, unfortunately, money was going to be taken from the teachers' wages to cover the cost and that certainly wouldn't help to attract bright young girls to become teachers, or bright young men, come to that. Rebecca sighed.

"That's just 'ow I feels meself," said a woman's voice and Rebecca came out of her reverie to find two regular Monday evening customers who came in for a drink on their way home from a long day working in the laundry. "Nothin' we can do about anyfink, eh? 'Ave to just get on wiv it, we do."

"Hello, Elsie. Bessie. Usual?"

"Warm in 'ere, it is, after being out there," remarked Bessie, loosening the shawls wrapped around her. "It was nice gettin' out in the cold after being' in the steam all day, but didn't take long to get ourselves froze, did it, Else?"

"Ooh, it's wicked out there, that icy fog is. Rather 'ave snow, I would, than that icy fog. Don't know 'ow lucky you are, Rebecca, just 'avin' to come out your back room there and in 'ere to work."

"I know how lucky I am not to have to go out in the cold," laughed Rebecca. "But it's not as easy as it looks, keeping a place like this going, believe you me."

"Oh, I believe you, ducks. I ain't envyin' you there. Just 'avin' me little joke, I am."

"You couldn't do 'er job, anyway, Else," said Bessie. "You 'ave to 'ave brains to be a woman running a beer-shop. You – you'd 'ave all the profits drunk in no time, you would."

"Speak for yourself - that ain't a nice thing to say." Elsie took a long draught from the mug of beer Rebecca had served her. "Ooh, that's better. Thirsty work, that is, in the laundry. 'Ere y'are, Rebecca." She handed her coins across the bar. "Johnnie get off all right this morning?"

"Oh, yes, today was the day, weren't it?" Bessie added, handing her money to Rebecca and sipping her drink. "Oh dear, you're going to miss 'im, ain't you?"

"'Course I am, but we all have to learn how to provide for ourselves, don't we? It's hard, but he's in good hands."

"Would've been nicer if it were 'is father 'e was apprenticed to…" Elsie shook her head sadly.

"Of course," said Rebecca, "but we all have to go on, don't we? However much it hurts." She hurriedly changed the subject. "How's your Betsy getting on?" She wasn't really terribly interested in Elsie's daughter's progress in motherhood but she really didn't want maudlin behaviour around her today. It was going to be hard enough to adapt to Johnnie being gone as it was, not much more than a year after his sister had left, without getting maudlin about things over which she had no control.

"Well, you'd think she'd 'ave no trouble with a baby of 'er own after lookin' after 'er brothers and sisters all 'er life, but she's 'opeless, she is."

"She's a very colicky baby, Elsie," said Bessie. "That's very 'ard on a young couple. I remember 'ow my Ernie took on when Tommy 'owled all night them first few months. An', talking about my Ernie, I got to get on 'ome and get 'is supper, I 'ave." She drained her mug and put it on the bar. "I'm off. See you tomorrer, Else. 'Night, Rebecca." She re-wrapped her shawls around her and, carrying her basket, hurried back out into the cold night air.

"It's 'er milk I thinks meself," continued Elsie. "She don't eat enough, does Betsey, so it stands to reason the baby ain't getting fed proper. Bloody starvin' that baby is, if you ask me. I've told 'er, I 'ave–"

"'Scuse me a minute, Elsie," Rebecca interrupted, glad of an excuse to do so. "I've got these gentlemen to serve."

She was glad to see that Elsie had found somebody else to whom she could expound her views on new mothers and their babies by the time she was free again to listen to her. The talk about the baby had made her feel glad that Ben and Jennie were moving to a house of their own before their baby was born in May. They'd lived here – first just Jennie then, after their marriage, Ben, too – for so long now that it was almost as if they were her family, but a baby in the house, bringing back all those memories of the days when her own children were babies and John was alive, and happy being a father, would be too hard to bear, especially now that both the children were gone from home. She wondered how Johnnie was feeling in the attic bedroom at his grandmother's house and sent up a silent prayer that he would be kept safe working on the river.

January 2007

"I'm sending an email to Kate and Claire to tell them my school's closed today because of all the snow," said Carolyn. "What time is it in England?"

"Well, you can figure it out, honey. How many hours difference?"

"Five."

"So, okay, it's quarter to eleven, add five and...?"

"Quarter to twelve, quarter to one–" Carolyn counted on her fingers "–quarter to two, quarter to three, quarter to four. Right?"

"Ah-ha. They'll just be getting home from school over there, I should imagine."

"Uh-uh," said Carolyn, shaking her head. "Claire will because she's still in the Infants – that's what they call kindergarten and grade one – but Kate's in the Junior School and that doesn't finish until four o'clock, she told before."

"I see. Well, you write your email. Then, you and Jamie can both get your coats on and we'll all go and see what we can do about clearing the driveway."

"Okay. I'm going to tell them that this is a very sad time for us and that we're going to go and put some flowers on Daddy's grave with

Grandpa and Grandma and Aunt Julie and Uncle Paul and Ryan on Saturday."

"Oh."

"What's the matter, Mommy?"

"Nothing, honey. You carry on with your email. I'll go and see what Jamie's doing."

Holly went through to the hallway and up the stairs. She'd known that the children were possibly as preoccupied as she was herself now that the first anniversary of their father's death was imminent, but Carolyn's matter of fact statement had jolted her. Was it a normal attitude for an eight-year-old or was it a call for help? She wondered, once again, about getting counselling for them. She'd refused it when the Police Association representative had told her it was covered, of necessity, and made quickly available under the police force's health insurance program, but it was a debate she'd been having with herself all along.

However, the three of them had made it this far the old-fashioned way, surviving the various milestones with the support of family and friends. Of course, they were sad, but wasn't being sad part of the grief process? Too much was made of so-called professional help being needed to work your way through things today. Some people disapproved when she said the children were not getting counselling as if declaring her guilty of bad parenting. Yet, at the first parent-teacher meeting of the school year, Carolyn's teacher, not knowing Holly's thoughts on the matter, had talked about how well adjusted Carolyn was and how fortunate it was that Holly seemed to have been able to get good counselling for her. Holly had explained that they had not had counselling and the luck was in having a very supportive family which had helped them, far more than any therapist could have done, to meet the challenges of the situation, without the awkwardness and *evasion so often seen in people not knowing how to behave towards those who were bereaved. The teacher had looked at her rather oddly and nodded and, since she obviously wasn't sure about what to say next, Holly asked her for ideas on scheduling homework, not that Carolyn really had a problem but she knew that, in most people, being asked for advice was a good antidote to negative reactions.*

She had found herself to be very much her mother's daughter in this hardly modern-day decision, which surprised her. She'd spent most of her adult life feeling that her mother was unhealthily intro-verted, something which Holly's own neediness seemed to have been a key feature in changing during recent months. Pat's unexpected desire to reunite with her family, and the subsequent spending of Christmas and the New Year in England visiting relatives, had saved the holiday season from being a nightmare for Holly and, quite prob-ably, for the children, too. While there wasn't the same emphasis on having professionals help people to 'work through their grief' when her own father died, Holly wondered now just how Pat had managed so well. She remembered the two of them falling over themselves to be nice to each other. At twelve, she had just reached the age when peer pressure dictated the need to be diametrically opposed to every-thing your mother wanted for you, then her father was diagnosed with lymphoma and given six months to live, so adolescent rebellion had been put on hold and eventually altogether forgotten.

As her newly widowed mother's only child, it had seemed trivial to play at being defiant, petulant or manipulative. In hindsight, it had probably been grief that made her feel that way and grief that influ-enced Pat's lightening up on how a twelve – by then, almost thirteen-year-old – should behave. For both of them, their grief was a private thing, not something to be analysed by outsiders, and they had come through it – changed, yes, but without major catastrophe.

Surviving Justin's death was different, though. Unlike her father, whose life had wound down amid the pain of cancer and discomfort of chemotherapy, her husband's vibrant being had been suddenly, irrevocably snatched away...

"Want me to help you shovel the driveway, Mom?" Jamie's voice broke into her thoughts. "It's stopped snowing now."

"That's what I was on my way to ask you about. I just told Carolyn that we'll go out and see what we can do after she's finished emailing your cousins. There was freezing rain before the snow started last night, so I don't know how much of it we're going to be able to move."

"I just did fifty push-ups so I'm in shape to shovel the tough stuff."

"That's good. I have to make my bed first," Holly said, going into her room. Jamie followed her.

"I can help…"

"Did you do your own? No school – you do your own, remember. That's the rule. Tell you what, you help me and I'll help you. Deal?"

"Deal," said Jamie, holding out his hand to hi-five.

With the children marooned at home for the day, Holly decided it might be a good time to broach the subject of Jamie's tenth birthday. They were all still in shock last year in the weeks following Justin's death and Jamie had turned down even the idea of taking a few friends to a restaurant, saying that he'd rather they just have Ryan and his parents over and have a birthday supper at home. She hoped that bringing it up now might take the children's minds off the first anniversary of their bereavement. Since she didn't want him to relate his birthday to his father's death for the rest of his life, she decided to attempt Carolyn's 'next item of business' attitude which had so startled her.

After they had cleared as much ice and snow off the driveway as they could, Carolyn's friend, Marie, walking carefully down the icy driveway of the house opposite, across the road and equally carefully up their own driveway, suggested she and Carolyn stay out and build an igloo.

Holly didn't expect them to stay out for long in the cold and was right. She and Jamie had taken off their coats and boots and were having a discussion about what to have for lunch, when the two little girls came rushing in saying they were frozen and were going to do their nails with Carolyn's Spray Nail Studio instead, but they'd have lunch first because they were starving as well as freezing.

Holly helped them off with their boots and snowsuits, shook off the snow and told Marie to call her mother and let her know she was staying. Then, Marie's mother wanted to speak to Holly and, by the time they had finished discussing the weather, the children and surviving a snow day, Holly found the girls had apparently forgotten about their hunger and gone upstairs to Carolyn's room. She hung their wet clothes near the register to dry and went into the kitchen. Jamie had put soup to warm on the stove and made a plate of tuna fish sandwiches, and was wiping down the countertop.

"Thank you, Jamie. You didn't have to do all this."

"Thought I'd save you the bother," he said with the bashful shrug typical of an almost ten-year-old.

"Well, that's really nice of you," she said, going into the family room and picking up the travel section from Saturday's paper, which she'd left on the coffee table, and bringing it into the kitchen. "Maybe we can take look at this before we set the table."

She moved the soup and turned off the burner, then laid the newspaper on the kitchen table and opened it to the colour spread in the centre.

Jamie put down the dishcloth, rubbed his damp hands on his jeans and came over to see.

"Winterlude," he said. "That's in Ottawa, isn't it?"

"I thought we might go for the weekend of your birthday."

Jamie was looking at the pictures of children on the giant snow slides at Snowflake Kingdom, but didn't say anything.

"I thought that–" she paused. "Well, now that you're getting older, maybe you'd rather do something special instead of having a birthday party."

"What are the Ice Hogs?" he asked.

"They're the Winterlude mascots. I think they're supposed to be some kind groundhog that hibernates in the summer instead of the winter. Something like that, anyway. I don't expect you to be hugely impressed by people dressed up as strange animals, though. There's all kinds of entertainment on and around the Rideau Canal, which is used as a giant ice rink in the winter. They build ice sculptures and snow sculptures and, of course, we'll take our skates. What d'you think?"

"Will it stay cold enough? I mean, it's won't be much fun going to a winter carnival if global warming makes the temperature go up and everything starts to melt."

Holly laughed. "Oh, I think the weather will co-operate," she said, thinking how such a possibility would have been the last thing to consider when she was his age, and gave him a quick hug. "But, we'll have to take our chances because I'll need to book a room pretty quickly. People come to it from all over, you know, and I expect most of the hotels are already booked up. And train tickets, too. I don't think I want to drive all that way in the winter so I thought we'd go by train."

"Yeah? Cool. How long does it take?"

"About four hours," Holly told him. "So, you think it's a good idea? We'll have to arrange for you and Carolyn to get out of school

early on the Friday and there's no hockey game on that Saturday, although you'll miss practice..."

"Can Ryan come, too? He's never been on a train – except for the GO-train to the Exhibition, and on the subway. He's never been on a proper train, I mean, where you sit down and have lunch and stuff. And there'll be two beds in the hotel room, so there's a place going for spare... and it is for my birthday and..."

Holly had half expected him to ask if Ryan could come. It would make a nice post Valentine's Day weekend for Julie and Paul, anyway, she thought, and she rather owed them since they so often asked Jamie along on outings as company for Ryan.

"We'll see what Aunt Julie says, but I expect so. Don't say anything about Ryan coming while Marie's here, though, because you know what'll happen. I'll possibly have to have a serious talk with Carolyn, when she does find out about bringing a friend not being an option for her because it's your birthday not hers, but we don't need to make poor Marie feel rejected, unnecessarily."

"She'll get it – Carolyn. She gets to come even though it's not her birthday, so she'll know I'm the one to get the special consideration, not her. Right?"

"Er, I'm not sure I follow your logic there, but I guess so. Anyway, what d'you think?"

"It sounds more cool than having a dumb old party. I wish my birthday was later, though. Maybe in April, like Ryan's is."

"Now why would you wish that?"

Holly knew that he meant because April wasn't as close to January as February was, but thought that an open question might be best if he wanted to talk about it.

However, he just pointed to a picture of an ice castle bathed in blue light and asked. "How do they make it look like that?"

"It's just filtered light. Remember it's built from ice – completely transparent."

"And that's how we'll see it? It's not just a photo made to look like that on a computer?"

"You'll understand when we see the real thing. Now, let's put this aside and get some plates and soup bowls out here. I'm starving."

August 1863

"There they are," Sam said, pointing towards the North Kent Railway ticket barrier as he and Phoebe entered the London Bridge station concourse. "Johnnie got 'ere before us." He stopped and held up his hand. "He's seen us – may as well wait 'ere."

Disregarding her brother, Phoebe ran towards Emma, who moved ahead of her own brother and the two girls laughingly hugged each other as they met amid the Sunday crowds on their way into and out of London for the afternoon.

"It's an awful mess out there," said Phoebe, "coming from our direction with the viaduct being built and the drainage work... Sam don't credit that I come this way every day and thinks he knows better, so I give into him and, of course, we're late."

"Never mind about that," Emma replied. "I'm only too happy to see you."

"We're all pleased to see each other," said Johnnie, coming up to them, "ain't we now? 'Ow are you, Phoebe? I see Sam's too lazy to walk over 'ere. 'Ope 'e ain't too lazy for scullin' – we got all them bridges to shoot going down to Battersea Park. Still like your job all right, Phoebe?"

"'Course I do. It's hard work but I'm getting paid more than what me *and* Ma used to get from the Golds' slop shop and I can pick up and take back finishing work for Ma so she don't 'ave to spend time doing that, with Harry an' all."

"And that's the best bit," said Emma. "She has to look after the boys instead of you."

Phoebe smiled and happily thrust her arm through Emma's the way they did when they were little, and they followed Johnnie through the bustle of the station to where Sam was waiting by the entrance.

The Walkerstons had moved house to Southwark the autumn before and Phoebe's life had changed for the better. All their lives had, with the exception of poor Will who could no longer work at the New Packet. Emma's ma had written out a character for him and Pa had asked around the pubs until a job had been found for him cleaning up and washing beer mugs before and after school but, of course, he didn't get his tea and time to do his night lessons like he had when he worked for Johnnie's ma. Apart from that, Pa getting taken on as mate on a Watermen's Company steamboat was a good thing, especially for her, Phoebe thought. Her father's one-time apprentice master, who had done well for himself with the Company, had been promoted to captain and, since there was not a man on the crew experienced enough to be mate, he had told the owners that there was a good man working for the Woolwich Company who wouldn't be averse to working from London Bridge. So, Pa had got his wish to move to London and Ma was happy because it meant Pa staying on a regular wage rather than plying at the stairs which she thought would give them no more income than it had in Woolwich. Sam had got a job as an errand boy, but would be bound to his father in a few months when the call boy on the boat got his freedom and was promoted. The wherry and its licence had been made over to Barney, with a monthly instalment plan, and they'd rented a little house in Southwark – a whole house, not rooms. Well, there were still only two rooms, but Phoebe had a narrow bed to herself in an alcove in the children's room and Ma and Pa's bedstead in the part of the downstairs beside the scullery was just like a separate room. They had their own privy and there was a sink and larder as well as a boiler for washing day in the scullery, which had a door to go out to their own little back garden where Pa had potatoes and cabbages growing. Best of all, through somebody one of his uncles knew, Johnnie Kentson had put her in the way of being taken on for training on the new sewing machines at a Cheapside clothing manufactory. Ma had complained about her working without bringing in more than a few pence, at first, but she was trained now and getting a full wage and handing over most of it

"She's got it light compared to me before we removed to Southwark," she told Emma. "Will and Georgie see Charlie to school – infants' is right beside the boys' and girls' schools in the Borough Road – and Harry's such a little sweetheart, he's no trouble at all. But, what about you? Twelve pound a year and all found – you're rich, you are. And that's such a lovely frock you've got on. Very flash, it is."

"Thanks, Phoebe. I've brought you some silk trimming and a bit of lace. I'll show you when we get in the boat." Emma stopped and surveyed Phoebe's dress. "You've really made that dress look nice. You're very clever with a needle, you know, despite not having learned about fashion properly. You seem to have a natural eye for what matches."

Emma was now an assistant in the establishment where she had apprenticed and was able to buy very cheaply the left over scraps from the dresses they made, as well as full lengths of dress material that was no longer in demand. The dress she was wearing was a result of such opportunities, as were the flounces that Phoebe had added to the dress she had made over from a gown she'd brought at a broker's shop.

"Come on, you two," shouted Sam. "We'll be 'ere all day at this rate."

Phoebe shrugged as if in apology for Sam, just as she had done all her life, and the two girls followed their brothers under the new viaduct still being built to carry the railway line to Hungerford Bridge and over the river to the new Charing Cross station.

"Same old Sam," said Emma. "I wouldn't have known you, I haven't seen you for so long, but once you opened you mouth, I'd have known you blindfold…"

"Sorry, Em. It's lovely to see you and you're lookin' lovely, more lovely than ever, but you know me – hurry-scurry, time and tide don't wait – swift Sam…"

"Right you are. Cheeky little begger as you always were, for all you're a head taller then me now."

"I'm reformed, Em. Got a full time job now and I'm getting bound on the steamboat soon as I turn fourteen. I ain't the little boy setting up the skittles no more–"

"Skiff's at the usual place," broke in Johnnie. "Be'ind St. Saviour's." Then for Emma's benefit, he added, "We just go across here and cut through the churchyard. Hops warehouse watchman's keeping an eye on me sculls so's I don't 'ave to carry them over 'ere with me. It don't 'urt 'aving a family that's a name on the river." He grinned apologetically as he said this, but Phoebe knew he was proud of being a member of a lighterage family operation. "Actually, this old bloke remembers me coming up with Pa when I was a litl'un. Dock labourer 'e was then. I leave the skiff there when I go to Sam and Phoebe's 'ouse, see, Em."

They followed Johnnie through St. Saviour's churchyard and the alleyways behind it to get to the river then, settled in the skiff's stern, the two girls exchanged news of their lives since they had last seen each other at Easter. It was then that Emma had been promoted from improver to assistant in time for what they called the season, which ran until July and was a very busy time for the fashion houses – even the comparatively modest one in Lewisham, and Phoebe had just finished her training and had been taken on at full pay. Emma's news about the gowns worn by the cream of Greenwich society was more interesting than Phoebe's telling of poor women from the East End who supported their families on the seven or eight shillings a week they earned as machinists, but they were both eager to hear about the life of the other.

"I s'pose you're really looking forward to your holiday now," said Phoebe.

"After working up to ten and eleven o'clock at night regular the last few weeks, you can be sure I am," Emma replied. "Now that I'm an assistant, I don't have to do the cleaning and wait for the last two weeks of the slack time any more, and I get three weeks instead of two. Did Johnnie tell you Ma and me are going to go and see her brother, my Uncle James? My other uncles and aunts, too, but we'll be staying at their cottage because there's only the two younger two boys living at home now, so there's room for us."

"No. I haven't seen much of Johnnie. It's been a busy time for him, too, I think. He come over Tuesday, just the day when I 'ad to work through to nine, as luck would have it, and 'e likes to leave 'fore it gets too dark to find 'is way across the Pool around all them boats. 'Course 'e was prob'ly out there in the middle as I come over the bridge but the light was failing so I wouldn't 'ave been able to see 'im, would I? No, it was Sam told me 'bout the arrangements for us four to go out together this afternoon."

"Oh. I thought he would've seen you and told you that he was down at Woolwich and spent Saturday night at home last week and came over, with Ma, to see me on Sunday afternoon."

"That must've been a nice surprise."

"It was. Ma brought a picnic with her and we walked across Blackheath into Greenwich Park. It was a lovely afternoon, just like today. I hope the nice weather'll last for the next few weeks for my holidays. Ben and Jenny and Sarah are going to look after the beer-shop. It's a long journey – ferry over, then a train up to Stratford, then another one and there's a two mile walk from the station, which I don't s'pose will seem so bad after sitting in trains all day 'cept we'll have a lot to carry, but I expect one or other of them'll be there to meet us. Ma's written already to tell them what time the train gets there. We haven't been since – since before my pa died because Ma would never leave the beer-shop, but Ben and Jenny have persuaded her, at last, that she needs a holiday and they can look after things with Sarah's help – you remember Sarah, Eddie Jones's wife?"

"'Course," said Phoebe. "I didn't forget everybody soon as we left."

"I know. It's me that's been away so long now. Be three years soon, won't it? But now that I'm earning instead of Ma paying my way, she doesn't need to work so hard. She doesn't seem to know how to stop, though. That's the problem. When we were little, pa would stay to look after the beer-shop and she'd take us to see our relations every year after Christmas, and we'd have a second Christmas there. We'd go to my uncle's first because it was easier to get to from the railway, then we'd go by chase to Ongar and then there was a long walk to Gran's house. Later, after she died, our other uncle and his wife and family stayed on there, so we still had the long walk. We loved it, though – it's proper country up there."

"I remember you and Johnnie going on train journeys and trying not to be envious 'cause of it being a sin. Maybe, once you've been on your holiday and she sees 'er relations again, your ma'll decide to go there more often now that you and Johnnie are off on your own. It's not like it's such a journey as it used to be. I used to go over to the beer-shop to see her a fair bit after Johnnie left – when I could get away from me own ma, that is – and she told me about 'ow she come to London by stagecoach and barge back in the olden days, like."

"She used to like you going in to see her of an evening, she did. Told me you write to her, too, and she's really happy you've got a job now 'stead of being a slavey to your ma."

"Ma's all right – she just doesn't know any better. That's 'ow they were brought up in her family with the girls doing all the work – 'cept Esther, the youngest – remember her?"

Emma grimaced and nodded.

"Ma's more relaxed now with Pa on regular pay and me and Sam bringing in a wage and Will earning enough to pay the school pennies and get his boots mended when needs be. Before Pa got on the steamboats, she never knew what he'd bring in and needed to get the shirts and drawers done so's she'd 'ave enough to feed us all. Anyway, I managed to get me education – with your help, didn't I? So no 'ard feelings there. It's not like I could ever 'ave got into a fashion house like you did – that costs money – so the factory'll 'ave to do for me."

"It was lucky Pa bought the lease on the beer-shop when he did or Ma would never have been able to pay for me to get a place in a high fashion establishment. So, now it's up to me to persuade her to take more time for herself. 'Course the trouble is it's part of her, isn't it? The beer-shop? She doesn't know any other life now."

"I think you're right. But she's happy with it – wouldn't know what to do with herself without. She says her reward is seeing how well you've done. She was so proud when you got moved up to improver before you'd done your two years and then, again when you got made an assistant. Over the moon she was. Remember?"

"I remember. Now that the season's over, maybe you and me can go down to Woolwich more – you getting the train from London and me getting on at Lewisham like we did at Easter. That's one of the best things about being an assistant – not having to be back in time to go to evening service of a Sunday but, while the season's on, you're just too tired to take advantage of it. We all go to morning service, have dinner and go to our rooms and sleep. So, after my holiday, we'll start going regular every two or three weeks and see how everybody's getting on – girls who were at school and all."

"I'd really like that, Emma. Me and Ma went in June to see me gran and grandad and ma's other relations. I kept thinking I'd go again by meself and see your ma but, you know how it is with there only being enough time to make the journey of a Sunday – like there ain't enough Sundays to go round."

"Well that's settled then. We'll go in September for certain." Emma looked around her. "You ever been on this part of the river before, Phoebe?"

"I came down with Johnnie and Sam one Sunday last month. Johnnie was teaching Sam to shoot the bridges and Johnnie and me were being the passengers for Sam to see if he could do it without us getting soaked."

"And did he?"

"We got a bit wet, but it was a warm day and it didn't take long for me frock to dry. We only went as far as Westminster Bridge. Sam's good at it now – ain't got us wet, 'as he? And we must be past Lambeth Bridge now 'cos that's Lambeth Palace over there." Phoebe pointed to the river bank. "Should've noticed really 'cos Lambeth Bridge is a hard one to row through – that's what they mean by 'shooting'. The water gets rough in between the arches, see? When there's lots of them, it's harder to get through. Anyway, we'll soon be at Battersea."

"It's very beautiful, you know. Lottie, the second hand, that I work under, went with her young man and she says it's like being in the Garden of Eden. The flowers are so lovely and everything's laid out in designs. She says the best is the tropical gardens. There's even palm trees. Makes you feel like you're in foreign climes, she says. And they've got all sorts of ducks and geese from other countries in the lake there."

"Pa said it used to be fields and marshes, and there was a very disreputable tavern that they tore down," Phoebe said, eager to display her own knowledge. "Used to be thieves and murderers all over and duelling in the olden days – Duke of Wellington fought a duel there, Pa says but 'e don't know who with. Anyway, seems they thought they'd clean it all out and build a public park for people to get exercise on their day off, like."

"Well, I hope we'll be getting some exercise. We can always walk round by ourselves if those two decide they want to watch the cricket. Johnnie says they play there on Sunday afternoons so, I imagine, they're expecting to sit and watch."

"I dunno about that, but you and me – we're going to see the flowers and the lake. I want to see the palm trees..."

* * * * *

Johnnie gave a final wave in the direction of the North Kent train as it steamed away carrying Emma back to Lewisham.

"Let's have a mug of coffee before we get off 'ome," he said "Not 'ere, though. It's better at the stand by the steam pier."

"Right you are," Sam said, falling into step with him as they made their way down the station concourse.

Phoebe followed until Johnnie remembered that they were almost grown up now and treating her the way boys did a girl when they were younger really wouldn't do. Phoebe was a young lady now and quite a pretty young lady at that. He turned and waited for her to reach his side. Then he held out his arm to her. Phoebe gave him a startled glance but took his arm and they walked on with Sam in the direction of the London Bridge steam pier. I must've grown again, he thought, she didn't used to seem so small when I would push Harry and Charlie in the cart for her back before I started working on the river. You didn't notice yourself getting taller when you wore rolled up canvas trousers most of the time. Ma had brought him a new corduroy suit at Easter, which had always been the time of year for getting new clothes although, in recent years, Emma had looked after her own dresses. While most of his working clothes were inherited from other family members, Ma had continued buying shirts for him and ordering his good trousers from the not too expensive tailor, who was a regular customer in the beer-shop, and everything always fitted right. He wondered how she did it. Just the way of mothers, he supposed. And tailors...

It was nice walking along with Phoebe on his arm. He felt like a gentleman. He glanced at her but couldn't see her face for her sunbonnet. Sam, on his other side, was chattering on about how the afternoon's excursion had taken him back to a day when they were children and Johnnie's ma had taken the four of them on the Woolwich ferry over to the Pavilion Gardens to see the man in the balloon basket. Phoebe, he suddenly realized was panting a little from the exertion of keeping up with his longer stride. He slowed down.

"Sorry," he grinned, "ain't really used to escorting a lady, yet."

"What?" she smiled. "And there was me thinking you and that cousin of yours, James William, was walking out with girls every evening."

"Some 'ope. We work most evenings in the summer – can't afford to waste the light."

Sam was still talking about the man in the balloon at the Pavilion Gardens. "Remember?" he asked, turning around slightly ahead of them, causing both Johnnie and Phoebe to come to a quick stop to prevent themselves from colliding with him. He looked at his sister's hand through Johnnie's arm, then stared at Johnnie.

"We ain't children no more, Sam," Johnnie said, defensively. "You got to learn to treat your sister like a lady 'stead of bargin' on ahead and leaving 'er be'ind."

"What? Oh. I–I s'pose so…"

Phoebe gave an embarrassed laugh, detached herself from Johnnie and walked towards the coffee stand. "Come on," she urged, "let's get our coffee. The steam packet'll be in soon. Maybe we should wait and walk home with Pa, Sam."

"Don't think 'e'll appreciate our company after working a twelve hour day and us being at leisure going off to Battersea Park like swells."

"Pa's not like that," Phoebe said. "Ma won't be very happy with us, but Pa knows we work 'ard, too, and wouldn't grudge us our day off. P'raps we'd better not wait though. Harry'll be wanting me to read his story."

Johnnie bought the coffee and handed them each a tin mug. They walked over to lean against the railing beside the river. Phoebe turned to him and said, without meeting his gaze. "Thanks for buying us the coffee, Johnnie."

They all sipped their coffee and Johnnie wished Sam wasn't there. It had suddenly become very important to be alone with Phoebe. "'Appy to do so," he said. "You walk over London Bridge, then, to go to work?" he asked her.

"Yes. It's a longer walk the other side by way of Blackfriars, and it's been closed, anyway, for the refurbishing. Can't waste money on the tolls at Southwark, so I come this way. I sometimes walk with Pa, in the morning, when 'is crew's on, but I'm usually finished before the last run gets back in the evening."

"You're right, Johnnie," Sam interrupted. "This is nice coffee. I'll 'ave to remember when I start working out of 'ere with Pa. Get paid, you know, call boys do, not like some apprenticeships."

Johnnie wondered if Sam expected him to get into a conversation about money which he didn't feel inclined to do, so he just nodded and finished his coffee. He knew he wasn't going to be able to talk to Phoebe alone but, with the evenings starting to draw in now, he could see about walking home from work at the clothes manufactory with her on nights when there was no unloading, which was about all that could be done on dark evenings.

"Well," he said, looking out over the darkening river, "I'd better let you get 'ome, then. 'Ere, you take the mugs back, Sam." He took Phoebe's mug from her and handed it, along with his own to her brother.

"'Course, Johnnie. Thanks for the treat," Sam said, walking off to the coffee stand.

Johnnie turned quickly to Phoebe. "You finish at seven?"

Phoebe nodded and they started to walk over to the High Street.

"Well, I might see my way to meeting you sometimes. I could walk up and catch you as you walk down to the river, like. All right?"

She nodded again. "I'll watch for you," she said.

"Watch for 'im why?" asked Sam, rejoining them.

"Never you mind, Sam Walkerston," Phoebe replied. "Johnnie and me was 'aving a private conversation. 'Ere, we'd better be getting 'ome. Ma's going to give me an earful, me not being in to get the lit'luns to bed."

"Georgie and Charlie are probably still out playing, so there's only 'Arry," Sam replied, looking cross at her outburst. "You go on though. I got to 'ave a private conversation with Johnnie, meself."

Phoebe glared from one to the other. "All right, I'm going. I don't care what you do," she said and walked quickly away along the road.

"'Night, Phoebe," Johnnie called after her, then began to walk swiftly through St. Saviour's churchyard to the alleyway between the warehouses to reach the wharf where the skiff was tied up. Sam followed him, but Johnnie did not slow down.

"Dunno why she'd want to spoil things acting like that," Sam was muttering to himself.

Johnnie stopped. "It weren't her that spoilt things, Sam," he said sharply. "It was you acting like a child. You don't always have to know everything what's going on, you know."

Sam hung his head.

"If you really must know," Johnnie continued, "she was saying as 'ow she'd watch for me 'case I 'ad time to come up and meet 'er after work some eveningwhen we're not working so late. That's all."

"Why's she go and make a scene about it then? Could've just told me 'stead of biting me 'ead off."

"'Cos it wasn't none of your business, that's why," Johnnie said, starting to walk on.

"What you want to meet 'er from work for anyway? You ain't getting sweet on 'er, are you?"

"And if I am, why not? We ain't children any more, are we? Least she's not and I'm not. I don't know about you."

"Well, 'cos she's Phoebe," Sam obviously had heard only the first sentence, "me sister… jus' Phoebe, you know…"

"Let's not argue about it, Sam. I got to get going. It's getting dark and there ain't no moon out yet. You'd best cut down Church Street there and go under the new viaduct."

"All right. We're still mates, ain't we?"

Johnnie clapped him on the shoulder. "'Course we are, Sam. Now, go on. G'night."

"'Night, Johnnie."

Johnnie stood and watched Sam go. It wasn't often you saw Sam Walkerston looking chastened, he thought. He crossed the deserted wharf, waving to the night watchman to let him know that he wasn't some vandal or layabout hanging about the warehouses, untied the skiff and jumped in.

Sculling briskly across the Upper Pool, he thought about Phoebe. Odd how protective he'd felt back there when she'd stormed off. It was only Sam's presence that had prevented him from running after her. Of course, the problem only came about because of Sam's presence in the first place, so there would have been no need, anyway, in that case. He hoped Sam wouldn't tease her, then remembered the way he had asked if they were still mates. No, he was unlikely to say anything to her and might even apologise. He knew that he had acted childishly when Johnnie had countered his suggestion about being sweet on her, so, you never knew, maybe he'd even start realizing that his sister was a young lady now. Forget Sam, he told himself. Think about Phoebe.

She liked him, he was sure she did. She'd always been Emma's friend rather than his when they were growing up but, during the year or so after Emma had gone to Lewisham and he was still in the upper class, he'd quite often walked with her as she took Georgie to school and back. Ma had told him that she had been quite concerned about his welfare those first few weeks of his apprenticeship and would stop by the beer-shop to hear how he was getting on. She did like him. She did, he was sure she did. Maybe that comment about him and JW walking out with girls every evening showed a bit of jealousy. Could be, he mused. Of course, he hadn't been entirely truthful in his reply. While they really were mostly too busy to do more than have supper and go to bed after work in the summer months, it didn't preclude dollymopping in the Wapping High Street now and again when they had enough money. He experienced sudden shame at comparing that to walking out with a respectable girl like Phoebe and wondered why. It wasn't like he'd ever want Phoebe to service him up against a warehouse wall. No, he wanted to walk with Phoebe on his arm like they had leaving London Bridge station. That was nice. It had made him feel confident, a man of the world. He wished he'd walked with the girls in the gardens at Battersea Park instead of watching cricket with Sam.

He was still picturing himself walking in Battersea Park with Phoebe on his arm as he reached the Kentson wharf, beached and tied the skiff and put away the sculls. It was quite dark now but the moon had risen and the river looked the way he liked to see it – sort of at rest on a Sunday evening. Walking between the warehouses to get to the High Street, he decided to go home and chat with Gran before she went to bed instead of joining the fellows at the Prince. Gran would be eager to hear about their afternoon in one of the new parks for the people which she thought were such a good idea.

* * * * *

It was such a stupid, stupid, childish thing to have done, Phoebe thought, feeling really annoyed with herself. Stupid to have been goaded by Sam's questioning. Johnnie hadn't meant any harm, she was certain of that now. It was just Sam's behaviour that had made her jump to the conclusion that the two of them were making fun of her. She shouldn't have stormed off like that. Johnnie must have been thinking that she was such a child after him treating her like a grown up lady. He probably wouldn't even bother about meeting her from work now. She felt like crying with vexation but swallowed hard instead as she turned the corner into Surrey Street.

"Georgie! Charlie!"

Ma was standing at the open door of their house shouting for the boys to get in and get ready for bed.

"There you are," she said when she saw Phoebe, "I sent them boys to get a jug of beer, for your pa's supper, 'alf 'our ago and they still ain't got back. Don't tread on the step now."

Respectability was measured by how well scrubbed your doorstep was on this street and, never having had her own doorstep before, Phoebe's ma had developed a keen competitive spirit as soon as they had moved in. They were all exhorted to step over the doorstep, from the street, into the doorway or, in the case of the younger children, to jump from the cobbles into the house.

Harry, in his nightshirt, ran to Phoebe as she stepped inside.

"You're late 'ome," he said. "You said you'd be back in time to read me story."

"You're still up, Harry, so I must be in time," Phoebe said, taking off her bonnet with one hand and holding the other one out to Harry. "Come along, let's go up."

Georgie and Charlie came clattering in as the two of them reached the top of the stairs and they could hear Ma scolding them.

"Ma said she'd throttle them," observed Harry. "What does throttle mean?"

"Choke, but I don't think she meant it, do you?"

Harry shook his head, although he still looked puzzled. "Will they get spanked?"

"Depends what their excuse is, I should think. Never mind them – you get into bed and I'll get the fairy tale book."

Phoebe went over and hung her bonnet on one of the hooks in the alcove where she slept, then took the battered copy of *Hans Andersen's Wonderful Stories for Children* from the shelf above the hooks for the boys' clothes on the adjacent wall. She'd found it at a broker's stall at the market when they still lived in Woolwich. The stories had captured the imaginations of all three younger boys and, while Georgie and Charlie claimed they were too old for fairy tales now, they still listened when Phoebe read to Harry and quite often, like him, fell asleep before the end of the story.

"We got to the part where the swindlers showed the empty loons with the pretend cloth, to the man with no clothes on," said Harry from the bedstead he shared with the youngest two of his older brothers.

"Looms," corrected Phoebe, sitting on the bed beside him, "and don't call 'im the man with no clothes on. 'E's the emperor."

"The emperor with no clothes on, then," said Harry.

"All right. Now lie down or I won't be able to read. You know the rule."

"I will, but don't let me fall asleep 'cos when you get to the parade part, I want to say that bit when the boy says it–" Harry sat back up, feigning surprise "–*but 'e's got no clothes on!*"

Phoebe wondered how much of the story the three-year-old understood and how much was a case of memorizing the parts he liked. While Georgie and Charlie had liked her reading to them at his age, she didn't remember them getting as involved in the stories as Harry did. Charlie, of course, had not heard so many of them as Georgie because they'd moved on to the Marryat books to maintain Georgie's interest in reading, which was probably why he liked fairy tales now, although he pretended he didn't because he didn't want Georgie to think he was a baby.

"All right, Harry, lie down again now," she said and began at the part where the swindlers showed the supposedly beautiful cloth to the emperor. Georgie and Charlie came up and she stopped to tell them to get ready for bed quietly and that she was watching to make sure they washed behind their ears. Keeping an eye on the two of them at the washstand, she continued the story until Harry said very sleepily, "But 'e's got no clothes on!" Then fell asleep before she finished the remaining paragraphs.

The older two boys were in bed by this time and Charlie pulled a crumpled chapbook edition of *Tales of Robin Hood* from under the bolster, opened it and held it up for Phoebe to see. Phoebe stood up and put her finger to her lips.

"I'll come round that side," she said in a low voice and she squeezed between the side of the bed and the foot of Sam and Will's bed and sat down, taking the book from Charlie, carefully inserting her thumb at the page where Charlie's had been. "If you make a lot of noise and wake Harry, I won't read another word. All right?"

"I'll be quiet," said Charlie. "So will Georgie."

Georgie turned onto his stomach and buried his head in the bolster. Ma must have spanked them, Phoebe thought. They both appeared very chastened and had washed their faces and put on their nightshirts without a word. She decided to let them maintain their dignity and not ask about it, however, and began to read from the page Charlie had indicated. It was a story about Robin Hood and Little John helping some boys to find their injured father, in Sherwood Forest, before the Sheriff of Nottingham wrongly accused him of being a thief and threw him into gaol.

When they were asleep, Phoebe put on her apron and picked up the urn to take down with her ready to fill with fresh water, after throwing the dirty water over the vegetable bed in the yard. Downstairs, she found that Pa had come in and was eating his supper at the table.

"I've cut bread for you and the boys when they come in," said Ma, as Phoebe turned to go towards the scullery, "and there's the rest of the chicken here. You'd better cut yourself some before they get in or you won't get none. I've put the drumsticks aside for them but you know 'ow they are when they're 'ungry. I'll put whatever's left in the stock pot and make a nice chicken stew for tomorrow."

"Thanks, Ma." She put the urn down beside the scullery door to be dealt with after supper, and joined her parents at the table.

"Litl'uns all asleep, then?" Ma asked.

Phoebe nodded and cut a little of the meat that remained on the chicken they had had for Sunday dinner, Pa's share having been kept aside to be warmed up and eaten for his supper.

"Where is Sam, anyway?" continued Ma. "I wasn't expecting Will yet, but Sam should be in. I thought you was together."

"Him and Johnnie were talking private after we saw Emma off, so I walked home by meself. I expect he went to meet Will on the way since it must be nearly time for him to finish for the evening."

"I dare say you're right. 'Ope 'e isn't getting 'isself into trouble with that rough lot around there, though."

"Better not be," said Pa, draining his mug of beer. "And 'ow did you youngsters like it down Battersea, then?" he asked, refilling the mug.

So Georgie and Charlie did manage to get the beer home of a piece, thought Phoebe as she watched him, the spankings must have been just for not going straight there and back. "It's lovely, Pa," she said. "You and Ma should go one afternoon when you're not working. I can look after the lit'luns next time you have a Sunday off. Emma and me left the boys to watch the cricket and we walked round all the gardens and the lake. Different feeling it gives you, a lake when it's the busy river you're used to seeing. Really pretty it is, too."

"River don't smell so bad down there, either, I bet," Pa said. "Johnnie let Sam scull all the way down?"

"They both sculled part of the way there and back. Sam's pretty good now."

Poor Pa, Phoebe thought, as she continued to eat her supper. He'd really much rather be back in his wherry than working on the steamboat. Should've been born fifty years sooner and he would have been in his element.

MARCH 2007

"When do we get to have the pancakes? I'm hungry and I'm getting cold."

Cranky, too, thought Holly, feeling exasperated with her daughter. Julie and the boys were already at the evaporator display where one of the Mountsberg staff was explaining how the sweet sap was boiled in the tank until all the liquid had evaporated, leaving the syrup behind.

"If you're cold, Carolyn, how about we run to catch up with the others? We'll get warm if we do that." She didn't wait for an answer. "Come along," she said, holding her hand out. Carolyn, with a show of reluctance, took it and they both ran up the path to the interpretation centre.

"Over here, Caro," called Ryan from the other side of the shed, through billowing steam, as they went inside.

Holly led Carolyn around the group of parents and children to the spot where Julie and the boys were watching the young guide ladle syrup from the bottom of the tank to demonstrate how it was forming there.

"This is the modern way of doing it," Jamie started telling them.

"I know," said Carolyn crossly. "I remember from that place we went to before Daddy died."

The sap bubbling in the tank was all that could be heard in the silence that followed. Carolyn looked around her, then straight at Holly, while Jamie looked on horror-stricken. He hated the sympathetic expressions on peoples' faces when they knew he was a boy whose father had died. Holly, who had let go of Carolyn's hand as they entered the building, took her by the shoulders and walked her outside. Jamie followed, biting his lip, Julie and Ryan behind him. Julie acknowledged the consoling smiles of some of the other visitors with a small nod as she passed them. Outside, nobody knew quite what to say.

"How about we skip the kettles and go straight over to the pancake pavilion," Julie suggested, finally. "We can come back later."

Holly nodded and turned to the children. "All right?" she asked.

"Yes," replied Carolyn, "I told you I was hungry."

Holly decided to ignore her rudeness under the circumstances, and they walked quickly along the snow-trampled path to the pancake pavilion. Once there, the children recovered more quickly than their mothers, and started discussing whether or not to have sausages and bacon or just pancakes and syrup. Holly took their gloves and put them all in her bag before they were lost.

"I'll get it," Julie said, when they, at last, reached the cash register. "You paid the admission."

Outside again, they seated themselves at an empty picnic table. Holly didn't really feel like eating pancakes and wished she'd just bought coffee. She had a feeling that Julie's sentiments were the same. The children ate hungrily, however, and Carolyn seemed to quickly recover her normally cheerful disposition. Jamie still looked a little uneasy but the three of them watched other children playing in the hay and exchanged occasional comments about how they would climb up on the bales themselves when they had finished eating.

"Having breakfast food for lunch is part of the sugaring off experience, I suppose," Holly said to Julie, "but I can't say I really feel like eating it."

"Best try to get things back to normal, though," Julie replied and nodded towards the children. "It seems to have gone down well with them, anyway."

"Can we go now?" asked Ryan, finishing his milk. "To play in the hay, I mean."

"I think you'd better sit still and get your lunch down first," his mother told him. "You'll throw up if you don't and you wouldn't want that, would you?"

Ryan shook his head.

"Put your gloves back on now that you've finished eating and we can play I-spy for a bit," suggested Holly, handing out the gloves. "Just for ten minutes so that nobody gets sick in the straw."

"I bet you can't get this one," said Julie, overdoing the enthusiasm but capturing their attention. "I spy, with my little eye, something beginning with… 'S'."

Jamie eventually guessed 'sugar shack' and, drowning out the comments from Ryan about how that should be 'S-S' not 'S' and that you could get free samples at the candy making demonstrations there, he continued the game.

"I don't know what got into her," Holly said, after the children had been allowed to go and play and she and Julie were collecting up all the sticky paper plates and cups ready to put in one of the receptacles placed nearby for the purpose. "She'd been claiming that she couldn't remember going to a sugaring-off before ever since we made plans to come here as a Spring Break expedition."

"I expect being here brought back memories and she didn't know how to deal with them."

"I wish she'd just talked about it instead of having the sulks and acting like that. She's never done anything like that before."

"I know," Julie agreed. *"She's usually such a sunny-natured kid. She seems all right now. I think it was best to get out of there and come over here – get their minds on pancakes. It is the highlight of the day, after all. I hope you didn't think I was interfering."*

"No. I'm glad you had the presence of mind to get us away from all those people looking at us. I didn't know what to do." Holly broke up the remnants of her pancakes with her plastic fork. *"It's best I talk to them about it by themselves – Jamie was embarrassed enough by the attention. The grief manuals tell you these kinds of things can happen with children and it doesn't mean anybody's getting dysfunctional or anything."*

"Odd it should have happened now, isn't it?"

"Yes. Jamie was the one I always worried about most. With Carolyn, I wouldn't say there was no impact, but she wasn't showing any long term effects. She seemed to accept Justin's death, apart from the first few weeks, of course, better than any of us. She was the one who would say 'Daddy wouldn't want us to be sad' and 'Daddy would want us to be happy' – things like that when either Jamie or I were having a bad moment. Still does... Well, you know – you've heard her."

"I think she really had forgotten the details of going to wherever it was for the sugaring off when she was what? Five? And, then something here reminded her of being there with Justin – something that really made her miss him and want him back. It probably involved just the two of them. Maybe, you and Jamie had gone on ahead for some reason."

"It must have been something to do with tapping the trees. That's when she first started lagging behind and I suggested you take the boys on so that we wouldn't have them getting into arguments. Actually, I think Jamie and I did go on to see something else that time at Bruce's Mill. Yes, I remember – it was the kettles steaming away on the campfires – well, that's what he called them. Campfires. We laughed about it."

"Choice is bonfire or campfire," Julie laughed. *"After all, what else would a kid know? And bonfire doesn't fit exactly, does it? Much more likely to be a campfire with the big black kettle steaming on top of it. Anyway, cheer up. Carolyn's over it. She'll probably talk about whatever she was feeling later on – bedtime, most likely. Maybe it would be a good idea to skip the kettles and looking at any more tapped trees, though .We should go over to the farm, perhaps. Animals always make kids happy, and there's a play barn over there, too. And, let's not forget about the birds of prey – they won't want to miss the owls."*

"Good idea. We probably won't be allowed to forget the candy making, though," Holly said, rising and picking up the paper plates and cups to put in the bin.

Later, Julie turned out to be right. Carolyn did bring up the subject herself, and at bedtime, too. She'd had her bath and Jamie had taken possession of the bathroom. Carolyn was in bed, reading her latest Beverly Cleary 'Ramona' book, when Holly put her head around the door to see if she was ready to go to sleep yet. The children always read in bed until they were sleepy.

"Mommy," she said, looking up from the book, *"I'm sorry I was mean to you."*

"Mean to me? You weren't mean to me."

"At the sugaring off – at Mountsberg, when we were in the trees."

"You weren't mean to me, honey," Holly said, crossing the room and sitting on the bed beside Carolyn. "but I think something upset you, didn't it?"

"No. I was being mean to you. I remembered, you see, about when we went to that other place for sugaring off when I was just a little kid." She put the book down and twisted the edge of the sheet. "Daddy carried me on his shoulders because, well – I think it was, maybe, a long way for a little kid to walk ?" She stopped and looked at Holly for confirmation.

"Yes, I expect so," Holly agreed.

"We were looking to see how much sap was in the pail and I asked him why it looks like water if it's syrup or something like that – I don't remember exactly. I mean I didn't remember at all before I looked in that one, today, but it was something like that because Daddy said that it wasn't just water, but sweet water, just like you and Aunt Julie and the other parents were saying to the kids today. Then Daddy took his glove off – it must have been colder than it was today because you must really have had to wear gloves if Daddy was wearing them, right?"

Holly nodded. Sometimes Justin would have to be persuaded to wear his gloves so that the children would wear theirs without complaint.

"He took off his glove," Carolyn continued, "and dipped his finger in the sweet water and held it for me to taste." She stopped and her eyes filled with tears.

Holly pulled her towards her and hugged her tight. "It's hard having to remember, honey, I know. Just cry – it's best to cry out the sadness. Here let me get you some Kleenex."

She continued to hold her until Carolyn's sobs died down and she began to sniff, then got up to fetch the box of Kleenex from the dresser.

She handed some to her and Carolyn wiped her eyes and blew her nose.

Holly sat down again. "Better?" she asked.

Carolyn nodded. "But that's not the really bad part," she said.

"Oh?"

"No. You see, I looked in the pail – today, I mean, at Mountsberg. It was a lower down one than the one when I was on Daddy's shoulders but I'm bigger now so it was sort of like I was in the same position and it was just like he was there saying, 'It's sweet water – here, taste it. You'll see.' Then, you came along and he was gone and I was cross because you were still alive and Daddy was dead. I'm sorry." She put her arms around Holly and buried her face in her neck. "I'm sorry," she sobbed.

"It's all right, hon. I didn't even know you were being mean to me. I just thought you were cross about something. It doesn't matter. Really, it doesn't." Holly pulled some more Kleenex from the box and wiped Carolyn's eyes, then held it for her to blow her nose again. "It's called a flashback – what you had. It happens sometimes to people who've had something disturbing happen to them, like– like their Daddy dying. Something triggers a memory just as the sweet water did for you. It's hard to bear, but it happens and we have to bear it. You should have told me, though, instead of… well, instead of acting mean."

"Does it happen to you?"

"Yes. And sometimes I get mad that somebody else is alive and Daddy's dead – just like you did. So you mustn't feel bad about being cross because I'm alive and he's dead. Okay? What's more important is for you to be as happy as Daddy would have wanted you to be. You know that, don't you?"

Carolyn nodded.

"So," Holly continued, swallowing hard, "what's Ramona up to in this book?" She picked up the book. "I bet she doesn't get to go to Winterlude or to a sugaring off during Spring Break, or to the Rogers Centre to see the Blue Jays play..."

"Ramona's an American girl, not a Canadian one," said Carolyn, taking the book, then handing it back to Holly. "She wouldn't do those things, anyway. 'Cept they have sugaring off in Maine and Vermont and places like that, don't they? It's just like Canada, there, isn't it? We learnt about it at school but, I don't think Ramona lives there. Will you read it to me, Mommy? I know I'm old enough to read to myself, but it's much better when you do it..."

February 1865

Johnnie peered through the front window of Phoebe's house, to make sure somebody was up, before he knocked on the door. He could see Phoebe giving her three youngest brothers their breakfast bowls of porridge. There was no sign of the latest addition to the Walkerston brood, a baby girl named Minnie who had been born last year. She was probably asleep in her cradle, alongside her parents' bed, in the curtained off part of the room at the back of the house. At his light tap on the window, Phoebe and the boys all looked up. Phoebe put her fingers to her lips, hushing them. Johnnie stepped sideways to the door which Phoebe opened.

"I won't come in…"

"It's all right. I'll step out and close the door to keep out the draught. Georgie's on his honour to keep the others quiet. What's wrong?"

"It's me ma," Johnnie told her, unable to keep the catch from his voice. "We was unloading in the Docks until late last night, then went to the tavern so I didn't get 'ome till late. That bloody Sally could've sent some one to find me but she ain't got no brains, the stupid dollymop ain't. I know you don't think well of me calling 'er names like that but she knows Ma's ill, so you'd think she would realize that a letter from Woolwich weren't just someone passing the time of day. And Jenny – why did she post it, anyway? Ben could surely 'ave found someone to bring it up the river…"

"Calm down, Johnnie. Maybe she thought it'd be quickest – the post's supposed to be quickest, after all, and *it* has to come up the river, too. She must've got it in the post before the last packet sailed Friday…"

"'Spect you're right and it would've been fastest, too, if bloody Sally'd got someone to bring it over to me at the Docks," he paused, shaking his head. "It's bad, Phoebe. Jenny says she was posting a letter to Emma at the same time. She wouldn't 'ave told us to come if it wasn't really serious. Emma probably managed to get there last night. I'm going down on the parliamentary 'cos first steamer don't sail until nine today. I just run down 'ere to let you know I wouldn't be over this afternoon."

"When's the train leave, then?" asked Phoebe.

"'Alf an hour. It's later of a Sunday – been any other day, I'd be 'alfway there by now. Been any other day, there'd be a working boat I could've been on at dawn…"

"I want to come, Johnnie. Is that all right? If she's really going to– to die, I'd like to see her. I can go over to me auntie's after, if you and Emma want to be alone with 'er…"

"'Course it's all right. I'd like you to come. What about them, though?" Johnnie asked, nodding towards the window to indicate her little brothers.

"I'll get Sam up. Him and Pa ain't working today. Georgie's old enough to look after the others really but Ma always insists on one of us older ones to be in charge. Look, there's not much time – let me talk to Sam."

Johnnie walked up and down in front of the house until Phoebe came back out wrapped in a thick shawl against the cold morning air, and wearing her bonnet. She was followed by Will, dressed for the outdoors in cap and jacket.

"Will's coming, too," Phoebe said. "We'll get a train or steamer back in time for him to get to work by five. Sam'll see the lit'luns don't play up."

"What did Jenny say, Johnnie?" asked Will, as the three of them started in the direction of the London Bridge railway station.

Johnnie had forgotten how attached Will had become to Ma during the time he'd worked for her in the beer-shop. "Says it don't look good," he told the boy. "She thinks there's not much time left and for me to come quick as I can. She wrote the same letter to Emma and was getting them in the post so's we'd 'ave them by morning – that's yesterday morning, 'course. Only, like I was telling Phoebe, I didn't get mine till midnight last night. I was ready to scull all the way down in the dark, but Jim told me not to be so blooming daft."

"I should hope so," cried Phoebe. "Be nice if you got yourself drowned on top of everything, wouldn't it?"

"I know," said Johnnie, "but it's hard being unable to do anything in the middle of the night like that. Jim and Sally made me go to bed – said I wouldn't be any good to anyone if I didn't get some sleep."

"You don't look like you slept much, though. Maybe you can 'ave a nap on the train."

Johnnie made no comment but didn't think it likely he'd sleep on the noisy crowded uncomfortable parliamentary. They concentrated on walking briskly on to the station without speaking again until they were at the South Eastern ticket office where the last of the people in the queue were moving off to the ticket barrier to board the train. Phoebe stepped quickly up to the wicket and asked for three tickets to Woolwich. Johnnie knew she didn't want him paying for Will's and her own ticket, leaving himself short of money. He went along with it because, while he would have preferred to pay for the tickets, he didn't want to embarrass her by drawing attention to the fact that she was paying. She'd probably put all the savings that she kept under her mattress, unknown to her mother but not to him, into her little drawstring bag to ensure that she and Will could pay their way.

The train was at the platform waiting to begin its first journey of the day into the Kent countryside. Even on a Sunday, parliamentary trains were crowded because they were the only ones many working class people could afford. They walked up to the front carriage, where there'd be more likelihood of finding three seats together because people tended to fill the back ones first to ensure that they got a seat. They found three empty places in the same compartment in the middle of two facing benches. Johnnie and Phoebe sat one side and Will on the other.

More travellers crowded in as the station master announced the stations the train would be calling at through his speaker trumpet. Then, the engine ahead of them disgorged steam and the guard blew the whistle. The noise became deafening as the train moved off out of the station. It was impossible for them to speak to each other. Phoebe stared into space, looking sad. Johnnie knew she was thinking about his ma. Will tried to see through one of the small windows. He had only travelled by train once before. Johnnie closed his eyes. He appreciated their concern, knowing that they had both become close to Ma after he left home to take up his apprenticeship. She'd be glad to see them – if she was strong enough… He felt his stomach lurch with panic as the thought that they might be too late flashed through his mind. He mustn't think of it, he told himself.

Emma must have gone to Woolwich as soon as she had read her letter from Jenny which, he knew would not have been until the workshop closed for the day at half past four on a Saturday, although she may have had some understanding with the owner of the establishment about any correspondence arriving for her while Ma was ill. At any rate, she would have been home by yesterday evening at the latest. If only Gran were still with them, he thought, she would have ensured that he got his letter in time to be on his way yesterday. Gran, unlike stupid Sally, always found out and remembered where they were working – right up until her old heart gave out last October. He wondered if Sally had withheld the letter on purpose. He knew she would like to be rid of him and have his room to rent to lodgers. Since Gran had died, she'd given up all pretence of being their domestic servant and moved into Jim's room permanently. She had talked Jim, who she seemed to have completely under her thumb, into renting Gran's room and the smaller room that had been hers and told him that they could make even more money renting Johnnie's attic room to an entire family. Jim had explained that the room was Johnnie's as one of his binding conditions until he won his freedom. The house would soon look like a common lodging house, as sordid as those in the courts and alleys between Great Hermitage Street and the High Street – the area into which Gran had always warned her grandchildren not to wander. It was enough to have her turning in her grave, Johnnie thought angrily.

"Are you all right, Johnnie?" Phoebe asked, speaking into his ear. It was the only way to be heard over the din of the rattling carriage. He turned to her and nodded. She smiled at him and said something, the word 'sleep' being the only one Johnnie could make out. He nodded again and faced front. He did sleep a little after that, very lightly while dreaming that Jim and Sally were on the train with him instead of Phoebe and Will, and that Sally kept saying that nothing could be done now and he must wait until morning. He awoke with a start to the glow of the single lamp in the carriage as they slowly negotiated the long tunnel at Blackheath. His neck felt twisted and he realized that his head must have been resting on Phoebe's shoulder. Phoebe was slight – not that he was especially big, young Will being almost as tall and their brother, Sam, noticeably bigger than he was, but his weight must have been uncomfortable in the already crowded conditions. He sheepishly tried to convey an apology but Phoebe just smiled gently. She really did care for him, he thought.

They had been walking out for more than a year now. This consisted mainly of him meeting her from work, whenever he was finished for the day himself, and walking home with her. Her mother expected her to come straight home from work in time to get the younger children to bed except when she was able to work overtime. When that happened, he always met her as she came out of the factory and they'd go and have their supper at one of the more respectable riverside taverns. Until, the winter months, this had meant that there was little time to sleep after seeing Phoebe home and walking the two miles back to Wapping. An early dawn meant a workday beginning at five, but it was not a good idea to use the skiff to cut down on the time it took to get home at that hour of the night. It was worth the loss of sleep to feel, if only for a few hours, like grown up young people who would one day get married and have children. They saw each other on Sundays but usually in company with one or the other's family members and, sometimes, he would visit her house on a Saturday evening when she was still expected to look after the younger children while her parents had their night out. There had been occasions, on a few Saturday nights last summer, when her pa was working on the evening steam packet runs, and her mother had looked after the children herself so that he and Phoebe had been able to go out to one of the various entertainments in the area or walk down to Surrey Gardens in Walworth. Here, they could be private on the opposite side of the lake from the rebuilt music hall, occupied now by parts of St. Thomas's Hospital until they decided where the new hospital was going to be built. Not that Phoebe had ever really shown how much she loved him on those few Saturday night occasions when they could be private – either by the lake or at her house after the children were asleep. She never would take her drawers off but, seeing how gentle she was with him being so upset about Ma, he could see that she really did care.

* * * * *

Emma was in the scullery, filling a kettle with water, when she glanced out of the window and saw Johnnie, Phoebe and Will, cross the yard from the door in the fence behind the skittle alley. She put the kettle down and ran to the scullery door, happy to see that Phoebe had come with Johnnie.

"Phoebe, I'm so glad you came," she said, hugging first Phoebe, then her brother. "It's awful. I told Jenny I could manage and not to come over – at least, I told Ben to tell her. She's been over to look after the lodgers' rooms the last few mornings and even stayed the night Friday, bringing the baby with her, and Ben's ma had little Becky. And she stayed looking after the shop for the day. Ben was here by the time I got here, half past six it was, and had sent her home. I told him Johnnie'd be here soon as he could and we'd manage between us, but he said she'd probably insist on coming over later today – that worried about Ma, she is. Says Ma's been like a big sister to her since she came here to live after Pa died, so it's the least she can do. I've just put the porridge on, hoping, if I thinned it, I might be able to get her to eat some, so I'll just put some more oats in so you can have some breakfast, too. I don't suppose you've had any with getting here so early."

"Phoebe was about to, but I interrupted," said Johnnie, "and we got Will out of bed."

"Let me look after it," said Phoebe holding out her hands as Emma took a bag of oats from the larder. "I don't want me and Will coming to put you to more work."

"You don't mind me coming, do you Emma?" asked Will. "Your Ma was good to me when I was working here before we removed to Southwark, and Phoebe thought you wouldn't mind."

"'Course not Will. Ma'll be happy to see you," Emma told him. "She's always saying young Freddie White isn't the worker you were, or Johnnie before you, of course. Or Alfie, your uncle, before that, even." She handed the oats to Phoebe and, picking up the kettle she had been filling, led the way out of the scullery. "Look, why don't you all sit down and have a cup of tea and take a breather? I know you must have run all the way down from the station. The pot's been keeping warm and I'll just top it up." She put the kettle she was carrying onto the stove and took a pot holder to the one that was simmering there already and poured a little water into the teapot. "I'll just take this water up and get Ma freshened up so she'll feel better. I've given her the medicine the doctor left for the pain."

"Let me come and help you," said Phoebe, putting the oats on the table and taking off her shawl and bonnet and handing them to Johnnie who took them back to the scullery to hang on the hooks there. "It'll be easier for you – another woman, I mean. Will knows how to look after the porridge. All right, Will?"

"'Course I can. Good at making porridge, I am."

Emma smiled, glad again that Phoebe had come with Johnnie. Johnnie, coming back in, exchanged an uneasy look with Will. "It's all right, Johnnie. You know Ma will want you seeing her look her – well, best she can… You and Will have a cup of tea while Will's stirring the porridge." She led the way up the stairs. "I'm really so glad you came, Phoebe," she said when they reached the landing out of earshot of the boys. "Boys don't understand what there is to do when someone's ill– dying…"

The door of the room which was once her childhood bedroom opened and the lodgers, a widow and her daughter who were both workers at the paper cartridge factory, came out.

"Mornin', Emma. 'Ow is she this morning?"

"Not so well, Mrs. Benson. You remember my friend Phoebe who's come to help me, don't you?"

Mrs. Benson nodded to Phoebe. "'Allo, dear. You tell your ma I was askin' after 'er, won't you, Emma? As per usual, me an' Betty are off to 'ave our Sunday breakfast with me sister over the river. Looks like we're getting a nice early spring day, it does."

"Yes. I hope it stays fine for you," Emma said, and quietly turned towards her mother's bedroom door. Phoebe stood aside to let the women go downstairs, then followed Emma.

"I'll look after their slops and putting their fresh water out for you after breakfast," she said. "You'd think they'd look after it themselves, under the circumstances, wouldn't you?"

"They would, but not until they get back and it isn't nice to leave chamberpots and washbasins like that all day long," Emma said, wrinkling her nose. "Ma wanted to get a charwoman in, but Jenny insisted on looking after things." She opened the door quietly and looked across the room to the bed where Ma lay with her eyes closed. "I'm back again, Ma, and I've got some hot water here that I'm going to put in the washbasin and we'll give you a nice sponge down and you'll feel a lot better."

"I'll get the basin," Phoebe said, going over to the washstand.

"Phoebe's come to see you, Ma," Emma continued as Phoebe brought over the washbasin and put it down on top of the commode beside the bed. "And Johnnie's downstairs – we told him you'd want us to help you tidy up a bit before he comes in to see you." She poured the hot water from the kettle into the basin and nodded to Phoebe to fetch the jug of cold water from the washstand. "And they brought young Will with them, too. Now you haven't seen him in a while, have you?" Phoebe poured cold water into the basin until she indicated that it was cool enough. "Quite grown up he is now. Looking after the porridge I started making for you and me, he is. Enough for us all, he's making."

Ma opened her eyes and smiled at up her, then turned towards Phoebe.

"Hello Phoebe," she said weakly.

"How are you feeling, Mrs. Kentson?"

"I've had better days, dear. I should have listened more to the doctor. He told me I'd end up collapsing if I didn't stop working and go to bed and he was right. But, like I told Emma, I look at it this way – I was never one for sitting around, and spending weeks in bed is not for me. Better I go this way..."

"You just save your strength, Ma," interrupted Emma, "so me and Phoebe can give you a sponge bath before the water gets cold." She passed some of the towels that were piled on the washstand to Phoebe and pulled back the covers. "You put those under her and I'll do this side."

"It feels like we've changed places," Ma said to Phoebe. "She's the mother and I'm the child."

"Lucky you trained her well," Phoebe said.

"She's going to make Stephen a fine wife, just as you'll be a fine wife to Johnnie one day."

She closed her eyes again. Emma wasn't sure whether it was due to flagging energy or embarrassment at the two girls washing her. She and Phoebe worked gently but quickly together and soon had her comfortable in a clean nightgown. She brushed her mother's hair while Phoebe put the jug back and hung the damp towels on the washstand to dry out.

"Are you all right, Ma?" she asked when she'd finished. "Want to see yourself in the glass?"

"I don't think so, dear. It's a fact, really, that I'd rather not."

"Well, I think we should give you a few minutes to rest while we have our breakfast, and then we'll send Johnnie and Will up to see you. All right?"

"That'll be nice. Tell Johnnie to wake me if I've fallen asleep."

Emma picked up the washbasin and poured the water into the bucket which Phoebe brought to her. Phoebe picked up the kettle and the two girls went back downstairs. Johnnie jumped up from the table as soon as he saw them coming down.

"'Ow is she?"

"I told her we'd let her rest for a little after the sponge bath we gave her. So you can go up when the porridge is finished and take some to her. She might eat some with you there, not wanting you to see she's so ill. How's it coming, Will? I'm really glad to have your help."

Will looked a little bashful, not being used to praise.

"It's just about ready," he said. "I'll put it in bowls for us and then you can thin the rest with some milk for your ma. And the other kettle's boiled if you want to make fresh tea. That's what you wanted it for, ain't it?"

"I'll make it, Em," said Johnnie. "Can't let young Will get all the praise, now."

Phoebe took the bucket from her and carried both bucket and kettle out to the scullery, filling the kettle and bringing it back in with her. Emma sat down at the table, where Phoebe soon joined her, and the two boys served the breakfast.

"Nice getting waited on, ain't it?" laughed Phoebe, then became more serious when she saw Emma's face crumple. "You all right, Em?"

"Yes," Emma said, blinking hard. "It's all right. Johnnie pouring the tea just reminded me of Uncle Jim the morning when Pa died. Remember, Johnnie, how he made us porridge and tea just like this and none of us could eat anything?"

"I remember," replied Johnnie, "but this is different, Emma. Ma's not dead yet and she needs us. We've got to keep our strength up. She don't need weepy children around her worrying her about leaving us before we're ready to look after ourselves. There'll be lots of time for sadness later."

Emma was surprised. Johnnie had never spoken so firmly to her before. Well, that's what comes of being the bossy older sister, she thought. Your little brother suddenly turns into a man. She was glad, though, to hear him sounding so grown up, and smiled. "I know – it's just reaction from trying not to look sad when I'm with her." She ate some of her breakfast. "This is very nice porridge, Will. Thanks for looking after it for us."

"I'm glad I could do something to 'elp," replied Will. "That near a year I worked 'ere for your ma were the best time of me life, you know. I used to make the tea for 'er and me soon as I got 'ere from school, then I'd get on with the work, then 'bout seven she'd tell me to sit at one of the empty tables and do me night lesson and when she'd see I was 'avin' trouble, she'd tell me to bring it round be'ind the bar and she'd explain it to me. Always told me I must get me education and not skip out of the upper class like Sam did and to make sure me brothers went all the way through, too. So, 'ere I am in the upper class and I sometimes wish I still 'ad 'er to 'elp me…"

"Just make sure Georgie and Charlie and Harry follow your example, Will. Little Minnie, too. That'll be Ma's reward," said Johnnie. "She loved being able to help people to learn. I still miss sitting by the bar there, doing me night lesson meself, you know. It was all so safe and comfortable, weren't it, Em?"

Emma nodded, but didn't say anything. She stood up and went over to the stove.

"I'll just get her porridge ready and you and Will can go up and see her, Johnnie. She'll probably seem drowsy – it's the medicine does that – but try and get her to eat a bit and to have a cup of tea." She thinned out the porridge with some milk until it was more of a gruel while Johnnie poured a cup of tea, stirring sugar and milk into it. He gave it to Will to carry. "There, just be careful now," she said, putting a spoon in the bowl and handing it to Johnnie.

She sat down again, as the two boys went upstairs, and finished drinking her tea.

"'Ave you decided what to do about the wedding, Em?" asked Phoebe.

"I talked to Ma about it last night. She says it's not fair to Stephen to put it off because of her– her dying, and wants us to go ahead as planned," Emma told her. "It's not going to be exactly as planned, of course. We'll just arrange with the vicar at Lee to call the bans and to marry us quietly there. I don't want to come here, to St. Mary's, without Ma being here. Stephen won't mind and his family aren't coming all the way from Yorkshire, anyway, so that's what we'll do. I still want Johnnie to give me away, though, and you to be my maid of honour…" she broke off. "Oh, Phoebe, I know Johnnie's right about not getting weepy yet, but – see, Ma says she's ready to meet her Maker. She says Pa's waiting for her and she's ready to join him…"

Phoebe put out her arms and Emma fell into them.

"It's all right, Em. You need to cry. You've been 'ere, by yourself, looking after 'er all night. It's a strain. You said yourself 'ow wore out Jenny was after Friday night. And it must've been such a shock to see 'er like that. I mean getting so weak so quickly. Johnnie said she wasn't 'erself last Sunday, but she was up and around… 'E's probably shocked 'imself now."

"It wasn't just that, Phoebe," Emma said, wiping her eyes. "It was the way she got all the arrangements made while she was still strong enough to do it. She's had the lease transferred to Ben and Jenny and had Ben get his own licence and she's had the boat ownership put in trust to Eddie until Johnnie's of age. She says, since Eddie's the one's using it and he's working out of Woolwich, that's the best plan because of Johnnie wanting to come back here and not to work up there when his apprentice-ship's finished, see?"

Phoebe nodded. "'Ope that doesn't cause trouble for Johnnie with the Kentsons."

"That's what I thought, too. But it was Pa's own boat, not the family's. She even went down to the funeral undertaker Tuesday morning – Jenny went with her while Sarah was minding the shop – and she ordered her coffin… Oh, Phoebe, can you imagine go-ing to order your own coffin?"

They looked at each other, then hugged again.

"Don't cry, Emma. Your ma just wants to make everything easy for you and Johnnie."

"I know. She's so brave. And in pain all the time – you saw how swollen up her stomach is."

"Yes. 'Ere, I'm going to warm the tea and we'll 'ave another cup. 'Ow about that?"

Phoebe picked up the teapot and took it over to the stove where she poured some water from the simmering kettle into it and stirred the leaves around.

"When you go home, Phoebe," Emma said, watching Phoebe pour the warmed up tea through the strainer, "can you stop at Lewisham and go and see Stephen for me? I know it means wait-ing for another train, but I have to stay and I need to get a note to the Mrs. Kinsey. If you take it to Stephen, that way I can let him know, too, and it'll be better if he takes it to her – as my soon-to-be husband, I mean."

"Of course, I can. I have to get Will back in time to go to work, but your Ma has the timetable somewhere that we can check and make sure we have time to get from the station to the cottage and back. I think it's in the dresser isn't it? Or, maybe it's in the pile of things people might ask for on the bar in there." She nodded towards the door into the beer-shop.

"It's a bit awkward, really. You knew we decided to go ahead and get married because I was getting promoted to second hand and would be able to live out, didn't you?" She didn't wait for Phoebe to reply. "Now, I'm worried that I won't get the promotion – taking leave without permission, I mean."

"They wouldn't do that to you, would they? Your ma's dying. Your place is here. Emma, you've been there since you was just turning fourteen working your way up – apprentice, improver, assistant – they know 'ow 'ard you've worked. Of course it'll be all right."

"I hope so. It is best I get Stephen to take the note, though, don't you think?"

"Oh yes. There's always more respect when you 'ave an 'usband to speak for you, ain't there?"

"D'you think so? Anyway, I'll write a letter to Mrs. Kinsey and a note to Stephen, explaining everything and he'll go round and tell her and give her my letter. You do remember the way to the cottage, don't you?"

"Well, I was only there the once, but I think so. Write the address on 'is note so's I have it in case I take a wrong turn and get us lost. Now, we'll just finish our tea and I'll go up and do the boarders' rooms..."

Emma nodded absently. Stephen, who was a carpenter, had rented the cottage and was in the process of getting it ready for her to move into after they were married. She had made curtains for the windows and it was going to be a lovely little house, but Ma would never see it now. She would never come to tea or sit in the little garden or play with her grandchildren or... Emma took a deep breath. I've got to do what Johnnie said – save the tears for later, she thought.

"Thank you, Phoebe" she said. "You're a good friend."

* * * * *

Upstairs, propped with pillows into a sitting position in her bed, Rebecca was thinking what a good friend Phoebe was to both Emma and Johnnie. Her son, over the initial shock at seeing how weak she had become, had sat on the side of the bed and told her how Phoebe had dropped everything and insisted on coming with him this morning and how glad he was since she was so helpful to Emma. Young Will sat on the little wooden stool beside the bed. Quite the young man he was now – eager to please like his sister. Shy, at first he'd been, coming in with a cup of tea for her, Johnnie telling her how he had made the porridge and she must eat some and keep her strength up. She had wondered, as Johnnie placed the pillows behind her, how much strength needed keeping up when you were dying. She managed to eat a few spoonfuls of porridge but it was such an effort to raise her arms and she wasn't ready to let anybody feed her food to her. Skip that part, she would, and get on with the business of dying… Holding the cup of tea was too much of a struggle as well, and she asked Johnnie to take it from her before it spilt all over the bed furniture.

Now, Will was telling her all about the beer-shop, in Southwark, where he worked and how it wasn't half as nice a place as the New Packet but it was a job and they were happy with him. He'd be fourteen next year and if some other opportunity came up before his pa got firm word on an apprenticeship for him on the river, he'd be taking it up. So, whichever way you looked at it, he wouldn't be there for much longer. His chatter brought back memories of those months after Johnnie left and Will, coming in after school, had filled the gap to some extent. He'd been just turning ten then – more than three years ago now which, of course, meant that Johnnie was almost halfway thorough his apprenticeship already. Her son had changed since his grandmother's death, though, and she suspected there were difficulties with that Sally. She knew Sally had got Jim renting rooms and wondered if she had her eye on Johnnie's bedroom, which was part of the terms of his apprenticeship. Ordinarily, he would have talked to her about it – both the children had always discussed their problems with her – but she knew that they didn't want to worry her now. Sally hadn't waited long to convince Jim that he should rent out his mother's old bedchamber and the one that had officially been her own, although everybody knew she was spending the nights in Jim's bedroom.

These last few weeks, she'd no longer been able to hide the pain and weakness she was having from Ben and Jenny, and one of them must have told Emma and Johnnie, despite her asking them not to, and Johnnie had, obviously, decided not to let on about his own unhappiness. It was Phoebe, the last time she was here, who'd let slip about Sally renting rooms and, as soon as the words were out of her mouth, she'd admitted she wasn't supposed to have said anything as Johnnie didn't want to worry her.

The pain was starting to come back by the time Will told her he was going back downstairs to see if the girls needed help with anything, as he was thinking that she and Johnnie likely wanted to have a chat together.

"The porridge was lovely, Will," she said. "You'll make some lucky girl a good husband one day."

The boy blushed and backed out of the room.

"Would you like to try and eat a little more, Ma?" asked Johnnie. "Or sip a bit more tea?"

"I don't think so, love. P'raps you can just put two teaspoons of the new remedy the doctor brought into the little cup for me – it's easier to drink that way... That bottle on the washstand. Then take the extra pillows out when I've drunk it so I can lie back."

Johnnie measured out the medicine and sadly watched her drink it. It was likely almost all laudanum, he knew. He took back the cup and arranged the pillows so that she was lying flat again.

"Does that feel easier?" he asked.

"It will do in a minute," she said. "Got to get it down first," she added with a smile. "Things ain't so good for you at Gran's – Jim's house, I s'pose I should say – any more, are they?" Johnnie, sitting on the stool Will had vacated, grimaced and bowed his head. "Look, son, I know you don't want to worry me..."

"It's all right, Ma. I just 'ave to get used to things. Gran sort of ruled the house right up to the end and what she said went... But things never stay the same, do they? And we all – well... we 'ave to get used to new things, don't we...?"

She knew he was thinking of more than just the changes since his grandmother's death.

"I can see what Sally's up to, Johnnie. You don't have to tell me..."

"I'm going to talk to Uncle Thomas about it. Stan, who's lodged there since Tommy got married, is getting married himself in May, so I'm going to see about Jim paying me a bit so I can move in there and pay me board to Auntie Sarah. Jim and Sally'll be getting more for my room than he'll be paying me so I can pay Auntie Sarah and it should work out right. What d'you think?" Rebecca felt a surge of joy at the question. He was no longer holding back because of her illness, but being her son again – discussing the problem with her, wanting her advice. "I can always use the money Gran left me if 'e don't want to pay me, though it's supposed to be saved for when I get married and 'ave an 'ome of me own, like – that's what she said…"

"Jim's responsible for your keep," Rebecca said, although, with the remedy beginning to have the required effect on the intensity of the pain, it was also starting to make her feel as if she were floating away and it was taking some effort to think coherently. "That's part of being an apprentice master. It was me insisted you have that room because I knew you'd like having Eddie and them share it with you when they were up there – 'specially at first, with being away from home for the first time, I mean. Like you said, we all have to get used to changes, though…"

"And it's not like there's the same need there used to be for lodging men there now that there's not so much business up and down the river what with so much of the fruit and veg and, even the 'ops, now, going by train, so you can sort of see why Sally thinks it's such a waste me 'aving the room to meself when she could be renting it to an 'ole bloomin' family."

"No longer what it used to be, the river… Remember all the cargoes your pa would take up? All through the season – I don't think he expected the railways to take over so much, as quickly as they have…"

"Nobody did, Ma," Johnnie said.

His voice was starting to sound far away and she knew she was speaking not above a whisper herself. She had to make an effort and let him know she thought moving over to Thomas's and Sarah's house was the best plan. She was always afraid that the medicine would send her to sleep for the last time and there would still be things left unsaid.

"Talk to your Uncle Thomas, Johnnie," she whispered, hoping he could hear her. "You're right – that's best with Jim being so much under Sally's influence, now. And, Johnnie, you do what you have to do…"

* * * * *

The second class compartment was a welcome improvement on the journey they had taken this morning on the parliamentary, Pheobe thought, as she and Will settled themselves for the short ride to Lewisham. Quieter, too, because the carriage was built better – likely an old first class one refurbished, that's what they did, so she'd read in the newspaper. Pa always brought home any newspapers left behind on the steam packet. Anyway, it didn't rattle so much and the window was big enough to see through. She thought of Johnnie walking back down Beresford with his cousin, James William, and wished she could have stayed with him and Emma.

James William and his mother, Johnnie's and Emma's Auntie Jane, had arrived, with their Uncle William while she, Emma and Will were checking the times of the afternoon trains. Jim had told his brothers and sister about the letter Johnnie had received and, after a family conference the three had taken the train to Blackwall where William's son-in-law, who worked on the river police boats, had picked them up and taken them the rest of the way to Woolwich. It wasn't something that the river police were supposed to do, of course, but it was quick and the men were in the habit of helping each other out when the need arose. James William had thought it a great joke that they'd have to pretend to be suspected felons if a supervisor spotted them, but that wasn't really likely to happen on a Sunday when river policing was left to lowly constables. Johnnie had come back downstairs while she was making fresh tea for everybody and told them that his ma had taken her medicine and was sleeping. He was glad to see his uncle, you could tell. She had poured cups of tea for them all, then told Emma quietly that she and Will were going over to their Auntie Mary's house and would be back after dinner. They'd bought some meat pies along the way so that Auntie Mary wouldn't be upset at them for arriving unexpectedly when she hadn't made enough Sunday dinner to go round. As it turned out, though, their grandparents were there and Gran and Auntie Mary had made lots of food to eat but she had left the pies, so that they could have them tomorrow and she and Will were under no obligation which was something their ma was always telling them they must never be. Ma said this so often that, as a child, Phoebe had imagined obligation as a huge cloud of soot above her head which would descend upon her if she ever dared to take more than she gave, whatever the circumstances.

Ben had arrived to open up by the time Phoebe and Will returned to the New Packet from Auntie Mary's house, and the men were all sitting at the bar, William instructing Johnnie on all he would have to do after his ma died. Emma was at the table in the back room writing the notes for Phoebe to take to Stephen on her way home. She told Phoebe that she had tried to get her ma to drink a little broth but that she had been sick and then asked for the remedy again, whispering that the pain was tearing her apart already despite only having taken it a short while before. Her Auntie Jane, who was very upset, was sitting with her, Emma said.

They had stayed with Emma, telling her that their own relations had said to give her their sympathy and, if there was anything they could do to help, Emma was to send over to them. Emma had said that the best help now was for everyone to pray that the good Lord would take her mother soon so that she would have to suffer no more pain. She didn't want to lose her but nobody should have to suffer the pain that cancer caused. Phoebe had wanted so much to comfort her but what could she say? Miracles didn't happen when you needed them, did they? She was glad that her aunt was there to help and comfort Emma now.

"It's not fair, is it?" Will said suddenly.

He was sitting in the corner seat and she was next to him so it was easier to talk to each other than it had been on the journey this morning, although conversation still required a certain amount of repetition and was virtually impossible in the tunnels, of which there were a number between Woolwich and Lewisham.

Phoebe shook her head.

"Why should it happen to Mrs. Kentson?" Will continued, but didn't really expect an answer. "She's the nicest lady I've ever known..."

"Better not let Ma hear you say a thing like that."

"But she really is," he declared staunchly, his changing voice sounding throaty. "I remember when I was little – when Georgie was a baby and you and Sam was at school – Ma would go to Mrs. Kentson's school what she 'ad in the beer-shop – Tuesday mornings, it was – for ladies what wanted to learn to read and write..."

"I remember. It would end when they let us out of school for dinner and we'd all walk 'ome together from the beer-shop, bunch of us, there was, what with all the women in the Buildings who'd go. Ma stopped going after Charlie was born – said she was too busy and that I knew enough reading and writing by then to get 'er by."

"Me and the other children would play with Emma and Johnnie's old toys in the corner with that fence thing their pa built to stop lit'luns running out the door when nobody was watching. Mrs. Kentson would give us rock buns and a little milk. I heard later – when I was older and working there – that some of the women would come for that more'n for the learning because they couldn't afford to buy milk for their children, like."

"Probably true. I only remember ever having a cup of milk at Emma's house, meself. Never at our house till I was working full time and paying for me keep after we'd moved to Southwark. We'd 'ave stewed tea – leaves used over and over, we did."

"Phil–phil – what's the word? We learned it at school…"

"Philanthropist," said Phoebe.

"That's what she was. Always 'elping people. Give me that job, after Johnnie left, 'cos she knew Ma wanted me working and that I didn't 'ave the gall like Sam to get them messenger jobs he'd get hisself around the wharfs. Give us me tea she did – rock buns, sometimes there'd be biscuits and always butter on the bread. Used to feel like a real toff, I did. Only ever 'ad butter on the bread for Sunday tea at our 'ouse, didn't we?"

"She was brought up in the country, Mrs. Kentson was, and it was butter and cheese and milk and gleanings kept them from starvation there, Emma says. The farm labourers are paid in food more'n in money, see? So, it's always what's first with her when it comes to feeding children."

"What's gleanings?"

"Left over harvest. Fill their baskets with the grain left on the ground they would, the women and children. Johnnie and Emma done it with them once when they visited their aunties and uncles that are still there working on the farm. Grind it themselves into flour and there'd be oatmeal, too, for making porridge and they'd go out picking berries to make jam with. Then, when the farmer would slaughter a sheep, all the workers would get a bit for their families. It was all their pay, see. Only *money* to be made was from doing gardening and charring and things like that for the rich people."

"'S'pose that's why they all come, from the country, to London to make their fortunes," said Will. "End up in the courts and alleys just as poor, though, don't they?"

The train entered the long Blackheath tunnel as he spoke and Phoebe indicated that she could no longer hear him. She could see him nodding in agreement in the gloom. He was right, she thought sadly, Mrs. Kentson was the nicest lady he had ever known. She hoped, one day when Johnnie finished his apprenticeship and they got married, that somebody else's child might say that about her. She wanted so much to be as nice a lady as Johnnie's ma, and she wished so much that she didn't have to die.

April 2007

"Kate sent me a picture of her whole family at their grandad's house with their Easter eggs, Nana. So I want to send her one of all of us, okay? We'll take it after you give us our Easter eggs..."

"Carolyn!" Holly exclaimed.

"Leave her, Holly. Of course, we have Easter eggs for her and Jamie. Where is Jamie?"

"He's just coming. Something came off the Mars Mission Claw-Tank thing which he brought with him to show Ray. He wanted to stay in the car and fix it before he brings it in," Holly explained, taking off her coat and hanging it on her mother's hallstand. "Give me your coat, Carolyn. Put the bag down before you take it off."

"Here, Carolyn, I'll take the bag," said Pat.

"Don't look into it, Nana," Carolyn said, handing over the shopping bag which contained Easter cards she had made and printouts of the pictures which Kate, with help from her mother, had emailed to her earlier in the day.

Holly took Carolyn's coat from her and hung it up, just as Jamie appeared on the other side of the storm door, carefully carrying the Lego MT-51 Claw-Tank which Pat and Ray had given him for his birthday a few weeks before. "Here's Jamie, now," she said, opening the door. "You go along with Nana, Carolyn. Jamie and I will be along in a minute."

Holly held the Lego toy while Jamie took off his coat and handed it back to him when he'd hung up the coat.

"Careful," said Jamie, taking it back. "It's the hardest part to do, you know, harder than the alien ship and the base."

"Yes, Jamie, so you keep saying. Go along and show Grandad."

Jamie had received several of the Mars Mission toys for his birthday and had not seen Ray since he built the Claw-Tank. They went along the passage to the living room where Carolyn was giving her grandparents the cards she'd made.

"Wow! You finished it," said Ray, looking up from inspecting his handmade card as Jamie brought in the Claw Tank. "I really thought you'd need help with that one – it looked so complicated on the package. Bring it over here. You just hang in there, Holly, and leave these two to Pat and me for a bit. Relax. Have a cup of tea. Pet the cat, whatever…"

Holly grinned and watched Jamie kneel down by the coffee table where he carefully placed the toy. Since Justin's death, Ray had shown a lot more interest in Jamie's activities than he'd previously done. Holly was never sure whether it was because he thought he should stand in for the boy's father or because Jamie was older now and more interesting. She certainly appreciated his continual encouragement, and the interest he shared with Jamie in Lego was certainly genuine, both the Windsor Legoland and the California one being proposed destinations at some point in the future, the Windsor park having been closed for the winter when they were in England at Christmastime. She had originally taught the children to call him Grandad Ray, thinking that, as they grew older, it would make it easier for them to understand that he was her stepfather and not their true grandfather. Quite early on, both children had dropped the Ray part, however, regarding him as their grandfather, period, and making Holly feel rather petty for differentiating in the first place. Ray was a good husband to her mother and good to the children and she knew that her initial dislike of him, all those years ago, was unfair and unfounded and often wished she hadn't been so bitchy towards him.

"How about we get those Easter eggs before we forget?" said Pat.

"Forget!" exclaimed Carolyn.

"No. Of course, I wouldn't really forget now, would I?"

"No, but I have to show you the pictures from Kate first…"

"We'll go out in the kitchen then, and get Mummy and me a cup of tea – you, too, if you like – and we'll look at the pictures? Then, when Grandad has finished inspecting that Lego thing of Jamie's, we'll bring in the Easter eggs." Pat picked up the cards Carolyn had made. "I'll just put these lovely cards up on the shelf first. We've got friends coming over to play bridge tonight and they'll be able to see what a clever granddaughter we have."

In the kitchen, Holly sat at the table and motioned Carolyn to do the same. Her mother added water to the teapot, from the kettle which must have boiled and been turned off as they arrived, and brought it over to the table where she had already placed a tray of mugs, a sugar bowl and creamer.

"I was going to take it into the front room," she said, "but we may as well have it here and leave them to their Lego. Ray got Jamie the trike and the accessory set. They're supposed to be in Jamie's Easter egg bag, but I know he's got them in there – been playing with them himself. Don't worry," she added, turning to Carolyn, "there's a little toy for you, too."

"You shouldn't spoil them, Mom," Holly said. "An Easter egg is enough."

"If I can't spoil my grandchildren now and again, what's the point of being a grandmother? Right, Caro? It's bad enough getting old and having to adjust to being retired…" She poured the tea and then continued. "There I go sounding like a grumpy old woman. Can't have that, can we?"

"You aren't grumpy," said Carolyn. "Mommy's being grumpy saying you shouldn't give us presents."

"No, Mommy's just looking out for you. She doesn't want you to grow up to be a brat but she doesn't need to worry. You won't. Anyway, I don't know why we're worrying about such things when we could be looking at those pictures of yours."

"Not mine. Kate's," said Carolyn, trying to smooth out the sheets of paper she had rolled up while they were talking. Holly took them from her and gently rolled them the other way until they sat flat on the table. "There you see, Nana," she continued, sliding the sheets over to Pat. "Mommy put them all together on one page to print them out – two pages, actually. And we printed these two on photo paper for your album – they're the best."

Pat picked up the photos which, fortunately, Carolyn had not rolled. "You and Kate have become good friends, haven't you?" she said.

"We're email buddies. I email Claire, too, but mostly Kate. Claire's still young and not good at email yet. She has to be helped."

"I expect you're looking forward to when they come over here."

Vicki, her parents and her two little girls were coming to visit at the end of July and Carolyn had big plans for her cousins' holiday. Holly was looking forward to seeing Vicki again. Her husband, Peter, being a landscape architect, was unable to get away in the summer and Vicki was accustomed to either going away with her parents or just having them take the children somewhere for a week or two during the summer holidays.

"They'll be able to play with my friend Marie, across the street – you've seen her – and we're going to go up to the cottage with Aunt Julie and Ryan so they'll be able to play with my friend that I play with up there, Shelley Coulson, whose cottage is next door. It's going to be soo-oo fun, Nana."

"I hope they'll be able to take some time out of that busy schedule to do some sightseeing," said Pat.

"Of course, we'll do that, too. You know there'll be–" she stopped. "You're just teasing me."

"Yes, I am. So, how about I make up for it by giving you your present?"

"Only if she plays with it quietly while I show you what Vicki sent to me," put in Holly.

"Yes! Yes, yes, Mommy."

"Only the present – not the Easter egg," said Pat, getting up and taking a package from one of two bags on the counter.

"Floam," cried Carolyn. "The whole critter kit. Just what I need. Thank you, Nana."

"You're welcome. Now don't make a mess. I'm not actually sure what this stuff is," Pat said to Holly. "I hope it's not too messy."

"It's okay. She's an expert with it."

"So what is it you have?"

Pat sat down again and Holly reached into her purse. "Here," she said. "Vicki went to the Heritage Centre in the Royal Arsenal in Wool-wich and found the baptism records for John Joseph's and Rebecca's children, John and Emma." She handed the copies she'd made from Vicki's scanned images to her mother. "It makes them more real some-how and they have the correct birthdates – Emma's I had from the

IGI, but I only had the BMD record for John, which is wrong because, being born at Christmas time, he didn't get recorded until after the New Year which put him into the next quarter which, in this case, was the next year. She found John Joseph's death record, too, but didn't get further than the 1850s, so we don't have Rebecca's. She wants to go again when she has the time and see what else she can find. It's very time consuming, though. She says you need to set a whole day aside, to ensure you actually end up with something to show for your labour."

"Would have been nice if your grandad – great grandad, that is – had known about his grandfather and great grandfather wouldn't it? His father, who was never around much anyway, told them nothing – just that he was in Barnardo's, the original Barnardo's Home, which, for some reason, he took pride in. From that, Dad thought he was an orphan. Well, it looks as if his mother, perhaps, was dead, but you found his father–"

"–on both the 1891 and the 1901 census with the name spelt wrong, but it's definitely him. And he remarried in 1896, too, although the woman was listed as his wife on the 1891 census. So we know, for sure, that Phoebe was either dead or divorced by 1896 when John remarried, but there's no sign of her anywhere after 1871 when she was a machinist in Wapping, her husband was in the army – stationed in Aldershot, and their child was listed at her parents' home."

"He may not actually have lived with them. Remember the census – just as they do now – called for whoever was actually sleeping in the house that night to be listed. He could just have happened to be there then."

"Mostly you find children listed at both locations in that situation," said Holly. "Remember, I told you one of the earlier Kentsons had two of his grandchildren listed at his house and they were also both listed in their respective parents' homes."

"Not very good at following instructions, were they? The Kentsons?"

"It wasn't necessarily the householder's fault. I think the information was manually collected so, asked for your children's names and ages, what do you say? Reading about living conditions at the time, I should think Phoebe lodged closer to where she worked and the boy possibly lived with her parents, bunking in with her younger brothers. The odd thing is that this is five years after the boy was born and the women had babies every year or two, so did the couple never see each other after he went into the army or what? Would he have been posted overseas in the late 1860s? There weren't any long wars going on, were there?"

"It was a cavalry regiment and a lot of them were in India, weren't they? It seems to me there were always regiments in India and not too many wives would have gone in those days – except officer's wives, of course. It would have been pretty grim for common soldiers' wives being in tents with all the men, expected to do all the laundry. Or, maybe they made the natives do it out there... Anyway, he must have been shipped off somewhere in the army and she lived with her parents or in lodgings and then, perhaps, she died in one of the cholera outbreaks or something. Maybe the boy got turned out of his grandparents' house or ran off and Barnardo found him on the streets – that's how the first Barnardo's homes began – older boys that Barnardo found on the streets and taught to mend shoes and I remember being told he learned to do that there, although he seems to have made his living in a number of ways."

"It's sad, isn't it?" Holly said, more as a remark than a question. "I wonder what happened? I mean John – the second John was destined to carry on the family lighterman tradition yet seems to have married Phoebe right in the middle of his apprenticeship, which they weren't supposed to do, then upped and joined the army."

"Well, judging by the wedding date and the date of the boy's birth, he didn't have much choice about getting married – the working classes were big on respectability in those days and her parents would have insisted on the marriage. The boy probably saw the army as an escape from all the aggravation. She likely gave up her job – no day-care centres in those days, although, I think there were charity-run crèches available so that poor women could work instead of going on the streets…"

"You're such a realist, Mom," Holly said, laughing. "It was a nice romantic scenario with the two of them growing up in Woolwich, then meeting again when they both lived in London…"

"Silly – as both you and I know, romantic scenarios aren't eternal, are they. The Kentsons seem to have had pretty bad luck, though, haven't they? The family history, really – isn't it?"

Holly knew that her mother meant all the cases of one or other of the partners dying, and children experiencing the loss of a parent. She nodded, but it was not something she wanted to talk about.

The silence was broken by Carolyn wanting them to look at the pink and purple dog she had modelled with the Floam. After that, Pat decided it was time to give the children their Easter eggs and they all went into the living room and took the family Easter photos Carolyn wanted to send to England.

May 1866

Emma lifted the sleeping baby against her shoulder and gently patted her back to bring up the wind, then laid her in the perambulator ready to go out. When the tap at the door came, quickly buttoning the front of her dress, she crossed the room to open it, putting her finger to her lips. Phoebe stood there alone.

"Did Johnnie go straight over to the green?" Without waiting for Phoebe's answer, she drew her friend inside hugging her in the process. "It's so nice to see you. You're looking a bit peaky – are you all right?"

"Yes, of course. Probably just the train being so hot and stuffy."

"Take off your bonnet for a few minutes and we'll have some lemonade. The greengrocer was selling lemons off cheap yesterday because they wouldn't keep any longer, he said, so I bought some and made two jugs. A glass will cool you down before we go. Susan's been fed and I've put her in the perambulator ready to go out. I'll get the lemonade and you can get the glasses – you know where they are. I have the jugs on the cold slab in the larder."

They were going to spend the afternoon watching her husband, Stephen, play cricket on the village green. Johnnie and Phoebe had come, by train, to Lewisham, the boys walking on to the green, from the station, while Phoebe had come to the little cottage first to walk over with Emma and the baby. They had done this a few times last summer, since Stephen played for the local working men's club in the North Kent league every Sunday afternoon, but this was the first time this year and the first time since three-month-old Susan's birth in February.

Susan had arrived on the first anniversary of Rebecca's death which Emma thought of as a connection to her mother but, despite Stephen's wish that they name the baby after her mother, she was superstitious enough about it to prefer naming her after his mother instead. She wasn't sure what she thought might happen but, somehow, it felt as if it would be tempting fate. It wasn't just because Susan was born on the anniversary of the day her mother died but the knowledge that the sister, who had died before she and Johnnie were born, had also been named Rebecca.

"I like the perambulator," Phoebe said, when Emma came back in with the jug of lemonade. She had fetched two glasses from the dresser and placed them on the table.

"You should have seen the mess it was when Stephen brought it from the rag and bone man. He's so clever at mending things. He paid next-to-nothing for it, yet pushing it around, I feel like the Princess Alexandra taking one of the little princes for an airing."

"I expect it's her nursemaid does the pushing, not her."

"She's very devoted to her babies – plays with them and everything. At least that's what I read somewhere." She sat down and poured the lemonade. "There you are. Sit down now and drink that."

Johnnie and Phoebe had come to see Susan soon after she was born and, again, when they had stood as godparents at her christening in the little church in Lee where Emma and Stephen had been married last year. Emma had attended services there, with the dressmakers from Mrs. Kinsey's establishment, since she'd first become an apprentice, it being one of Mrs. Kinsey's rules that the girls attend church on Sunday morning and, during their apprenticeship, the girls were required to go to Evensong as well. People had joked about Susan's birth coinciding with the beginning of the busy spring and summer 'season', providing Emma with a pleasant holiday and, indeed, after four years of working eighty hour weeks during the 'season', having the time to appreciate the rebirth of trees and plants and the warm weather was a luxury. However, it was scarcely a holiday with a newborn baby to learn to look after. She loved being able to cook meals following the recipes she'd collected instead of having to hurry home to make a quick supper, after working all day. Yes, she was enjoying being a housewife and mother but, to some extent, was still adjusting to the slower pace. She looked expectantly at Phoebe as they drank their lemonade.

"What d'you think of it?" she asked, finally. She was very proud of finding lemons selling so cheap that she could buy enough to make the lemonade, following the recipe in Mrs. Beeton's *Book of Household Management* which had been her mother's last gift to her – her first wedding present.

"Lovely," said Phoebe. "Just what I needed. You're becoming quite the housewife, aren't you? I'm so happy for you..." Tears suddenly sprang from Phoebe's eyes and she put down the glass and buried her face in her hands.

"What's the matter?" cried Emma, horrified. She jumped up and put her arm around Phoebe's shoulders. "What is it, Phoebe? What's wrong?"

"I'm not looking peaky, like I said, from being on the train on such a warm day. I–I... Oh, Emma..." Phoebe spluttered and felt in her pocket for her handkerchief. "Oh Emma, what am I going to do?"

"What do you mean? What's wrong?"

"I don't know how it happened. I washed meself out with bicarb right after. Laura and them say that does the trick. Now she says she can get a remedy for me but I don't know about that. I've 'eard that can make a baby to be born as an idiot 'stead of it coming away... I don't know what to do."

"Who's Laura?" asked Emma, puzzled. Then it dawned on her. "You're going to have a baby?" She sat down again. "Is that what you're saying, Phoebe?"

"Yes!"

Phoebe collapsed into more paroxysms of tears while Emma stared at her. "Have you told Johnnie?"

"No," Phoebe sobbed. "I ain't told anyone 'cept Laura – she's a girl I work with that seems to know about these things but, Em, I can't do what she says."

"You have to tell Johnnie," Emma said firmly. "And he'll have to marry you."

Phoebe looked up. "You know 'e can't. It's in the binding – '*He shall not commit Fornication, nor contract Matrimony...*' it says."

"I know, but they do – your own father did. Must have done, seeing as he was only nineteen years old when you were born. You told me so yourself."

"It's a bit different being a waterman's apprentice in Woolwich, 'specially when the apprentice master's the mate you've lived next door to all your life. You can keep it quiet and, more important, pick up your own fares and have something to live off of. A London lighterman can't do that – it's a different thing all together, 'specially if you're a Kentson."

Emma was glad to see that explaining the situation from Johnnie's viewpoint had, at least stopped Phoebe from crying but she still thought her brother should be told about his impending fatherhood as quickly as possible. If Phoebe didn't tell him, she would. She took Phoebe's hand. "There has to be a way," she said. "How far along are you?"

"I don't know exactly. Well, I suppose I do..."

"Of course you do. How long since you had your time of the month?"

"That was the problem. I've never got it regular, like, so I didn't realize it was such a long time since I 'ad it, till I started being sick in the privy of a morning… That's when I told Laura and she said about the powders, but that I'd 'ave to be quick about it or else it wouldn't work. Maybe it's even too late already."

She looked as if she was going to start crying again.

"When did you and Johnnie – well, you know…?" Emma asked gently.

"It was the Saturday before Susan was born. Johnnie and me went down to Woolwich the next day remember, it being close to the time when your pa and your ma passed away, to put some flowers on the grave from all of us, you not being able to make the journey yourself just then. Anyway, the night before, I put Harry and Minnie to bed as usual on a Saturday night, with Ma and Pa gone to the pub. Will 'ad taken the boys to this little gaff down Walworth where they do turns that're all right for boys – 'though I think Charlie's too young, meself, but Ma said 'e could go – and Sam's got a mate who passed 'is two year test in January, too, and his pa lets them 'ave 'is wherry, over at Vauxhall, of a Saturday night. Sunday, too, sometimes, but the boy's pa was working to-day so Sam come over 'ere with Johnnie and me."

Phoebe stopped and took a deep breath. Her aitches, which, at other times, she made a great effort to remember, always tended to disappear under stress, Emma knew. She poured her a bit more lemonade.

"Here, drink that before you start getting all upset again."

"They'll be wondering where we've got to…"

"Never mind. We have to get this remedied first or you'll feel miserable all afternoon. Johnnie came over and the children were asleep…"

"Yes. He was upset. Sally'd got Jim to spin 'im a yarn again 'bout the money it took to run the house and he'd have to pay your Auntie Sarah for his board out of the money in the savings bank. That's another problem, Emma. That money's s'posed to be for when we get married but, since Johnnie's been boarding at your Uncle Thomas's house, half the time Jim doesn't give him the board money he's s'posed to and he has to take the money from the bank – the money your Gran left him – to pay 'is rent. So I was trying to help him feel better and, before you know, well… it 'appened, didn't it? I remembered what the girls said about the bicarb, but I s'pose I didn't do it right. You need a rubber bag to do it proper and I could only sit in it, see."

Emma nodded. Her own knowledge of such things was a limited as Phoebe's. She decided not to make matters worse by voicing the thought that her brother should have been in possession of more information, such things being more accessible to men than to respectable young women.

"You could get married in Southwark and keep it quiet. There's no need to let tell the relations. Go on living at your ma's…"

"Me ma'll kill me."

"But she must have been in the same fix herself when she was expecting you!"

"That's not the point. I'll 'ave to stop working and won't be able to pay for me keep…" Phoebe wailed. "Don't you see?"

"Phoebe, you must have paid for your keep many times over by now, all the time you've spent looking after little brothers – most of your life, in fact. She owes you."

"I doubt she thinks so. And how will she like minding the baby when I go back to work – and let's hope I can get me place back after the baby's born. I'll 'ave to pay every penny over to her for me keep and for the baby's and for her minding him. Johnnie's not going to have a living wage for the best part of three years yet and, because of Sally, the money he does have will be all used up long before that."

Emma thought of how Stephen had rented the cottage and spent months mending windows and doors and building furniture, determined that they weren't even going to touch the money Gran had left her. It was still intact, earning interest in the savings bank. Stephen said it was only to be used for an emergency, but it was unlikely they'd have one because he was a skilled carpenter and, as a second hand, not only had she been able to contribute a very respectable amount to their household before stopping work to have Susan, but wouldn't have any trouble getting a job later on. In comparison, Johnnie and Phoebe would have a very impoverished start to marriage, living separately and pretending not to be married.

"If it comes down to it," she told Phoebe, "I can lend you some of the money Gran left me. She didn't leave the girls as much as the boys, but I still have it. We had enough savings to get us started.

But, I'm going to write to Uncle Thomas and tell him what's happened – not the baby. I mean about Jim and Sally. Uncle Jim used to be so nice – he was always our favourite uncle when we were children. I'm sure Uncle Thomas and Auntie Sarah wouldn't dream of taking the money if they knew it was from Johnnie's inheritance."

"That's the whole problem, Em. Johnnie don't want them to know. He says Sally's already caused enough trouble in the family and it's awkward for 'im, being as he's apprenticed to Jim." Phoebe paused and took a deep breath, then carried on more calmly. "Jim does give him the board money when he has it. It's just that Sally runs things in that house, not him. The three of them – your three uncles, I mean, are all operating for themselves now. So are their cousins, Joe and Bill. It's not like it was before your gran died. They didn't dare change from running things your grandad's way while she was alive. Johnnie's working on Jim's boat like he was a freeman and not getting paid above the odd tips an apprentice gets. Money's all paid over to Sally who says your gran taught 'er to keep the books, but she really just picked it up prying into everything like, didn't she? "

"I didn't know things were so bad. Uncle Jim didn't even come to Ma's funeral last year and Ma told me about Sally wanting to rent out Johnnie's room, but she was dying, wasn't she? So I told her not the worry about it. Johnnie could look out for himself. And, I suppose I thought he had…"

"Well, with your ma had passing away and you were getting married and setting up a home, then expecting. You had enough to keep you busy."

"It's no excuse, though. I never even talked to Johnnie about it and you never mentioned it, so I thought everything was all right.

Anyway, the more important thing is for you and Johnnie to get married and get ready for the baby, so first thing we have to do is to tell him. Come on, we have to get over to the green. Stephen'll be pretty disappointed if he's scored a century or something and we weren't there to see him…"

* * * * *

The three of them were silent on the journey home. Even the usually irrepressible Sam seemed to be buried in his own thoughts.

Johnnie had been horrified to find that Phoebe had been keeping the news of the baby from him. He'd felt pretty annoyed that she should have told Emma while he had to hear about it with both his sister and Sam looking on. He was thankful that Stephen was fielding, out of earshot, at silly mid-on. He forgot his anger, however, when Emma had explained how worried Phoebe was about their future while he was still an apprentice, not to mention about how her mother was going to react, so that she didn't know where to turn, so why shouldn't she come to Emma who had been her bosom friend since the day she started school?

Sam had immediately pointed out that their ma could hardly kick up a fuss when you didn't need to be a mathematician to figure out that she'd been in the same situation, herself, some nineteen years ago, to which Phoebe replied that their ma had had two older brothers earning their keep and sisters working, too, so it wasn't like her ma needed her wages like Ma needed Phoebe's, with Sam being apprenticed and Will making very little yet as a carman's van boy. Then Sam had said that, if the marriage had to be kept secret, Phoebe would still be handing over her pay, anyway, except for when the baby was actually being born and Phoebe replied that you didn't just drop a baby and run back to work.

And who was to suckle the poor little thing if she had to be at a sewing machine in Cheapside ten, sometimes twelve or fourteen hours a day? Sam countered with the fact that lots of poor women had to work all day after having a baby, so how did they manage? Johnnie had finally found his tongue at Sam's including his soon-to-be wife, and mother of his child, with the anonymous poor and told them to stop arguing about what, as the baby's father, was his decision to make.

He'd felt funny saying that – 'as the baby's father'. It was like a sudden jolt – almost as if saying it had suddenly made it real. Until then, it had seemed as if they were all talking about some-body else. Yes, somebody else. Not John Joseph Kentson aged eighteen, apprentice lighterman. How could he be a father? In the fifth year of his apprenticeship, he did get a share of cargo billing when he partnered one of his uncles or cousins, but, the terms of his binding as Jim's apprentice provided only board and lodging – despite the fact that they worked as partners most of the time now. If he was off working for one of the others when Jim collected the bills due, he didn't even get enough to pay over to Auntie Sarah, who he had been lodging with for more than a year now because of Sally taking over Gran's house and renting rooms to people Gran would never have countenanced in her house.

At the sudden jolting realization that he and Phoebe really were going to be parents, he had quickly recovered and said he'd get work around the warehouses, when the nights drew in and he had the time, so that he could make good Phoebe and the baby's keep with her ma until she could work again, not that he wanted her to work, with the baby to care for, so maybe he should give up the apprenticeship and get daily work on the docks or see if JW's pa could find him a job in the warehouse, where JW himself was an assistant manager now. At that suggestion, Emma had, immediately, said that he couldn't settle for a labourer's wages when, in little more that two and a half years, he'd get freedom of the river and be able to make a good income. Phoebe had nodded her agreement, adding that she didn't mind their marriage being kept quiet and, as long as he could make enough money to pay over to her ma during her confinement (she had stumbled over the unfamiliar word), she could do what some women she knew at the factory did. There was a nearby crèche where they left their babies and young children, while they were working, and went over to feed them at dinnertime and teatime. She had smiled, then, and admitted that she was glad she had told them her secret because now that she was over the panic, she could think more clearly about what was best to do about it. His sister had quickly hugged her and said that she was sure that it would be wonderful to be sisters as well as bosom friends and that everything was going to work out right and she could see that Sam would help her to deal with their ma, to which Sam had nodded vigorously. He said he could help by giving his ma more of the fare money he made on Saturday nights instead of pretending he made less than he really did, but that he had to keep something for himself.

After that, they had watched the rest of the cricket match, then gone home with Emma and Stephen to tea where Stephen, apprised of the news of the upcoming wedding, had opened a bottle of his mother's elderberry wine, left over from presents they had received when Susan was born and which he had been saving for another special occasion. He proposed a toast to their having as happy a marriage as him and Emma. Looking at Emma, as her husband said this, Johnnie had hoped fervently that Phoebe would look as serenely happy in her marriage as his sister did. He knew how hard it had been for Emma with Ma dying just as she and Stephen were about to get married, how she had felt she didn't have the right to happiness with Stephen so soon after Ma's death, and he was glad of her present contentment.

The journey was not a long one and the train was soon beginning to slow down as it approached London Bridge station. He turned to Phoebe.

"Do you want me to come 'ome with you now and talk to them?"

"No," she said. "This wouldn't be a good time. Ma'll be in a bad mood from having Minnie and Harry to look after, and Georgie and Charlie likely played 'er up. She'll blame me because I wasn't there to help her. It'll be best on a Saturday night just before she and Pa go out–" she broke off. "Maybe not, though. She'll think that's how it happened."

"Well, it did."

"No need to spell it out for 'er, is there? What I mean is that we have to find a time when she likes me because I'm looking after the lit'luns, saving her from having to do it."

"With the light evenings, I'm working late. Even Saturday nights it's difficult to get over to your house before they go out – look at last night. I wasn't there until after nine."

Sam had obviously been listening from the seat opposite. "I got a better idea," he said. "'Ow about I talk to Pa about it? 'Im and me, we're together a lot, working on the steamer, walking back and forth from the steam pier. We gets along pretty well now that 'e treats me like crew 'stead of 'is child."

The engine let out a long, loud whistle at that moment as it came to a stop, belching steam. Johnnie indicated that they'd talk about it once they got out of the station and they disembarked, hurrying along the platform to the station entrance and out into the street.

"Let's walk over and sit in the churchyard," Phoebe suggested.

Johnnie nodded and they crossed the road to St. Saviour's and found a quiet grave to sit on. The graves were old. They had stopped burying people here, same as most of the London church-yards, because they were so full of bodies that there was nowhere to put any more of them.

"See," Sam said, looking at Phoebe. "Pa'll understand 'ow 'ard it is for Johnnie to find a favourable time for the two of you to talk to Ma and he'll respect you, Johnnie, for not wanting to leave it to Phoebe to tell Ma by 'erself. I can tell 'im that you want to ask for Phoebe's 'and– "Johnnie and Phoebe both giggled at his choice of words. He continued, "He'll guess why right off, won't 'e, what with you still having more'n two years apprenticeship to do, you'd 'ardly be asking yet, otherwise, would you?"

Johnnie shook his head.

"So, 'aving been in the same position, 'e'll sympathise with you and I'll get 'im to stop by the coffee stand at the steam packet dock 'fore we go 'ome, say, Tuesday night, and you be there to ask 'im. Okay?"

"Okay," agreed Johnnie. "But how does this help Phoebe with telling your ma?"

"You time it, Phoebe," Sam said, turning to his sister, "so you get the lit'luns to bed and, when Ma's laying the table, you tell her that Pa and me'll be a bit late 'cos we're meeting Johnnie at the dock so 'e can ask for your 'and, like. Then, same as Pa, she'll know why–"

"Oh yes. And, after she clips me round the ear, you and Pa come gaily in for your supper and what's that expression people are saying – pour oil on troubled water – and everything'll be all right?"

"But Sam's right, Phoebe," Johnnie said. "Your pa's been in my position – you on the way before he'd finished his apprenticeship, I mean. So 'e's the best person to help us with your ma."

"The problem with you two is that you're still missing the main point," Phoebe cried, jumping up. "It's not the baby that ma's going to be upset about or, even us getting married – 'though, she won't like it being kept quiet 'cos she'll see me marrying you as a step up. She don't know about Kentson Lighterage coming apart at the seams and used to always say, when we were children, about things being easier for you and Emma because you was better off then us. What the problem will be is that she's got used to me handing over me wages each week. It's all very well for you to say that you'll be able to earn enough money to pay her for board and lodging for me and the baby the first few weeks, but she's still going to be the one that's out after that, ain't she? I'll 'ave the crèche to pay for, won't I?"

Johnnie took her hand and pulled her down beside him.

"Look, I think you're worrying too much about your ma," he said. "I think we should follow Sam's plan, except you don't say anything to your ma. I'll come 'ome with your pa and Sam, and your pa can announce the news of the wedding to her, let her draw her own conclusions, then explain about keeping it quiet because we can't 'ave Jim or Waterman's Hall knowing, just like when she and your pa got married. She'll be relieved that you'll still be bringing 'ome your wages, you'll see. If me binding was finished, you'd be moving out altogether, then she would have something to complain about, wouldn't she? This way, she gets to 'ave your wages for another couple of years 'til you and me and the baby set up 'ome, and Sam and Will'll be earning more money to make up for it by then ."

Phoebe looked at him doubtfully.

"That's good thinking, Johnnie," said Sam. "The fact that you'll still be 'anding over your wages'll do the trick, Phoebe. You mark my words it will."

"Well, we'll see. I have to get home and look after putting Minnie and Harry to bed. I know Ma's counting on me to do that tonight so she can get the finishing done for me to take in tomorrow, so why don't you walk over to the wharf with Johnnie, Sam, and finish getting the plan worked out. 'Night, Johnnie."

Phoebe rose to leave.

"'Ere," cried Sam, jumping up. "Ain't you going to say g'night proper to your betrothed? Don't mind me. I'll just start walking on ahead."

Johnnie got up, smiling and shaking his head at Sam, and exchanging a glance with him, Phoebe relaxed and smiled after her brother as he moved off.

"It'll work out, Phoebe," he said, putting his hands on her shoulders and drawing her towards him.

"I expect so," she replied. "These things are just so much harder for a woman." She nestled against his shoulder, making Johnnie feel very protective, then raised her face, "I'd better be going."

He kissed her gently on the cheek. "G'night," he said. "Stop worrying – everything's going to be all right."

* * * * *

Phoebe hung up her dress, by the light of the gas lamp in the street outside the bedroom window, and got into bed carefully so as not to disturb her sleeping two-year-old sister. Ma had recently decided that Minnie was too big for the cot and should start sleeping with the rest of the children, so Phoebe wasn't yet used to sharing the narrow bed in the alcove. She secretly thought that, since she paid her way, she should be entitled to having the bed to herself but, in the present circumstances, she didn't like to say so. She wondered how she and Minnie were going to manage to fit into the bed as her middle expanded over the next few months, then put the thought from her mind.

Instead, she went over the afternoon's events and decided that she was glad her secret was out – at least, among her peers. Tuesday night would tell if she'd feel the same about Ma and Pa knowing. She remembered what Johnnie had said about Ma most likely being relieved that she wouldn't be losing her wages just yet awhile and realized that he was probably right. Except for when the baby was actually born and the weeks afterwards when she wouldn't be able to work, she'd be handing her wages over as usual – well, less however much she would have to pay at the crèche and, hopefully, Johnnie would be able to make it up by working on the docks or in the warehouses when the evenings drew in and they didn't work so long on the river. Would they give her back her place, she wondered. She'd worked there going on for four years now, including when she was a trainee, and was a good worker. They'd surely take her back – she knew three girls who had given birth and come back to work afterwards and she knew, for a fact, that the line supervisor thought she was a better worker than any of the three. Say the first or second week in December. That would be enough time to get the baby's feeding times regulated so that she could leave him at the crèche. The crèche was a much better idea than having Ma look after him and having to pump milk to leave for him. She'd be able to go in and feed him properly twice a day whereas there wasn't time enough for her to come all the way home. 'Course the reason she hadn't thought of it before was because it was run by a charity for poor women and she hadn't really classed herself as 'poor', but if circumstances prevented her husband providing a place of their own to live in and her ma needed her wages, then she was poor, wasn't she? She'd find out how to go about putting her name down for it. Ma probably wouldn't like it because she'd rather have the money it would cost but, hopefully, Sam would keep his word and help make it up and Johnnie would be able to carry on making a bit extra on the docks, at that time of the year, until the evenings started to draw out again, and the working day became longer for the lightermen. Georgie had Will's old job at the beer-shop and was earning the school pennies now and Charlie, competing with other young boys, for pennies earned handing out pamphlets and tracts, was contributing to the household, too, so it wasn't as if they were as badly off as in the days of her childhood when Ma was sewing shirts and drawers for the slop tailor at all hours.

Discussing the situation with Emma had helped her to think about it properly instead of getting into a state the way she had ever since she first began to suspect that she was going to have the baby. Once she got past Tuesday, she could even look forward to the next few weeks – getting their banns called, the wedding. It was a shame they'd have to keep it from Johnnie's relations… they'd probably suspect but, as long as they didn't officially know, it would be all right. That's what she remembered Ma telling her once, after a few pints and good company at the beer-shop had made her more expansive than usual. She'd said how Pa's apprentice master, whose family had lived side by side with Pa's for years, couldn't fail to know what was going on when she had

given birth to first Phoebe, then Sam, just up and around the corner in the room over her pa's butcher shop, before Pa got his
freedom. 'Course Woolwich was a world away from Waterman's
Hall really and the watermen there had their own ways of doing
things. Wapping was another story altogether, but she and the
baby wouldn't be around there. Johnnie hadn't taken her there
since before his Gran died and his troubles with Sally had begun.
Anyway, it would be as much as she could do to keep up with
looking after the baby and work for twelve hours a day, too.
Wouldn't be much like the lovely time Emma was having with
baby Susan, would it? Envy was wrong. She shouldn't envy her
friend. Emma deserved her good fortune and it was nice for her
to have the summer months to herself this year. Next Easter to the
end of July, with Susan weaned, it would be back to long hours
working on the beautiful gowns the society women of Greenwich
and Lewisham ordered during the Season, for Emma was determined to become a first hand and, one day, have her own salon.
She said that the first hand she worked under, had advised her
that, with just a bit more experience as a second hand, she'd be
eligible to be a first hand as soon as an opportunity arose, either
there in Lewisham or, maybe, moving on to a West End salon.
And, since Stephen, too, expected to move up in the world, they
would be seriously considering removing to Islington or Camden
Town or maybe, even, Regents Park in a couple of years – a nice
genteel neighbourhood, Emma had said.

Well, that's one thing she and Johnnie would not be looking
toward, Phoebe thought. Lightermen had to live near the docks
and the docklands neighbourhoods attracted all and sundry, but
not the genteel. She smiled at her own humour and wondered
what it was like to live somewhere other than the teeming river-

side. She pictured herself and Johnnie and the baby in a house of their own in a row of cottages like Emma's at Lee Green but knew that it could never be. The best they could hope for would be rooms in a house that wasn't actually in Wapping's presently cholera-stricken courts and alleys inhabited by unskilled labourers, transient dock workers, prostitutes, pickpockets and worse, and the poor who could afford nothing better. Although, nowadays, trains were bringing workers into London, she knew, from nicer homes in villages like Lee Green and more underground railway lines were going to be built north of the river, making it possible to live further away. She and Johnnie had gone on the underground railway all the way to Paddington, once, but she hadn't really liked it very much. Her ears had been ringing for days afterwards. Anyway, there was no point in imagining living anywhere other than with Ma and Pa until Johnnie got freedom of the river and that wouldn't be until more than two years after the baby was born, would it? Perhaps they'd go back to Woolwich then. John-nie had always said he wanted to go back and work his pa's old boat with Eddie Jones. It might be nice living in Woolwich if they could find a house somewhere nicer than the streets in the Dusthole, but still in easy reach of the river…

MAY 2007

"My cousin, Vicki, found some more baptism records for our ancestors," Holly said, putting down the phone.

"Old ones?" asked Julie.

"1840s and 50s. Our, I think, three times–" Holly hesitated, calculating mentally. *"Yes, that's right – our three times great grandmother and her brothers. She's going to scan the copies she made and email them to me. She found their grandmother's – Vicki's and my however many times great grandmother's – burial record, too. Remember I told you how you can get access to the parish records in Kent, where they lived, in what was the Woolwich Arsenal. It houses the big artillery museum now and a heritage centre. Anyway, you can book time and go through the records – on microfiche or microfilm, I imagine. I didn't ask her. She said it takes a lot of time but she likes doing it."*

"Wow! That must be pretty cool. How come you didn't think of it when you were there at Christmas?"

"We did, but there wasn't the time. On vacation with two kids, my mother and stepfather? Come on – you need to plan a trip dedicated to family history research to do that kind of thing. This is only the

second time – in nearly five months – that Vicki's been able to find an afternoon to devote to going through things there. She works part-time – in the mornings. Her mother went round to her house for when the kids got home from school. Anyway, she wanted to let me know and she'll probably email the pages after supper."

"Of course, it's evening there, isn't it? So, is this the one who married her childhood sweetheart, had a baby and disappeared? The baptism records?"

Julie had come over to Holly's house for lunch and they had been drinking their coffee and discussing plans for the upcoming Victoria Day weekend when Vicki called. Holly had recently been filling in some of the twentieth century gaps in her family history records by going through the scanned indexes of birth, marriage and death records on the internet but, like Julie, found the idea of researching old parish records more exciting. If it hadn't been for her mother getting itchy feet and coming to Canada, she'd have been born in England and could do so but, then, of course, she wouldn't be herself since her father lived on this side of the Atlantic. Anyway, you could order the microfilm and look at it in the basements of Morman temples all over the place and there was one not far away.

"Holly?"

"Sorry. Yes it is that one. You know we should find out how you go about searching parish records at the Morman temple. You can, you know. I read it on the LDS website."

"Yeah – just like your cousin, we'd never be able to find the time. That must be why so many older people get into it. You need to be retired to have enough time. Your mom might be interested in doing it."

"Mm," said Holly. "I might run it by her and see what she says. She's more of a realist than me. I get carried away with romantic notions about the ancestors, but she just bursts my bubble and lets me know how their lives would really have been in the grimy river-side slums."

"Well, she did spend her formative years in the general area and, from what I've read about it, it didn't really get cleaned up until the last twenty years or so."

"Well, not exactly. They put sewers in, and had figured out that polluted water made them sick, back in Phoebe's time. Yes, the gentrifying has happened during the last twenty or thirty years, just like Toronto and any other large port city, but building better housing started after the war because the slums in the docklands were all bombed and, in fact, London started working on modern day pollution control back in the fifties – way before the rest of the world caught on. But, as my mother, the realist, says, Phoebe probably got cholera or something like that living in a vermin infested garret or leaky cellar full of polluted Thames water."

"Let's not get quite so realistic. It's depressing."

"When I have time, I'm going to go through the rest of the nine-teen teens and twenties images on Ancestry and see if I can find a death record for John. He's on the 1901 census, married to the other woman so his has to be either in the non-transcribed records or else transcribed with the name mispelt."

"He may have lived into the nineteen thirties, you never know. And, you know what else?"

"What?"

"Well, if they did separate, remember it wasn't easy, and certainly not cheap, to get a divorce in those days. So, maybe, Phoebe didn't get cholera and die but is on a later census under another name – just like the woman her husband later married."

"One day, I'll find the answer. It's just a question of finding the time to search," Holly said. "Right now, it's May and there's baseball and soccer starting, Carolyn's costume to make for the ballet recital and a hundred and one other things that have to be done..."

"Talking about things that have to be done," said Julie, getting up, "I have work to do so I'd better be on my way. Paul should be picking Jamie up for baseball practice about six thirty. One of us'll let you know if that changes. Okay?"

"Sure. He'll be ready," Holly replied, following Julie to the door. "Nice not having to bother with coats and things again, isn't it? I love May – you know, the expectation of the whole summer ahead..."

"Me, too. See you later."

After Julie drove off, Holly sat on one of the rattan chairs she had cleaned and put on the veranda ready for the summer. The lilac between her property and the next house was in bloom and the scent wafted around the entire area creating, along with the sunshine, a feeling of well-being. She had an appointment at three to show a house and was debating on whether or not to bring the yards of tulle out here to sew onto Carolyn's leotard which she had stretched over a garbage can to make it easier to stitch. It would be the second ballet recital without Justin, just as they'd had the second Easter, the second Valentine's Day, the second Spring Break and, this past weekend, the second Mother's Day without him. Would she always count the various events, the important family days, as the years went by? Would there always be the desperate longing to have her old life back, to wake up and find these long months of widowhood to be just a dream, a nightmare? She shook herself and stood up. There wasn't time to work on the costume, she decided. She'd stack the dishwasher and turn it on to rinse the lunch dishes, then drop into the office on her way to pick up her clients. She could check the new listings and see if there were any alternative properties she could tentatively present, although she had a feeling that the Cape Cod was exactly what the clients were looking for. It would look nice on a sunny afternoon like this with the tulips all in bloom. Problem was the price...

She thought about her ancestors in their poky little one or two up and down homes, with scrubbed front steps, or so her mother had said, in the overcrowded residential areas of the great city that was growing faster than it ever had done before. Pat had told her that spanking clean steps and shiny door knockers were status symbols in those mean streets. She wondered how large families like the Walkerstons, whose birth records Vicki would be scanning to send to her later today, managed to live in two or three rooms without somebody doing somebody else serious harm. The front door would have opened directly onto the street and a smelly outhouse would have taken up most of the tiny back yard. Cheap, dusty coal would be burning in the stove, spewing smoke and soot into the fusty room where they cooked, ate and generally spent the hours they weren't working or sleeping – probably served as a bedroom, too, for some of the family. By the time Phoebe's baby was born, there would have been three teens, the three younger boys, the little girl and the parents, in addition to Phoebe and her son.

They seemed to have moved from Southwark to Stepney at some point between the baby's birth in 1866 and the 1871 census. Her father had, for some reason, given up working on the river – traded his wherry for a van, his occupation being listed as a carman, as was his son Will's. Since all three of the younger boys were listed as printers on later census records, the move, must have involved improved circumstances and the means to acquiring apprenticeships for them. Regardless, with two men's wages coming in, the boys old enough to earn money from odd jobs and no school fees after the 1870 Education Act, they would probably have been better off than they had ever been before. Yet, Phoebe appeared to have been thrown out to *live in lodgings. On the other hand, there was no way of knowing what had happened to Phoebe and John between their marriage, and the birth of the baby in 1866 , and John (and Phoebe's brother, Sam, too) being listed in barracks at Aldershot, while Phoebe lodged with a coal merchant and his wife in Stepney, in 1871. At some point during those years, John and Sam had given up their apprentice-ships and joined the army. She had been able to find out that their regiment had been in India until 1867, then returned to England by way of Abyssinia, where they'd fought some mad emperor's army up in the mountains, in 1868. She could find no reference, on the inter-net, to the 3rd Prince of Wales' Dragoon Guards between that homecoming and their being stationed in Aldershot in 1871. She'd found Sam, now married, out of the army and living in London's East End, on the 1881 census, but there was no sign anywhere of John or Phoebe, and their son was in the Barnardo's home. If John hadn't shown up in the later census records, married to somebody else, she'd have concluded that the boy had been orphaned... It would be nice to know the true story, but she probably never would.*

Holly looked at her watch. Better quit daydreaming and get a move on, she thought. It was probably just as her mother had said. Phoebe's father had insisted on the marriage but the two had been too young to set up home and have a real marriage, then John had escaped into the army and they'd gone their own separate ways.

February 1867

"I can't have it, don't you see that? Think 'ow you would feel, Steve, if you weren't making the money to support your wife and child?"

"Emma's gone back to supporting 'erself now, anyway, in't that right, luv?" Stephen turned towards Emma who had just come out of the bedroom after settling Susan for the night. He had grown up in Yorkshire, and Johnnie sometimes had trouble understanding his accent.

"That's not so much supporting 'erself as bettering 'erself, that is. Em takes after our ma – got to be learning all the time, and teaching, too. It's different with Phoebe. She's a slave in a garment factory."

"She'll still be a slave in a garment factory if you give up your apprenticeship and go into the army," said Emma sharply, piling supper dishes together to take out to the scullery. "You only earn enough to keep yourself in the army. You know that – you grew up in an army town. You didn't see any common soldiers getting rich, did you? I didn't. You'll be no better off than you are now and you'll be in India…"

"But I will be better off. What'll I 'ave to spend me money on in India? I'll 'ave enough spare to send 'ome for Phoebe and the baby. Now, everything she doesn't pay to the crèche, goes to 'er ma who's complaining it ain't enough. I've tried to give Phoebe enough so's she can make up the difference and Sam's been paying 'is way more than 'e did but with both 'im and me being apprentices, an' Will, too, come to that, it's not like we can make much money, so Phoebe's ma's not getting as much as she used to and she's got an extra child in the house."

"But, Johnnie, being in the army won't be any different than being apprenticed – especially at first when they're taking money out of your pay for your uniform and things."

Johnnie wished Emma had stayed in the bedroom.

"I can work my way up. Going straight out to India shows them you want to get somewhere. That's what the recruiting officer told us…"

"That's right – somewhere full of mutinous natives and monsoons and snakes and tigers and…"

"You know that's not what he meant, luv," said Stephen. "Maybe 'e's right and it would be better than a life working on the river. Didn't you tell me once that, when 'e was a litl'un, Johnnie always used to say 'e wanted to go for a soldier?"

Johnnie was glad of Stephen's support but he knew what Emma's answer to that would be, right enough.

"That's just a stage all little boys go through," she said, crossly.

"It were a sailor I wanted to be, meself, but being out in t' lighter with Johnnie them couple of times made me thank t' Lord that me da bound me to a carpenter," Stephen laughed. "But Johnnie really studied t' cavalry, din't he? Fixed on it, din't you tell me? Could be it's meant to be, then."

Emma didn't say anything. She pushed the crockery aside and sat down in the seat she'd vacated earlier.

"Look, Emma," Johnnie said. "You know I was only bound because it was expected. All the boys in the family were apprenticed to fathers or uncles or brothers. I didn't 'ave any choice, but it wasn't really what I wanted. That's not to say I wasn't 'appy with things the first little while, but you've got to understand. After Gran died, the business, as it was since Grandad's time, just – well, disintegrated, you'd 'ave to say. All three of the uncles are working for themselves now, and Bill and Joe are running their pa's boat and contracting for the customers 'e always looked after. It was Sally taking over the desk when Gran was fading that did it – remember the desk in the back parlour where Gran always did all the reckoning up for Grandad. With Jim choosing to side with Sally, who'd no business being there – Good Lord, she was the 'ousekeeper, not the mistress…"

"But mistress she is, isn't she? Uncle Jim's mistress."

Both Johnnie and Stephen chuckled.

"Well, they 'ave less polite names for it around the docks," laughed Johnnie.

"Ma knew she'd set her cap for Uncle Jim soon as she saw her," Emma continued unhappily, ignoring the interruption. "Look, Johnnie, I know that everything went as wrong as it possibly could and you've been having a rough time the last couple of years, but there's less than two years to go now and you'll have your freedom. Surely you don't want to throw it all away just because Sam wants you to join the army with him."

"It's not Sam. He's just fed up with being a call boy. I've been thinking about this for a long time now," Johnnie replied. "After Ma died, see, I thought, maybe, it didn't matter anymore. Her last words to me were 'Johnnie, you do what you have to do now…' and I never knew whether she meant about moving into Uncle Thomas's house, which is what we'd been talking about, or if she meant that she'd done her duty, by Pa and Grandad, having me bound to Jim but, now that she was dying, I was free to do whatever I have to do."

Emma was silent. She looked at her husband. Stephen poured the remains of the jug of beer they'd had with supper into his and Johnnie's mugs.

"That's all very well, Johnnie," he said, eventually, "but joining the army's like startin' over. You've spent over five year becomin' an expert on the river – you'd be just throwin' it all away. If you were talkin' of joining the navy, I could see it, but the army – well, I don't know about that…"

"The recruiting sergeant says we 'ave skills from working on the river that'll be useful in the cavalry…" Johnnie told him. "Don't really see how knowing how to reckon up your time and tides'll be any use in India, meself. Said something about sizing up the situation, whatever that means. Anyway, 'e's only interested in getting 'is bounty, and me and Sam, we ain't no mugginses, so we took it with a grain of salt, but it'd be true about signing on now and going out to India to show we're serious about making our way up the ladder, like. It's not as if theres's a war there, the army's just patrolling and they'll be changing regiments at the end of the year."

"That's stupid," said Emma. "By the time you get there, it'll be time to turn around and come back."

"Not quite as quick as that but I did wonder why they'd bother with recruiting now. Seems they need to get the numbers back up before they come 'ome. See that's what makes the 3rd Dragoon Guards our best bet – we get to 'ave service in India on our record without running much risk of getting them tropical diseases and suchlike. We'll be there for some months, though. A lot of the basic training is done on the way out, so we'll be leaving in just a couple of weeks. If we sign up, I mean."

"What d'you mean *if*?" Emma asked. "Your mind's already made up. I can tell. It's like when you were little and you'd say *if* you went up the common to watch them drill, you'd do whatever Ma wanted you to do when you got back. We always knew there was no *if* about it."

Johnnie grinned. "I used to pretend I wasn't sure if I was going so that nobody'd tell Sam if he came looking for me," he said.

"What about Sam? He's not old enough for active duty, is he?"

"'E already added a couple of years to 'is age when we was talking to the sergeant. 'Long as you don't look like a drummer boy, they'll believe you're as old as you say you are."

Emma stood up and picked up the pile of supper dishes and took them out to the scullery. Johnnie and Stephen drank their beer in silence until she came back to pick up the kettle of boiling water from the hob. "I still don't see how signing your life away for ten years is going to help Phoebe," she said.

"Twelve years for cavalry," Johnnie corrected. "It won't much change things for her at first 'cept I'll be able to send money, regular like, for 'er and the baby. 'Er ma won't 'ave Sam to keep so she'll 'ave it easier and won't be on at Phoebe 'bout an extra mouth to feed, not that the baby's an extra mouth yet, but that's 'ow she puts it. But, once we're back and the regiment's in barracks, Phoebe and Baby John'll be able to move into the married quarters with me and be entitled to rations. So, you see, it will be better."

"That depends on where the regiment's stationed. Remember Jenny's sister – married quarters for her in Devon somewhere, I forget where, was behind a strung up blanket in a corner of a barracks that slept thirty men."

"All the newer depots have proper married quarters and, with the reforms that parliament's bringing in this year, the recruiting sergeant said, they all will eventually, among other improvements – 'e listed them all off. Regimental depot's at Chichester at the moment – that's where we report to get kitted out. I s'pose that's where we'll come back to, but then we get moved on to wherever we're stationed next."

Johnnie decided against telling his sister that he hadn't actually mentioned the fact that he was married in the conversation with the recruiting sergeant. Sam had said he thought it better not to say anything until they had actually enlisted as they weren't too keen on common soldiers getting married in the army, so they'd likely not want one who was already married. Johnnie had no idea how Sam knew this but thought it best to go along with it. Anyway, Emma would misunderstand if he told her. She'd think he was trying to disown Phoebe and the baby. That was the trouble with Emma – she'd been acting like she was her guardian angel ever since the school mistress had entrusted the seven-year-old Phoebe, who was going to school for the first time, to her care, a charge his sister had taken very seriously then and still seemed to be doing now. He knew that her sympathies had been with Phoebe rather than with him last summer when they first knew that the baby was on the way and she, obviously, thought that he should stay on the river and not enlist in the army. She would think that the whole idea was a ruse to get out of his responsibilities if she knew that he wasn't going to admit to being married just yet. He watched her as she shook her head and went back to the scullery with the kettle of water.

"Give 'er a while to get used to the idea, Johnnie," said Stephen, getting up from the table. "If you're going to sleep 'ere and row the skiff back over come dawn, we should go down the pub and 'ave a game of shove 'alfpenny with me mates."

Johnnie had brought some lumber over for Stephen who had met him at the flour mill dock, where they'd left the skiff and transferred the lumber to a handcart to bring down to his yard. It was easier to wait for dawn than to row back up Dartford Creek and across the river on a dark February night, so Johnnie would doss down on the straw bed Emma kept for the purpose and get back in time for work in the morning.

"Can't stay late, though. I need to be up at the crack of dawn to get across before water's up."

"I'll need to be working on t' cabinet first thing meself, so we'll be back 'fore ten, you can count on 't," Stephen replied. He put his head around the scullery door. "Em – we're going over t' pub for a game of skittles, Johnnie and me. Won't be long."

Johnnie picked up the mugs and went into the scullery as Stephen moved over to get his cap and muffler from the coat hooks by the front door. "Here, Emma, I brought the mugs out for you." He put them into her bowl of hot water. "Look, I'm sorry you're disappointed in me, but I have to do what's right for me and Phoebe, and for the baby. Don't worry, I'll make you proud of me, yet. You *and* Phoebe."

Emma turned to him and he could see she'd been crying. "Just make sure you come back, Johnnie. You're the only brother I've got. I can't afford to lose you." She smiled. "That's where Phoebe's got the advantage over me – all those little brothers growing up into big strong men to look after her."

* * * * *

Baby John gurgled and brought up his wind again as Phoebe went to lay him in the wooden cradle that Emma's Stephen had made and which the two of them had given to her as what they called a baby gift. Phoebe had never heard of giving presents when babies were born, except for crossing the baby's palm with silver. It must be something done by people who were better off. The cradle was the most beautiful thing she had ever owned – except for the baby himself, of course. It was exactly the same as Baby Susan's and Phoebe liked to imagine Emma putting Susan to bed as she was putting her John into his cradle at night. It was the happiest time of the day. Until yesterday, of course, since when even her beautiful baby could not stop her feeling desperately unhappy.

Yesterday, Johnnie had met her after work. He and Sam had been there when she came down the stairs from the crèche, cradling the baby in one arm and her basket on the other, bracing herself for the long walk home. It had been nice to have Johnnie take the basket from her so that she could carry Baby John more comfortably. The reason he was there wasn't so nice, though.

The boys took her into a newly opened tea room on King William Street despite her protests that it was a shocking waste of money since they'd be having supper when they got home. Thankfully Baby John, who she rocked gently on her lap, remained sleeping as she was sure the lady proprietor would not have wanted a crying baby in there. Of course, she knew they had some sort of unpleasant news for her by the way the two of them were being so nice – sympathizing with how tired she must be, after the hard day's work and still the long walk home, carrying the baby.

They had found a way to make things easier for her, Johnnie said. Maybe not at first, but within the year she wouldn't have to work. She'd be able to stay home with the baby, maybe do a bit of finishing if she wanted to, like her ma did, to pay for extras, but she wouldn't have to sit at a machine all day long, getting swollen veins in her legs from working the treadle. Then, she discovered that when they said 'stay home', they didn't mean stay home at Ma's house or the house – even a room – of their own that they'd been planning to get when Johnnie won freedom of the river and began to earn money for himself. No, Johnnie wasn't even going to stay on and get his freedom. Neither was Sam. They were both going for a soldier and staying home meant married quarters in an army barracks. Putting from her mind some of the awful stories she'd heard, back in Woolwich, about married quarters, she had listened in horror as they'd told her that the reason this wouldn't actually happen until the end of the year was because they had to go to India first. She had struggled to remember what they'd learned about India at school and finally said, "But there are blood-crazed savages, who murder good Christians in their beds, out there in India."

Both Johnnie and Sam had laughed.

"That was ten years ago," Johnnie had said. "The 3rd's been on patrol to keep the savages in order ever since – they send out replacements so's soldiers whose time's up can come 'ome, but another regiment will be going out at the end of the year and the whole 3rd'll be back and in barracks somewhere in England for a couple of years until they're needed somewhere else. So you and the baby'll come and join us then."

They had carried on like that, not even noticing that she wasn't saying anything until Sam said Johnnie should come home with them. They could buy some pies on the way so that Ma wouldn't complain there wasn't enough supper to go around. So they'd, eventually arrived home and after they'd had supper and were finishing off the jug of ale while she and Ma did the washing up, Sam had told Pa what he and Johnnie were intending to do. The funny thing was Pa wasn't even angry at Sam proposing not to finish his apprenticeship. He'd even said something about the glory of defending the empire.

She didn't want to live in an army barracks, Phoebe thought now, as she lifted the baby against her shoulder to make sure he had no more wind to bring up. She sat down on her bed and gently rubbed the baby's back. She really didn't want to be a soldier's wife. She didn't want to live in an army barracks hundreds of miles away from Ma and Pa and Harry and the rest of her brothers, and little Minnie. Or, worse than that; have to sail away to another country in a couple of years. Johnnie had said that the regiment would be sent wherever it was needed. There were terrible diseases in those foreign places. What if Baby John were to catch something? She bit her lip. She was Johnnie's wife and it was a wife's duty to do what her husband wanted, wasn't it? There was one good thing about all this and that was not having to pretend that she *wasn't* Johnnie's wife anymore. If Johnnie was going for a soldier, the Watermen's Company and the Kentsons no longer mattered.

Phoebe rose and settled the baby in the cradle.

"Ma says it's time for you to put us to bed," came a piercing whisper from the stairs.

Phoebe looked up to see Harry dragging three year old Minnie by the hand.

"Is Baby John asleep?" he asked softly.

"Yes. Come along. You help Minnie put her nightgown on and I'll run down and get some more water so you can both wash your hands and faces."

Phoebe took her little sister's nightgown from the peg in the alcove where it was hanging with her own, and guided the two children into the space between the washstand and the bed where Harry slept with Georgie and Charlie. She undid the strings of Minnie's pinafore, which Harry would get knotted, and picked the urn up from the washstand. "I won't be a minute," she said, crossing to the stairs.

With Sam gone for a soldier with Johnnie, she thought, Georgie could move in with Will which would leave room beside Harry for Minnie. She'd have her narrow alcove bed back to herself again – until they came back from India when she and Baby John would have to go and join them and live in some horrid army barracks…

Downstairs, she went out to the scullery to pump some cold water into the urn, then over to the stove and poured in a little hot water from the kettle. Ma was sitting nearby, with the lamp beside her, darning stockings, while Georgie, who had just come in from his job at the beer-shop, and Charlie were doing their night lessons at the table. Pa and Will had gone to see a man with a van for sale – Pa was thinking of getting into the carting business with Will's employer, apparently, which explained why he hadn't been too upset with Sam last night, and Sam, himself, was out, with some mates, at a tavern somewhere.

"Charlie needs some help with his – what did you say it was called?" Ma asked the boys.

"'Is multiplication," said Georgie. "I can't explain it right to get it through 'is thick 'ead."

"I ain't got a thick 'ead," Charlie said crossly, kicking his brother under the table. "You just ain't no good explaining things."

"I'll help you, Charlie," Phoebe told him, "just as soon as I've got Minnie to bed. But Harry'll be waiting for me to read his story, so you'd better listen properly because I don't 'ave time to say it twice, do I?"

She washed Minnie and softly – so as not to waken the baby – sang some songs with her, watching to make sure Harry washed behind his ears as she did so. Then, leaving the two of them in their beds, Harry singing quietly to the sleepy Minnie, she ran back downstairs to help Charlie. He was not very good at arithmetic, but seemed to learn better from her than from the teacher or his monitor at school.

"You'd have made a good school mistress, Phoebe," Ma said.

She often said this when Phoebe was helping the younger boys with their night lessons which made Phoebe smile sadly since, if Ma hadn't stopped her going to school when Harry was born, she really might have been a school teacher. Of course, she wouldn't have been able to marry Johnnie and have Baby John but, of course, that hadn't been what they'd actually planned to do anyway.

Charlie finally seemed to have understood the nine times table. Georgie had confused him by saying that it was easy to remember because of the way the first number ascended and the second descended when he had only ever heard those words as part of the Apostles' Creed and couldn't see how they applied to numbers. Phoebe went back upstairs to read Harry his story, then wiped up splashed water around the washstand. She took the urn downstairs with her to bring more warm water up later, then sat in the chair on the other side of the lamp from Ma to mend her own stockings, then – if she wasn't too sleepy – to smock the front of the little gown she was making for Baby John.

"Litl'uns all settled, then?" asked Ma.

Phoebe nodded. "Harry says he's going for a soldier, too, when he grows big."

"'E'd better not, that's all I can say," said Ma. "Bad enough me oldest son talking like going off to India was like going down to Brighton, I ain't losing me youngest one, too."

"Can't we stop them, Ma?"

"I should 'ave thought at nineteen years of age, me girl, you'd 'ave learnt that when a man gets a bee in 'is bonnet, so to speak, there ain't much us women can do about it."

"Johnnie's gone down to Emma's tonight. Maybe she'll make 'im see that it'd be stupid not to finish 'is apprenticeship now with only the two years to go to 'is freedom."

"I don't think she'll make no difference, luv. They've got their minds made up, Johnnie and Sam. It's a pity they met up with that recruiting party…"

"It would've been different if it hadn't've been a cavalry regiment," said Phoebe. "That's what really got them going, if you ask me – brought back the times they'd go up the common and watch them drilling at Woolwich."

"They'll find watching soldiers ride their 'orses and practice their shooting a bit different from the 'ard work of actually doing it, won't they? They'll both be wishing they was back on the river. 'Specially out there in India, they will."

"They will, won't they? But it'll be too late by then."

* * * * *

Emma lay awake beside her gently snoring husband. On the other side of her, the baby made little grunting sounds in her cradle. Stephen stopped snoring momentarily as he turned over; then his even breathing began again. She knew her brother was just as soundly asleep as Stephen on the pallet by the banked up stove. She wished sleep would come to her. Men seemed to be able to fall asleep no matter what troubles there were, she thought, laying on her back staring up at the blackness of the night, her mind churning with questions and doubts.

She wondered if Ma was really telling Johnnie that he must do what he thought best that day on her deathbed. If only she were here to guide Johnnie. If only Pa hadn't died. If Pa hadn't died, Johnnie would have been apprenticed to him in Woolwich and the problems with their uncles, after Gran's death, wouldn't have affected him to the point where he had now chosen to throw away all that he'd learned about working on the river over the past five years, and start a new career. Perhaps if Ma had bound him to Eddie Jones things would have worked out. Johnnie would have stayed in Woolwich then. While they'd enjoyed visiting their grandparents and other relations as children, neither of them had really liked the mean courts and alleys sandwiched between the London Docks and the river. There were similar places, of course, in the Dusthole at Woolwich but, somehow, they didn't seem so bad. There weren't all those scary foreigners, either. No, she'd known, without him ever actually saying so, that Johnnie wasn't happy living in Wapping right from that cold January when he'd first gone off to be bound to Uncle Jim. It hadn't been so noticeable while Gran was alive and, when the Walkerstons had moved to Southwark, he'd been able to take a skiff across the river and see Phoebe and Sam regularly and had seemed quite happy.

Maybe he was right and that was what Ma had meant. Ma must have known how unhappy he was however hard he tried to hide it. Ma most likely would have preferred him to stay in Woolwich but had probably promised Pa, sometime during that terrible night when he died struggling to breathe, that his son would carry on the Kentson tradition and learn lightermanship in the family business. But, even if Ma had meant that Johnnie should let his own conscience guide him, she, surely, would not have wanted him to go for a soldier, would she?

In her mind's eye, Emma saw her mother at the bar in the beer-shop and, wistfully, thought of the times when she or Johnnie – sometimes the two of them – would climb up on a stool and discuss a problem with her. She remembered the day when she had told Ma that she wanted to be a dressmaker and not become a school teacher the way they'd always planned. Ma had told her that she'd need to be apprenticed to a good house if she wanted to better herself and not become one of the poor, exploited needlewomen you read about in the newspaper. She probably had thought saying that would make Emma think again but, instead, Emma had confided that she didn't just want to be a dressmaker. No, she just needed to learn dressmaking so that, one day, she could be a couturier, explaining that that was what an Englishman in Paris was calling himself. He was a draper who had gone to Paris and started his own dressmaking house just two years ago, and was now devising dresses for the Empress Eugénie, she had told her mother who had wondered where she'd learned such things. Emma had told her how, now that she was in the upper class, she had lessons with a needlework teacher, who came in just to teach the older girls. On learning that Emma made her pinafores to patterns that she drew first and that she contrived patterns for other girls, the teacher had said she had a talent and told her all about how her distant cousin, Charles Worth, had made such beautiful dresses for his wife to wear that customers at the draper's shop where he worked in Paris wanted him to make copies for them. He had set up his own establishment and called himself a couturier, which meant being a creator of fashionable clothes, not just a dressmaker, and had young women model dresses he made for prospective customers who would then order copies for themselves. He was creating a new industry that would be quite different from a dressmaker sewing a dress upon instructions from a customer, the way it was done now. Ma had been disappointed, she knew, despite being impressed by her own enthusiasm. However, on the advice of the needlework teacher, she had found Emma a place and paid a substantial apprenticeship fee.

"And it won't go to waste, Ma," Emma silently told the picture of Ma in her head. "I will devise ladies' dresses one day, maybe even for royalty. Once I get some experience as a first hand, I can get taken on at one of the houses in London that are following Mr. Worth's lead."

Perhaps if Johnnie had told Ma he wanted to stay in Woolwich and learn the trade from Eddie and carry on helping in the beer-shop, Ma would have braved the displeasure of the Kentsons – even Gran's, despite her long-standing admiration for the old lady. But, then, maybe Gran would have understood. Maybe Grandad had left the company in her hands because he knew that it was likely that his sons would not keep the business going the way he had shaped it, without her guiding hand. Perhaps, in truth, she was the guiding hand behind Grandad's success. Such a thing was often the case, she had heard. Anyway, there was nothing she could do. Johnnie was going to be a soldier.

Did he really have to join a regiment that was serving in India, though? That was the part that she really objected to, Emma thought. It wasn't fair to Phoebe. And it wasn't as if it was just her husband that Phoebe was losing, there was the brother with whom she'd grown up. Despite having had to care for all the other brothers and little Minnie, too, Phoebe must feel closest to Sam who had shared so much of her life. What did any of them really know

about India? Well, they knew there had been a rebellion of the –
what were they called? The Sepoys, or something like that. It had
been back when they were children at school, although, to this
day, she couldn't honestly say she understood what it was all
about. The boys probably knew better – boys in National Schools
were taught a lot more about what was going on in the world
than girls were. She did know that the government now control-
led India instead of the East India Company and that British
soldiers patrolled the country to prevent other rebellions from
breaking out.

Well, at least, going out there to be on patrol was better than
being sent out to fight barbarous natives and, it wasn't for so long.
The time would pass – look how fast the last year had gone by,
since Baby Susan had been born. Why, she'd soon be walking and
Emma was quite sure that some of the sounds she was making
were meant to be words… But, growing as she was, she'd keep
running over to the child-minder's house to feed her at dinner
time and tea time for a while yet. It was a shame she couldn't be
with her the whole day, but she must get experience at being a
first hand before she had another child…

Maybe, if Johnnie did send her money and she didn't have to
hand it over to her ma, Phoebe would have enough for train tickets for her and the baby to come over here more often of a Sunday…
If she brought little Minnie and Harry like she did that last time,
her ma would be all in favour of it and ensure that she had the
money for their fares…

June 2007

"Kids seem to be getting along well together," said the woman beside her. "Mine's the boy in the Harry Potter tank top."

Holly nodded, watching Jamie and the other boy, who were some distance ahead of them, racing each other to the refreshment station.

"How long have you been going it on your own then?" the woman asked, continuing to jog alongside her.

Holly was beginning to wish she had never concluded that it was in the children's interest for her to join the single parent families group. Everyone was either separated or divorced and assumed she was, too. A sign of the times, she supposed, but she hadn't joined in order to discuss deadbeat dads and that's all anybody seemed to want to do.

She should have listened to Jamie. When she had told the children that she thought it might be a good idea to join so that they could meet other single parent families like their own, Jamie had remarked that half the kids in his class had fathers who didn't live with them – some even had mothers who didn't live with them. One girl's father had died but it was when she was a baby and she didn't remember him, so it wasn't exactly like their own situation but what he meant, he said, was that it wasn't unusual to only have one parent so they didn't need to join a club for it. Holly, however, thought it would be a good for them to socialize, as a family, with other single parent families and had joined the group.

She had attended two of the weekly parent evenings which were of a motivational nature with a speaker, or facilitator, leading discussions on everything from child discipline and school problems to the inevitable topic of missing support payments. On both occasions, she had found that conversation, during the coffee and refreshments half hour, generally degenerated into a grouse and gripe session.

Participation in the Moms and Kids Run for cancer fund-raising had sounded more like the sort of activity she had envisioned but, even here, she found people, who had not been at the two meetings she had attended, latching on to her and moving swiftly to the topic of their wretched ex-partners. Jamie and Carolyn, on the other hand, seemed to be having a wonderful time which, she told herself, had been the main point of joining the organization in the first place.

"A year and a half," she finally answered. Since they were running there was no need to apologise for not responding right away. Much as it still hurt to say the words, she decided to be upfront about her own situation and, hopefully, head off the pleas for commiseration over some irresponsible ex-husband before they began. "My husband died a year ago last January."

The woman stopped and Holly felt obliged to stop with her.

"My husband died fourteen months ago," she said. "I'm so glad to meet you. My name's Tracey."

Holly smiled. "Mine's Holly. I'm glad to meet you, too. I just joined, and haven't met another person who's been widowed yet, so I was beginning to think I'd made a mistake…"

"You and me, both. I joined because I wanted Chris to benefit from being around other kids without fathers but find the group seems

to be more targeted to parents involved in marriage break-ups than...
well, people who have lost someone..."

"I was feeling pretty disillusioned myself," said Holly. "We'd better keep running or my daughter, for one, will think we're not up to it – you know, being so old... She's the one yanking her shorts up just ahead of us. I told her to wear a belt, but she knew best."

Ahead of them, the group of girls began to slow down and trot off the road to stop at the refreshment station.

"Low-rise, huh? I don't know why they brainwash little girls into wanting teenage clothes. It's enough to make me glad I only have boys."

"Tell me about it. It's hard to believe that an eight-year-old truly believes that she must wear 'coo-ol' clothes or nobody will be her friend. I thought it was some psychological problem surfacing when Carolyn first started complaining about her clothes, but her friends are all the same."

"My sister's having the same problem," Tracey said. "Her daughter, who's nine, wants to have her belly button pierced."

"Thank God Carolyn hasn't come up with that one yet. Ears, yes – we're constantly fighting that one out, but she hasn't hankered after any other piercings yet."

They ran on until they reached the picnic tables where volunteers were handing out donated bottles of water. Carolyn ran towards them with a bottle of water each for herself and her mother. The group of boys, with whom, Jamie and Chris had been placed, were already being waved on. Jamie turned and spotted Holly before he reached the roadway again. He pounded his fist in the air, indicating that he was ready to finish the run. Chris followed his gaze and waved to his mother, then the two of them ran off, with a few surreptitious backward glances, obviously informing each other that their mothers were talking together.

"I got you a bottle, Mom," Carolyn said, running towards them holding out a bottle of water.

"Thanks." Holly said, taking the bottle and opening it as she turned to Tracey. "This is my daughter, Carolyn. Carolyn, this is Mrs. –"

"Tracey's fine. Hi, Carolyn."

"Hi. You can have this bottle if you like. I can get another one when I go back."

"Oh, that's not fair," Tracey said, although she had little choice but to take the bottle Carolyn was holding out to her. "You got it for yourself."

"Yes, but I only came over to give one to my mom," Carolyn explained. "I can't stay because I have to get back to the other kids so as to be ready when our five minutes is up. Actually, I think I'd better go or I won't have time to drink it, so 'bye for now. See you at the finish."

Carolyn ran off, picking up another bottle of water as she reached the other girls who were clustered around the picnic table. She immediately fell into conversation with a girl who she had told Holly, at the start of the run, was in her class at school. Holly took a deep swallow of water and found she was so thirsty she could probably use second bottle, but decided it might not be too comfortable running the rest of the way with water slopping around in her stomach.

"She's very eager to please," said Tracey, after swallowing down half of her own bottle.

"They're both good kids. I get worried because everyone seems to think there should be adverse effects, and they should have had counselling despite the fact that they both seem to have adjusted well."

"I know what you mean. It's just the way things are today. Nobody's supposed to be able to weather a crisis by themselves. There's *always some social worker type, who hasn't a clue really, wanting to weather it for them. I'm afraid I get impatient with it all…"*

"Wow!" laughed Holly. "Somebody after my own heart. It's awful feeling something must be wrong because your kids haven't turned into bullies or victims of bullies, emotional wrecks, whatever! I'm lucky, though, I have my mother in my corner. My father died when I was twelve, so she's a good mentor to have, but I thought it was time that we got to know other single parent families. You see, my best friend was my husband's twin sister – we met through her, and her son, Ryan, and Jamie were born within a few weeks of each other. Naturally, they and their fathers did all the boy things together and, of course, Paul – Julie's husband – still takes them to hockey and baseball and everything but, I think Jamie sometimes feels a bit like I do with Paul and Julie themselves. You know – third wheel syndrome…"

Tracey nodded. "I know. My family's been great, too, but you're right, there comes a time…"

"Exactly. I'm so happy to meet somebody who understands. Oh-oh, they're moving the girls on and I'd rather keep right behind them. Jamie's okay up ahead, but Carolyn's a bit young and we don't know this area very well so it's best I'm where she can see me and vice versa."

"That's okay. Let's go."

They dropped their bottles in the recyclables bin and set off along the road. There was a little over a kilometre to go to the finish but some of the little girls were obviously tiring. Carolyn, however, was maintaining her pace. Holly knew that her daughter was not about to have her older brother call her a wimp and she was proud of all the pledges she'd collected which made her determined to complete her part of the bargain and finish the run.

"Do you just have Chris, Tracey?" she asked, once they were back running at a comfortable pace.

"No, I have a sixteen year-old, too. He has a job at the local Price Chopper. It's harder on him than Chris really. Losing his father just when a kid's supposed to go to war with his parents, I mean. Instead of being a teenage rebel, I think he feels he has to fill his father's shoes and be a father figure to his little brother." Tracey shook her head. "And be a comfort to me, too. He's always falling over himself to make the supper, look after the garden, things like that... It's hard to get him to just be a kid."

"That would be difficult for you," Holly agreed. "You must feel that you're pressuring him even though you're not, if you see what I mean. I was bit like that when my father died. I mean, you can hardly treat your mother the way you did before – you'd look like a real little jerk, so you overcompensate. I wouldn't worry about it too much, though. It didn't do me any lasting harm."

"That, I'm glad to hear. You see, it's insights like that which make it worthwhile joining a club for single parent families."

Holly smiled. "You're right. I'm glad I did, after all."

And she was, Holly told herself, thinking about it later as she made supper. She had talked quite spontaneously to Tracey about Justin's death when they sat down, drinking iced tea, while the children took part in the treasure hunt which had been arranged for them after the run. Other than the necessary talks with the children, she had never really been able to speak about it before, even with Julie or Pat. Usually, when the subject came up, she tended to freeze, and other people would uncomfortably, but considerately, change the subject.

Tracey, of course, remembered the media coverage of the shooting once Holly explained who she was or, rather, who Justin was, and said it must have been very difficult for them all having the kind of attention that comes with the murder of a policeman, while trying to deal with their grief, and that it made her grateful that her own loss had been less public. They talked about the terrible numbness of the first few months when you felt time passing while your own life seemed to be on autopilot, and wondered if you'd ever again see, feel or hear the world outside of yourself the way you used to. And they agreed that they must both have come through that phase since they were now looking for guidance and support in being single parents. Sometimes the conversation brought one or the other to tears, but that was a good thing, Holly decided. It was a relief, in fact, to cry in the company of a stranger who was experiencing all the things that you were yourself.

They were still sitting at the picnic table talking when the treasure hunt was over and everybody else had gone home, the three children patiently waiting for them, immersed in their own conversation in the nearby adventure playground. For some reason – Holly wasn't sure why – she told Tracey all about researching her family history and finding her great, great, great, great grandmother Rebecca and the record of her husband's death when their two children were just a little older than Jamie and Carolyn. Then, because Tracey seemed interested, how John, the son – Holly's great, great, great grandfather – had grown up and married his childhood sweetheart, Phoebe, fathered a son and then disappeared into the army, to resurface at the end of the century, married to somebody else; Phoebe disappearing altogether after 1871 without any death record being evident; their son showing up later as an inmate of the original Barnardo's Home in Stepney.

Tracey, it turned out, was a sociology professor and had some suggestions, which rather supported Julie's theory, about the mystery of Phoebe's disappearance from the census records and John's *reappearance married to somebody else. Apparently, divorce was virtually impossible for a woman – not only because she had no resources since what she owned was deemed to belong to her husband, but because, adultery being socially acceptable for men, but not for women, meant that a man could get a divorce simply by proving his wife's adultery, while the poor woman needed to be able to prove him guilty of more criminal aberrations. Then, she told her, such a divorce also prevented the woman from remarrying and she was forced to live common law which, of course, made it difficult to trace her. People were much more likely to live common law than to divorce and remarry, in any case.*

No organizations for single parents in those days, Holly had said wryly, so you just found yourself another man to whip the kids into shape, and they'd both laughed. Tracey also confirmed that, if Phoebe had been alive in 1871, it was not very likely that she died in a cholera outbreak since transmission of the disease by contaminated water was well documented by then and was being brought under control.

They talked about the different attitude that their nineteenth century ancestors had toward death – of the desire for ornate funerals and elaborate mourning, even among the poorest of people, while the higher death rate must have meant that death touched people far more frequently than it did today. Tracey said that you had to remember religion played a much larger role in the life of the Victorian family, to the point, really, where death was just another part of life.

Discussing the afternoon as they ate their supper, Jamie had said that Chris was cool even though he didn't play baseball, and Carolyn had decided that Chris's mother seemed like a nice lady and that she was glad that Mommy had found a friend to run with just like she and Jamie had done. They both agreed that they'd had a great time at the run and it was a good idea of Mommy's, after all, to have joined the club.

After the children had gone to bed, Holly checked her email and found a message from Vicki with an image attached of a page of British deaths registered in 1921. The name Phoebe L. Kentson of Lambeth, aged seventy-three, was circled. As Vicki pointed out, the name was the same right down to the initial, the age was right and Phoebe's parents and youngest two siblings had lived in Lambeth until their deaths, so there was every likelihood of Phoebe having done so, too. So, Holly thought, perhaps she did get recorded under another name on the census records, just as Julie, and now Tracey, too, had suggested, and didn't die after all. Yet, John had definitely remarried in 1896, and his bride had actually been recorded as his wife in the 1891 census five years earlier. Perhaps it had taken him that long to save up for a divorce although the second marriage could have been bigamous; Tracey had also mentioned that bigamy was quite common due to the inaccessibility of divorce. Although, after five and, probably, more years, why bother with a marriage service at all, legal or not?

Scrolling down the messages in her inbox and deleting the spam, she discovered a second message from Vicki saying she'd forgotten to let her know that she'd also been able to trace the life history of Johns' sister, Emma, who'd married in 1865 and had a baby girl the following year. Her husband had died three years later and she'd married again, twice – surviving both of these husbands, too. The third husband appeared to be a cousin – at least, his name was the same as her mother's maiden name. There had been three children from the second marriage, but two of them had died in their early twenties. Wasn't it sad, Vicki wrote, that she should have survived the death of three husbands and two adult children?

There was a P.S. The kids could hardly wait to get on the plane next week and they were all looking forward to getting away from the rain – bucketfuls, they were having just now.

So, Emma, too, had been widowed – three times. Holly thought of her own anguish and tried to imagine how the poor woman had survived bereavement so many times – her parents, her husbands, her children… It demonstrated what Tracey had said about death being just another part of life back then. That's how she would have managed, when the memories became too hard to bear – thinking of death as just another part of life.

She must remember that when her own memories surged, unbidden, through her mind. Justin was a part of her life, part of her and part of her children, and would never completely die.

June 1868

Phoebe turned into the narrow Holborn street where Emma and Stephen had been living for several months. As she always did, she wondered how they could have changed living in the cottage in Lee for this grim city street. Despite the fact that working as a first hand in a fashionable West End salon, together with Stephen's contract with a city cabinet maker, was the big step up in the world to which Emma aspired, Phoebe suspected that her friend had been pretty homesick for Kent when she wasn't too busy to think about it. Compared to her own one up, one down Southwark home, Emma's house was spacious and the neighbourhood, while not really genteel, was certainly a respectable one. But, it was still a city street with not a tree in sight. Emma had talked about how they were saving the money to buy a lease on a house further west – maybe close to Regent's Park, Primrose Hill, even… Now, with Stephen's death, those dreams were all over. Emma was taking Susan to Essex where they were going to stay in the little village where her mother had grown up. Her young cousin, Freddie, who Stephen had taken on as an apprentice, had arranged it with his mother and Emma had agreed that it would be best for both she and Susan to put their London life behind them for a while. Summer was here and she'd be able to help with the haying, as she and Johnnie had done on holidays there in the days before their father died. Two year old Susan would thrive in the country air…

Phoebe shook her head. Emma was no longer the spirited, sometimes bossy, young woman wanting to better herself and her family. She had been left all alone in the world. Except for Susan. And Johnnie, of course, who still didn't know about Stephen saving the children from the runaway horse and being killed himself. And she has me, too, she thought, we're sisters in marriage and closer than sisters by blood, aren't we? Emma, who she had always admired and, if the truth be told, envied – despite knowing that envy was a sin – Emma had been left fatherless as a child, motherless as a young woman about to be married and now she was a widow, too. It was just too much to bear. Phoebe felt tears pricking her eyelids again and blinked hard.

Reaching the front door of the house, she knocked gently. Emma opened the door immediately and moved back motioning Phoebe to walk around the bundles that stood on the floor ready to be taken to the station.

"Oh Emma," she said, throwing her arms around her friend, as the full import of Emma's leaving dawned on her. "This is such a sad day. I mean, on top of all the other sad days."

"It's best we go," Emma said, disentangling herself. "Freddie's gone to get a handcart from the workshop. He took Susan with him. They'll be back in a bit. I know you have to get to work but you can stay until they get back, can't you?"

"I wish I could come over to Bishopsgate Station and see you off properly…"

"You have to get to work. I understand. It's a long walk all the way over here and now you have to walk all the way back to Cheapside. I do appreciate it, Phoebe, but you shouldn't have… You're going to be so tired. What time did you get up?"

"It doesn't matter. I wanted to see you. You're my oldest friend and I don't know when I'll see you again."

"I won't be staying there forever. I expect I'll come back when my savings get low – it's not a place where there's much business in the way of high fashion dressmaking. Make do and mend is more the way of life… but, I just need to get away from all the reminders of Stephen, all our hopes and dreams…" Emma's voice cracked.

"I know, I know," Phoebe murmured, putting her arm around her again. "I was selfish to say that. Of course, you must go…"

Emma turned and faced her. "I'm really very lucky," she said, "being able to do this. To have the money to pay my way, I mean. Most people must carry on. They don't have the means to have time to recover. Death is, after all, just another part of life, isn't it? The people we love die, and we have to go on. I know that I have to go on, but–"

"–you're going to have a rest. It's right that you do. You have no ma or pa and your only brother is far away in Abyssinia. It's right you should go to your ma's relations in a place where life is quite different. Actually, Johnnie is very likely on his way home. That's what I wanted to tell you before you left. Ma had a letter from Sam which I read for her yesterday. He said they were due to board the next ship – after the one that the letter was going on, I mean – so, they maybe on their way home to England by now."

"What did he say about Johnnie?"

"Nothing much. You know Sam – never paid much attention to schoolwork and writes a terrible letter – but he said Johnnie was writing to both of us, too. Perhaps the postman's on his way with the one for you right now..."

"If he is, I'll have gone before he gets here. Train goes at half-past seven and Freddie'll be going straight to the workshop from the station. They'll want the handcart back."

"You said Freddie had found lodgings nearby, so he'll be able to fetch it and send it on to you."

"Yes, of course. Don't pay heed to me grumbling – I'm just feeling sorry for myself. Freddie and Jeb, who his apprenticeship's been re-assigned to... they'll be coming round here after work this evening to take the furniture–" her voice broke again and Phoebe knew it was because she was thinking about Stephen lovingly making that furniture "–to take the furniture to be stored in the workshop. The new tenants are moving in tomorrow."

"I'm afraid that, even if the letters do arrive for us, we won't be able to write back to Johnnie until they're back in barracks. At Chichester, Sam said. They'll march from Portsmouth soon as the ship docks."

"Well, at least we know they're both in one piece or they were when Sam wrote the letter and we'd have heard if the ship went down... It doesn't really matter about not being able to write yet. Johnnie never replies anyway. When did you last get a letter?"

Emma was right. Johnnie was not a good correspondent. Phoebe decided that she mustn't get upset despite her own long-ing for a letter from her husband.

"When they first landed in Africa and were going off to march across the mountains, but never mind. You'll write to me, won't you? And I'll write to you."

"Of course, Phoebe. I'm sorry, I'm not being very pleasant, am I? And you got up so early to come and say goodbye before you ₕₐₑₑ to go to work. I'll write tonight and tell you all about the journey. We'll never forget each other – remember how we swore that we'd always be friends when we were children?"

"Yes," said Phoebe. "I'll write to you tonight and let you know if there is a letter from Johnnie – if I get one, I mean. I have to be going. I'm so sorry about your distress, Emma. I 'ope you can find, at least, a little bit of 'appiness with your auntie and uncle in the country…"

Emma hugged her. "Goodbye, Phoebe, dear. Look after my little nephew. Keep him safe – his pa will come back one day."

"Goodbye, Emma," Phoebe said, fighting back tears. "I'd better be going. I hear Freddie trundling the hand cart along the road…" She disengaged herself and opened the door. "Hello Freddie. I'm just leaving – I have to get to the factory by seven and you 'ave quite a walk over to Bishopsgate, too, so I won't keep you. Hello Susan, you have a nice time in the country, my love." She bent and kissed the little girl who was riding in the handcart and hurried along the street without looking back.

She had managed to get her tears under control by the time she reached Farringdon Street, hurrying under the partly completed viaduct, where whole streets of houses had been demolished, and on to Newgate Street. It was all so sad. She had admired and envied Emma since that January day when she had entered the schoolroom for the first time and the teacher had put her in Emma's charge. Admired her because she knew so much more than Phoebe would ever learn – envied her for being able to go to school every day, and later, because her mother could afford for her to attend the upper class and to pay for her to be apprenticed to the dressmaker's salon, while Phoebe sewed slop and looked after her little brothers. Even more recently, she had been envious of Emma's happy marriage and home of her own with Stephen and Baby Susan, in comparison to her own, at first secret, then almost forgotten marriage and the overcrowded living conditions she and Baby John must bear in her parents' home. Yet Emma had lost her father, then her mother and now her husband while Phoebe, herself, had yet to experience true heartbreak. She had parents and a little son, brothers and a young sister and a husband who would soon be back from India and the strange war in north Africa. With Johnnie on his way home, soon to send for his wife and baby son to join him, her married life was about to begin at last. And Emma's marriage had so sadly ended…

Passing the prison, she fleetingly thought of how crowded the streets had been that day two weeks ago when the Fenian was hanged. He had killed and injured all the people living in the row of houses beside the Clerkenwell House of Detention trying to rescue Fenian prisoners by blowing up the wall. A little girl had been among the dead, a cousin of the very children Stephen had rescued from the path of the runaway horse. A strange coincidence: Stephen losing his life while saving the little boy and girl and the Fenian being hanged for killing their cousin. Then, the dreadful finality that was death brought her wandering thoughts to an end and Emma's words rang in her ears, as she reached Cheapside and hurried along the road to the clothing manufactory – *"Death is, after all, just another part of life, isn't it? The people we love die, and we have to go on."*

www.ingramcontent.com/pod-product-compliance
Lightning Source LLC
Chambersburg PA
CBHW051413170626
46809CB00006B/2144